HIS CURVY FANTASY

A SMALL TOWN CURVY GIRL ROMANCE

BOOK BOYFRIENDS WANTED
BOOK 11

MARY E THOMPSON

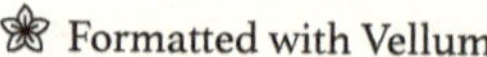 Formatted with Vellum

BOOK BOYFRIENDS WANTED

Pumpkin is in the air, and so is love. Fall becomes winter and enemies become lovers. This story has been years in the making, and it's finally here. Never miss a thing when you sign up for Mary's newsletter.

Romancing the Curves comes with subscriber exclusive freebies, sneak peeks, and a first look at everything Mary has to offer. Be the first to know about new releases and sales and all the curves ahead!

SUBSCRIBE NOW AT MARYETHOMPSON.COM

Happy reading!

For you... You made this book possible. Asking for it, waiting for it, and getting excited for it. You make me keep going on the tough days and make me smile on the good days. Thank you.

1

HUDSON

"No. Hell no. It's not gonna happen. You just need to quit asking." I glared at my supposed friend and resisted the urge to kick his ass.

"Come on, Hud. You know this is the best option. You can't pick up women at your own bar. And you're not gonna talk to them outside here because you never leave." James Rucker was one of my oldest friends and should have been on my side. Instead, he was leading the damn charge.

"I already told you I'm not interested in online dating. That shit is weird."

"That shit got me my wife."

"Trinity hated you."

"Exactly. She never would have given me the time of day if she'd known she was talking to me. Karissa is a genius for the way she designed the app. She created something that allows us to meet people and get to know them without it being all weird."

"What if I meet some freak?" I'd heard the stories. It wasn't just men that were freaks. There were some women that went nuts and did crazy shit, too. I didn't want some wacko following me home and stalking me.

"You might, but take it slow. You don't have to meet someone in person after talking to them once. Just sign up for the account, and if you can't figure out how to talk to someone, I'll help you."

I snorted and shook my head. "I can talk to women."

"Yeah? How about that one? Go flirt with her."

I looked in the direction James pointed and found a gorgeous woman at the end of the bar. She wore a plain white tee and jeans. I'd noticed her when she walked in. Ordered a whiskey neat. She was definitely my kind of woman, but a decade or so too young for me.

"She's half my age."

"So? You can't talk to a woman who isn't the same age as you? You know there aren't a ton of single women your age."

I glanced at the woman again. "I don't need to prove anything to you. Why am I even thinking about this?"

James lifted his drink off the bar and shrugged. "Fine. Don't talk to her. But don't blame me when you have a date that goes sideways because you haven't talked to a woman in more than a decade about anything besides her choice of drink."

I growled as he walked away. He wasn't wrong, but that didn't mean I needed to like it.

I glanced at the woman again. She was twirling her straw in her drink and looking around. She had a distinct not-interested vibe about her. Which was fine since I wasn't interested either. She was an experiment.

No. A woman wasn't an experiment. She was a person. Someone my asshole friend thought I couldn't have a conversation with.

I walked over, checking on the few customers at the bar before her.

She looked up at me as I approached and pasted on a tolerant smile.

"Need another drink?" I asked her. I groaned internally. I was proving James's point.

"I'm good."

"Are you waiting for someone?"

She casually assessed me. Her gaze slid down my body, dismissing me entirely before she returned her cool gaze to my face. "I am. A friend."

"Maybe it's someone I know. I know a lot of people. Pretty much everyone. Except you, of course."

She nodded and eased off her stool. "I think maybe I'll wait at a table."

I opened my mouth to argue that I wasn't trying to be a creep, but it was useless. She was gone, and I was definitely being a creep.

Dammit.

I hated when Rucker was right. He'd never let me live it down. Of course, that was assuming he knew.

I went back to work, ignoring the churning in my gut. I didn't like the woman thinking she might not be safe in my bar. She was just enjoying her drink, and I had to make it weird. Because of James. If he'd just left well enough alone, I wouldn't have talked to her. I didn't need to practice talking to women. It would be fine when I met someone.

Growling at my stupidity, I poured another whiskey and added a scoop of ice. The woman was sitting at a table by herself. She watched the door, her back to me.

I told Jonathan, the other bartender working with me for the night, that I'd be back in a minute and carried the drink to the woman's table. I set it down next to the one she already had.

"I thought you could use a refill." I clasped my hands together and smiled at her.

"I'm good. Thanks." She avoided my gaze, hers locked on the door.

"I just wanted to apologize. I wasn't trying to make you uncomfortable."

"And your apology is to get me drunk so you can take advantage of me? Or did you put something in this drink so you can be the hero and offer to take me home? What is wrong with you?" She glared at me, drawing back like she thought I was going to attack her.

"What? No. I didn't do any of that. I was just trying to be nice."

"Nice guys don't make women feel like they're about to be assaulted!" She jumped to her feet and grabbed the drink. She tossed it in my face before I had a chance to react. "Leave me alone!"

She raced toward the door, grabbing the arm of another woman the second she walked in the door. She pointed to me, and the two of them left.

I stood there watching them, whiskey dripping off my face and soaking into my shirt.

"What was that all about?" Neve asked. She was the server for that section and offered me a towel.

"I was just trying to be nice."

"How nice were you trying to be?"

I growled and snatched the towel from her hand. I stalked past the bar and straight to my office. I wiped my face and patted at my shirt, knowing nothing would erase the shame I felt.

What the hell did I do?

I yanked my shirt off and slammed my way into my bathroom. I shoved a paper towel under the faucet, wiping at the sticky liquor on my chest. Dammit.

When I was clean, or at least less sticky, I grabbed a new shirt and pulled it on. Jonathan could handle things for a little while. I needed a break.

Five minutes later, a knock on the door said my time was up.

"What?"

"You ready for that app yet?" James asked as he opened the door.

"Fuck you, asshole."

"Is that what you said to that poor woman before she threw a drink in your face?"

"Why is it my middle finger gets a hard-on whenever I see you?" I showed him.

James snickered. "Man, you're just asking for it tonight. What did you say to that woman?"

"Nothing! I didn't say anything. I asked how her drink was and if she was waiting for someone. I thought I could tell her if the person she was waiting for had been there or something. She thought I was hitting on her. I brought the drink over to apologize and she asked if I roofied it."

James doubled over, holding his gut.

He was going to need to hold his gut for a different reason if he didn't pull his ass off the damn floor real soon.

"This is even better than I thought. Dude, you need help. How in the hell did you snag Hillary?"

I shrugged. Hillary was my world. We met in college and fell in love. Everything was easy with her. She was assigned to be my tutor, and after I got over myself about needing help, everything with her was easy. We started talking and clicked. She was supposed to be my forever, but an icy road ended that dream.

"You're even worse off than I thought. I need to call in reinforcements." James had his phone out before he finished talking.

"No, please don't," I said as my phone buzzed in my pocket. Then buzzed again. And again.

Group text. Kill me now.

"Most of the guys are busy," James said a minute and dozens of texts later. "Ian's on his way."

What did I do to deserve this? Oh, yeah, I let these assholes be my friends.

James left me alone to sulk and stew while he went back out to the bar. His wife, Trinity, was with him, so I hoped she'd drag him back home, but when they both walked into my office a few minutes later, I knew I was in trouble.

"I hear we're signing you up for online dating," Trinity said, rubbing her hands together. "I can't believe he finally talked you into it."

"I never said that," I argued.

Trinity turned to James with narrowed eyes. "You said he was on board."

"I said he needs to be on board. He could have lost O'Kelley's. That woman accused him of trying to date rape her. I'm an officer of the law. I could arrest him."

"You wouldn't dare," Trinity said, getting up in James's face. "You know Hudson would never do that."

"Sure I do, but clearly the woman he was failing to flirt with didn't."

"You were trying to flirt with her?" Trinity asked in a voice most people reserved for puppies and babies. One I was not okay with having directed at me.

"Oh, God, no. Do not. I can't handle this," I told them,

standing from behind my desk with every intention of throwing them out of my office.

"Can't handle what?" Ian asked, letting himself in as I was trying to escort the others out. "Whoa, what's going on?"

"Hudson tried to flirt with a customer, and she thought he roofied her, so we're going to get him signed up for Karissa's app and teach him how to talk to women, since he's finally ready to date again," James explained.

"I changed my mind. I'm not ready to date. No more dating. I'm done. I'm good by myself," I said.

"Dude, chill. It's fine. We'll set it all up, and you can practice flirting with Blake. Trinity?" Ian looked at Trinity, and she nodded. "All the women will let you flirt with them."

"I'm going to kill myself," I muttered.

"It's not that bad, Hudson," Trinity said. "Dating isn't easy, but you're a gorgeous man who's kind and sweet. You already have half the women out there lusting after you."

"Hey!" James shouted.

Trinity shrugged while I smirked.

"It's true, babe. But you're the one I go home with. You can't be jealous." Trinity blew him a kiss.

"Sure I can. You shouldn't be calling my friend gorgeous," James pouted.

Trinity rolled her eyes. She tossed her brown ringlets behind her shoulder and focused on me.

"You never have trouble talking to me. Dating isn't so different from any other conversation. Why did you talk to the woman?"

I pointed at her rat of a husband. "James made me."

Trinity turned back to him with a scolding look on her face. "Why did you make him flirt with someone? And why did you tell him to be all weird and creepy?"

"I'm not taking the blame for that! I told him to talk to a woman about something other than what she wants to drink. He was weird and creepy all on his own."

I rolled my eyes. "I think it's time for you guys to go. All of you. I will figure out what I want to do. Right now, I need to work."

They protested, but I shooed them out of my office anyway. To keep up the pretense, I followed them out and settled behind the bar.

"You good, boss?" Jonathan asked.

I nodded and moved to the other end of the bar to take orders. At least I knew I could handle that.

O'KELLEY'S WAS CLOSED. The lights were off and the place was empty. I should have gone home, but for some reason, I was in my office looking up Karissa's app.

I'd downloaded it before, but I never created an account. I never wanted to. I wasn't ready to date. Still wasn't sure I was, but seeing my friends fall in love made me more than a little jealous. I wanted that again. Someone to come home to. Someone who was watching for me. Someone who would walk in and smile just because I was there.

Before I could talk myself out of signing up, I tapped to create an account. The first thing it asked for was a screen name.

Screen name. What the hell? How was I supposed to know what to pick? I didn't want to sign up for online dating. I wanted to meet a woman the way I met Hillary. In a casual, comfortable, normal way. I was being forced to do things this way.

I tapped the side of my phone for a minute, then rolled my eyes at myself and typed *HereByForce.*

Next.

Holy shit. Page one of seven. It was going to take all damn night to fill out the stupid survey.

I groaned and dove in. It was better than not doing it at all. And then when online dating didn't work out, I could tell them all I tried. That the only people who met online were freaks and that it wasn't for me.

An hour later, I was finally done. My eyes felt like sandpaper and my throat felt full of cotton. I needed water and a bed.

Home wasn't far. The cottage I bought a few years ago was more than enough for me. Three bedrooms, two baths with an eat-in kitchen and a living room. It was empty and lonely, but it was home.

I OVERSLEPT THE NEXT MORNING. I never overslept. I was always up at the crack of damn dawn, but I overslept. And worse, I had another dream about Anna.

I was not happy.

I showered and pulled on clean clothes, then raced the three blocks to O'Kelley's. Everything was locked up because I was the only one working the lunch shift. It was only ten minutes later than I was supposed to open, but that meant I was going to be playing catch-up for the rest of the day because I should have been there an hour ago.

No one was waiting outside, so I flipped the OPEN sign on and went straight to the back. I started up the grill and the oven and did a quick inventory of what we had on hand and what we were running low on. Charlie, the full-time cook and unofficial kitchen manager, would get me a list by the end of the week, but since I was in the kitchen, I wanted to know what I had.

I'd barely finished getting things started when I heard the door open. I checked my watch and saw it was already almost noon, which meant the small lunch rush would start soon.

I tied an apron around my waist, slid my ball cap on my head, and pushed through the kitchen door to see who was in the bar.

And froze.

Anna Charlotte.

"Do you have our lunch ready?" she asked. No hello, no how are you, no anything. Just barking like a rabid dog.

"What lunch?" I had no idea what she was talking about.

Anna crossed her arms and rolled her eyes. I noticed the second one much later than the first because crossing her arms meant plumping up those breasts that were featured in my dreams.

Son-of-a-bitch.

I adjusted my hardening cock and leaned closer to the counter so there was no chance she could see the morning wood I was sporting. Yeah, that was my excuse.

"Finley said she texted you a lunch order. She told me to come get it because you always have it ready. Her words, not mine. Clearly, she was wrong."

My brain took a few seconds to register what she was saying with those full, round breasts on display for me. Jesus, did the woman have to wear a shirt that showed off that much cleavage? I swear to God, I could see half her boobs. Not that I was complaining, but shit.

"I don't have my phone with me," I finally blurted. "What was the order for?"

"How do you run a business?"

"I do quite well for myself, thanks," I barked.

She pursed her plump pink lips and rolled her sharp brown eyes again. "Yeah, I can see that." She gestured around my vacant bar.

"Whatever. Do you want lunch or not?"

"Yeah, but I'm wasting my entire lunch break talking to you. I can't wait for you to make something. I'll figure something else out. And I'll make sure Finley knows we can't trust you to have food ready."

Anna stomped out with a huff and a sway of her too damn tempting hips.

The door slammed shut behind her, and I finally took a breath. Anna Charlotte was as far off limits as a woman could get. I really needed to get my dick on the same page as me on that one because it was never going to happen. Ever.

2

ANNA

I stomped back to Book Boyfriends Unlimited, fury and frustration trailing right behind me. I shoved the door open, wincing when it slammed against the wall. "Sorry."

Finley, my boss and friend, rushed around the end of a rack of books. Her dark bob and piercings made her look a little rough around the edges, but the baby on her hip softened the woman I knew to be more mush than metal. "Everything okay?"

I rolled my eyes. "Hudson did not have our lunch ready. Or even close. He hadn't even started it. Didn't know what I was talking about. I ran over to Cracked. Blake had Earl make something for us. I'm sorry I was gone so long."

Finley shrugged like it was no big deal, but she was the owner. And married to the man the entire town was named after. Money wasn't an issue for her. Not like it was for me. If I took a longer break, I didn't earn as much. If one of my boys was sick, I didn't earn as much. It was what I agreed to when I started working for Finley, so I wasn't upset by it, but it was my reality. One she couldn't possibly understand.

"You're fine. Thanks for running out to pick it up. This one is itching to move, so he's getting tough to take out."

I smiled at Finley and her son, George. He was a beautiful blend of both her and her new husband, Trent. His smile was all Finley, but his eyes sparkled like his father's. My boys were the same, a blend of my ex and me. I just hoped one day Finley didn't look at her son and feel the way I did about my ex.

"I'll eat quick so I can be available for customers."

"Anna, we're good. I should have called Hudson when I didn't get a text back. I'm sorry."

I shrugged and tried to play it off. Really, though, I was annoyed. Not just that Hudson was the same unreliable man I thought he was, but that my boss continued to push me into his orbit. I had no interest in spending anymore time around Hudson Grant that absolutely necessary. And even that was too much for me.

Finley cooed at George and waved me toward the break room in the back. I ate my lunch as quickly as possible, then relieved her from the quiet storefront. Fall had officially settled into MacKellar Cove. Our small town on the Saint Lawrence River was a popular summer destination, but as fall arrived and winter trailed behind it, the entire area got quiet. Especially places like Book Boyfriends Unlimited. Which was why I was looking at other jobs when Finley came back up front from eating her lunch and feeding George.

"What are you looking at?" she asked before I could close the tab on the computer.

"Nothing."

"Are you looking for a new job?" She sounded hurt, and a little worried.

"I'm just being realistic. I know you only hired me to

work here last spring because you were pregnant and needed someone to help during maternity leave. Things get quiet in the winter, so I just assumed it was only a matter of time before you had to fire me."

"I am not firing you," Finley declared. "I'm sorry I ever made you think I might be. Things will be quiet here until spring, but you've been invaluable to me. You have so many great ideas and you've really helped to increase revenue in the time you've been here."

My cheeks warmed with her praise. I wasn't used to people talking about the good things I was doing. Usually I heard about all the stuff I was doing wrong.

"Trent and I have been talking about rolling the bookstore under the MacKellar Investments umbrella. He likes the idea you had about opening up bookstores in some of the hotels and featuring local authors at each. We both think that's an amazing idea."

"Good," I said, forcing a smile. Yes, I was good at coming up with ideas that made other people lots of money, never myself. And eventually, they starting pitching the ideas as their own and didn't need me anymore. It happened all the time.

"I am not letting you go, Anna. I promise. I really appreciate everything you did for me, and I want to keep working together. Unless you're not happy here. Then I'm totally overstepping and being an ass. Is there something I can do to make you happy so you'll stay?"

I breathed a laugh and shook my head. "I'm very happy here. I'm also very realistic about what it looks like to work in any kind of tourist driven job here through the winter. I don't want to be a burden or make you feel like you have no choice but to keep me and then close the store because you lost so much money."

"Neither of those is going to happen. We're all good."

I forced another smile for her and nodded. I really liked Finley, but I'd only been working with her for a little over six months. I didn't know her well. She kept inviting me to her book club, but I dodged her attempts so far. She was trying to be nice. People didn't actually enjoy socializing with the help. That was another lesson I learned the hard way.

A customer came in and distracted Finley when she gushed over baby George. I let them talk and busied myself with inventory and online orders.

It wasn't long before Finley left for the day. Her hours were sporadic most of the time, which I didn't mind at all. I had a schedule because of my boys, and Finley was great about giving me time off to spend with them. Not that I took it. I needed the money more. But it was a nice thought.

WEDNESDAY HAD BECOME my least favorite day of the week. It was the day I worked until close at Book Boyfriends Unlimited, and my oldest worked at O'Kelley's. Joey got a job there a year ago, when he saw an overdue bill on the counter. I hadn't meant for him to find it, but he did. And he took matters into his own hands.

My kids were amazing. Both of them. That wasn't the first time Joey decided to help out at home, but it was the first time he did it in a way that wouldn't land him in jail. Thankfully, that didn't happen, but he was lucky and he knew it.

I locked up the bookstore and pulled my coat tighter around me. It was a few sizes too small and more than a few years out of style, but I couldn't afford to buy myself a new coat. Not when I had two growing boys who needed stuff constantly.

The walk next door to O'Kelley's was short, but I resisted every single step. I knew Hudson would be there. And I knew he'd have something to say about the way I spoke to him the day before about lunch. Not that I owed him an apology. If anything, he owed me one.

The warmth and the smells hit me as soon as I opened the door. It made me want to go inside and settle in for a while. O'Kelley's was the kind of place I probably would have loved to go to, if it weren't for the obnoxious owner and the fact that I wasn't and never would be a part of his crowd.

I scanned the bar for Joey, spotting him on the far side, clearing a table. The work was good for him, even though I was not happy when I found out he went and got a job without talking to me about it first. In the last year, his grades had improved, and he was more helpful at home. He was growing up.

Once I knew where Joey was, I headed toward the bar to find Matty. He always sat on the same stool at the very end of the bar closest to the kitchen. He told me he did his homework in Hudson's office when he first got there after school, then Hudson would let him help out at the bar. Matty thought it was fun to do things like fill salt and pepper shakers and stack napkins in dispensers.

As I walked over to Matty, Hudson approached him with a smile, the kind of smile he never showed me. Hudson said something to my son that had him looking up at Hudson like he was Matty's hero. Matty nodded, and Hudson lifted his hand for a high-five. Matty happily obliged. The two of them laughed, then Hudson started to move away.

He glanced toward me, and the smile on his face melted into a scowl. That was more like it.

I was comfortable there. With him hating me. It was good to see he was nice to my kid, but I didn't need him to be nice to me.

"Hey, Matty," I said, ignoring the man on the other side of the counter.

"Mom! Hudson said I can draw him a new logo for the bar. Isn't that awesome?"

My brows shot up. "That is awesome. You'll have fun with that."

"I know. It's so cool. And then everyone will see my art. Ms. Trinity keeps telling me it's good, but I know she's only saying that because she's my teacher."

"I'm sure—" I started, only to be cut off immediately.

"No, she's not," Hudson said firmly. "Trinity loves what you do. She showed me some of your art. That's why I asked if you would design me something. She was in here for lunch today and was bragging about how hard you're working and how creative you are."

Matty's cheeks pinked, and he smiled shyly at Hudson. "Really?"

Hudson nodded. "Absolutely. You're amazing, dude. Never doubt that. Never let anyone make you doubt that."

"Are you saying you think I'm making him doubt his talents?" I barked. He could not be serious.

Hudson lifted his cool gaze to mine slowly, standing up even slower. Inch by inch, the man towered over me, crossing his arms that made every woman in a mile radius drool, and pausing just long enough for it to be uncomfortable. "I didn't say a thing about you. If you think I might be, that's something you need to deal with yourself. Not blame me for."

I narrowed my eyes at him. God, the man made me crazy. And not in a good way. Well, not only in a good way. I wasn't an idiot. Hudson Grant was the biggest catch in town, maybe the county. He was strong and stable and stunning. But he was not the man for me. No one was. Been there, tried that, had the sons to prove it. I was not interested in rinsing and repeating any of it. Which was why my vagina was as dusty as an abandoned textile factory. But I wasn't complaining. I'd rather have a dried up vagina and an intact heart than risk my heart getting shattered again just for a few months or years of good sex. No sex was worth that.

"Is Joey done with his shift?" I asked, instead of addressing his insulting comment.

"Yeah, I'm done, Mom. I just clocked out, Hudson. I handed over things to Danielle."

"Thanks, Joey. Good work today. I'll see you Saturday to set up for the party. You can stay if you'd like, but you can't work past nine."

"Can we stay, Mom?" Matty begged.

"I'm not sure that's a good idea," I said immediately.

"That's not fair. Why does Joey get to do everything?"

"Joey's not coming to a party at a bar," I said, looking between my sons.

Joey blanched. "What? Why not, Mom? All of my friends are going to be here. It's a community thing. The whole town is going to be decked out for it, and this is only one stop on the way. Tierney and I... Why can't I come?"

"Ooh, Tierney," Matty teased.

"Shut up, snot-nose," Joey countered.

"Stop," I barked. "Both of you. Matty, leave your brother alone about his girlfriend. Joey, don't call your brother names."

"But he's—" Joey started.

"No. Enough. We'll talk about this party later. If you

have to work, I have no choice, but that doesn't mean I have to let you wander the entire town on a Saturday night."

"But, Mom," Joey whined.

"Go. Now. We're done." I pointed to the door, ignoring Hudson, who was still watching our argument.

Joey's shoulders slumped. He waved to Hudson, then dragged his feet toward the exit. Matty high-fived Hudson, then followed his brother.

I caught Hudson's gaze before I turned away. I didn't mean to. I didn't want to. The ass was smirking at me, like he brought up the party on purpose because he knew it would make my night hell. Jackass.

The drive home was tense. Both boys argued their case. In the end, I told them I'd think about it, which earned more groans and a *well, that means no* from Matty. I wanted to just say no, but I agreed to think about it, and I was going to.

"Do you know anything about this Halloween party on Saturday?" I asked Finley the next day at work.

"Yeah, it's amazing. The whole town comes. How do you not know about it?"

I shrugged, embarrassed to admit I never got involved in anything the town did. Between not having the money and not feeling like I was really a part of the town, I avoided most things.

"Yeah, so it's awesome. There's a hay bale maze through Catherine Park, and a lot of the shops will set up Halloween decorations and have special events. I've participated on and off, but since my shop isn't family friendly, I usually close for the night and go to the party. Hudson decorates the bar. He loves Halloween. Cracked participates. And Cove Bakery. So many places. Are you going to go?"

"I'm not sure. Hudson mentioned it yesterday. Joey's working to help set up, and he wants to go with Tierney. But Hudson said something in front of Matty, so now he wants to go, too."

"It's super fun. And low-key and great for kids. We're taking George. I mean, he won't remember it, but we're dressing up as a family and going."

"What are you dressing up as?"

"The Flintstones. It was Trent's favorite show as a kid."

"That's cute."

Finley chuckled. "I think so. What would you normally do on Halloween?"

I shrugged and shook my head. "Nothing, really. Our neighborhood doesn't trick-or-treat, and it never made sense to go somewhere else. If Hudson hadn't said something in front of Matty, I wouldn't have had to worry about this at all. He did it on purpose."

Finley snorted. "Maybe. But it's fun. Of all the things for Hudson to do, this is not bad."

"I guess," I argued.

"Did you ever sign up for Book Boyfriends Wanted?"

The sudden subject change was like having whiplash. "Um, no. Why?"

Finley shrugged. "I was just curious. I really think you should."

"I'm not sure dating is in my future. I don't really want to get involved with anyone again. After Nick, I have no interest in men."

"At all?"

"No."

"Not even for one night?"

"I thought it was a dating app."

Finley shrugged. "It's how I met Trent. We were matched on there and met at O'Kelley's and left together. We both knew it was for one night. I didn't even know his name."

"You're kidding, right?"

Finley laughed. "Nope. We didn't know each other at all. But I got pregnant and had to track him down. If it wasn't for George, I probably never would have seen Trent again."

I forced a smile for her because I knew she expected it. Her story was a bit like mine, except my story didn't have the happily ever after hers hopefully would. My story involved a lying, cheating asshole who made promises he never kept and got me to marry him. My boys would forever have a worthless ass of a father, and I'd forever be divorced and single with no hope of ever getting the happily ever after I once believed in.

"Anyway, you should totally sign up. All my friends who are attached found their guy on the app. It's like magic."

"That definitely sounds like something I should not do."

Finley laughed. "Oh, come on. It's quiet here. Let's do it now."

"Um..."

Finley waggled her fingers at me until I surrendered and handed over my phone. "Unlock it."

Damn. She was smart. I unlocked it and handed it back to her.

A few taps later, and she was downloading the app. "What do you want your screen name to be?"

"How about *I don't want to be here*?"

Finley snorted. "My friends made me do this. Perfect. Okay, let's find you a man."

My stomach churned. I'd rather go to the Halloween party naked. But Finley Jameson-MacKellar was not the kind of woman you argued with. Especially when she was your boss.

3

HUDSON

I TWISTED IN THE LAST OF THE RED LIGHTBULBS AND JUMPED down from the chair. It looked pretty damn good, if I did say so myself.

Halloween was always a fun time for me. Hillary hated it, but I loved it. It was a holiday that was all about fun. I didn't go for the scary parts of it since it was a good kid-friendly holiday, but I liked it. I wasn't sure what I was going to do for the bar this year, but Joey suggested a graveyard, and I was all-in.

The red and orange lighting was the first part of it. It cast an eery glow on everything, making the bar look like twilight was coming. I changed a few of the orange bulbs out for navy blue ones and liked it better. A little darker, which was always good on Halloween.

With the lighting decided, I had to position the head-stones. I found a ton online with hilarious names like Noah Scape and Izzy Gone. People were damn clever.

Danielle whistled when she walked in. "Hey, boss. The place looks great. You need any help?"

I nodded. "Yeah. I'm trying to figure out where to put the tombstones."

"Well..." Danielle set her stuff on a table and looked around. "Do you have a plan for what people are going to do? Is it business as usual tonight, or are you trying to get people in and out?"

I shrugged. "I dunno."

Danielle laughed. She'd been working for me for almost a year. She was smart and friendly and didn't take shit from anyone. She reminded me a lot of Piper.

"I'd say things should be business as usual, but maybe have family friendly stuff to one side. That way, the families who come through won't worry about getting beer splashed on them or anything like that."

"Good idea. How do we do that?"

Danielle sorted through the tombstones and separated the ones that were a little less appropriate for all ages. We moved those toward the side of the bar where the pool tables were. I'd been planning to line the walls with them, like decoration, but Danielle, and Joey, Jonathan, and Sam all worked together to create pathways and stations for guests.

"Well, damn, I never would have come up with all of this. Thanks, everyone," I said.

They accepted the praise and went about setting up everything else for the night.

Everything for the town started at five. Early enough that kids could enjoy it before the teenagers and adults got too spooky. Dinner rush was busy, and I was helping Charlie in the kitchen when I heard a crash.

"Want to go check that out?" Charlie asked me.

I shook my head. "Not really."

He chuckled. "You gonna anyway?"

"You trying to get rid of me?"

"Nope. Just know you're a control freak and need to have things done your way."

I opened my mouth to argue as the door swung open. Joey looked up at me with a shell-shocked expression.

"What happened?"

"Someone stepped in front of me when I was carrying a tray. I dropped it."

"Okay. Clean it up. You've done that before."

He nodded.

"Is there more to it than that?"

He shook his head.

"What's going on? Why do you look afraid to go out there? Did something else happen?"

He shook his head. "She's wearing this tiny little bikini thing and her... you know... popped out when she collided with me."

Charlie barked a laugh.

I sent him a glare and moved toward Joey. "Did you touch her?"

"No! Of course not."

"Did you say something to her?"

"No."

"Did you do anything inappropriate?"

"No. It was just right there. I bent down to pick things up, and she did the same, and it was right in my face. I just left."

I nodded, wondering what hell I was going to get from his mother for that one. It was after the dinner rush, and almost time for Joey to clock-out, and he was face-to-tit with some woman who likely had too much to drink already.

"Need me to take care of it?" I asked.

"No, I got it. It's my job. I'm sorry."

"You have nothing to apologize for. It sounds like it was an accident, and the woman was trying to help, but clearly wasn't aware of her state of undress. If she says or does anything, let me know and I'll take care of it."

Joey nodded and grabbed the dustpan and broom.

As soon as the door closed behind him, Charlie let out a belly laugh. "Oh, that poor kid! Nose-to-nipple and no clue what the hell to do with it! I'll go clean up for him. You were quick to offer that one."

I threw a towel at him and chuckled. "That's not why, and you know it. I've had plenty of women throw themselves at me. Not my style."

Charlie still laughed. "Yeah, man, but damn. Sometimes a woman makes it too easy. I like a little challenge."

"Is that what you tell your wife?"

He snorted. "Trust me, she's got more than enough challenge for me."

I grinned. "Keeps you on your toes."

"Damn straight. And keeps me coming back for more. I don't want anyone but her. I— What happened?" Charlie's tone changed too fast.

The hair on the back of my neck stood up. I turned and found Joey holding his wrist, a towel around his hand.

"I cut myself. I was picking up the glass and someone bumped into me." Joey moved toward me, red seeping into the towel.

It was one of those moments where I wanted to laugh because I thought he was joking, but the look on his face was too serious. If he was pranking me, he was damn good at it.

"Let's wash your hand first. If you need stitches, we'll call your mom and get it taken care of."

"I don't like needles," Joey said, his face paling.

"No one does, kid. Let's see if you need it first. Wash." I guided him to the sink and set my hand on his shoulder.

He slowly unwrapped the towel, revealing a small cut on his left palm, near his index finger. Blood seeped from the wound, trailing down his hand. I didn't think it was bad, but that didn't mean much since my medical training was nonexistent.

Joey winced when the water hit his skin, and again when I squirted soap onto it.

"Hey, boss, want me to get someone to finish cleaning up?" Charlie asked.

"Yeah. Thanks," I said.

I focused on Joey while he left the kitchen to find someone to clean up the rest of the broken glass.

Joey washed his hand, three times, then we dried it with a clean towel. I led him to the office where I had a First Aid kit. The cut was small, a quarter of an inch at the most. The bleeding had mostly stopped. He held it tightly together with his fingers, but I knew it would bleed again if he stopped.

I pulled my phone out and tapped Nico's name for a video chat. The phone beeped at me until he picked up, nearly invisible in whatever dark space he was in.

"Hey, Hud. What's up?"

"Joey cut his hand on some broken glass at O'Kelley's. We cleaned it up and are holding pressure on it, but I'm not sure if it needs stitches."

"Where are you? Laura and I are at a table."

"We're in the office."

"On the way."

Nico hung up, and I put my phone back in my pocket.

"You doing okay?" I asked Joey.

He nodded, but I could tell he was trying to be strong.

"You can be not okay," I told him. "The first time I got hurt playing ball, I wanted to cry it hurt so damn much. I pretended I was good, and it meant a longer recovery because my coaches all thought it wasn't as bad as it was."

"This isn't the same."

"Sure it is. You're working for me. I'm not going to make you go out there and carry things if your hand is bothering you."

"My mom's going to kill me," Joey mumbled.

His mom's going to kill me.

I was not looking forward to that conversation. Anna was a mama bear on the best of days. This was not one of those days.

A knock on the door was followed by Nico and Laura, and right behind them was Anna.

"Joey, what happened? Are you okay?"

"I'm fine, Mom. It was just an accident. I was cleaning up broken glass, and—"

"Why were you cleaning up broken glass?" Anna screeched.

"It's my job, Mom. Someone bumped into me. It was an accident."

"This is why I didn't want you working here. I never should have allowed it. I don't know what I was thinking."

Laura walked over to them and calmed Anna down while Nico approached me. "Sorry. She was talking to Laura and heard our conversation. She followed us back here."

"It's fine. She was going to find out eventually. I just want to make sure he's okay and doesn't need to go to the hospital or something."

Nico nodded. "Laura will check things out, and she'll get him patched up."

"Not you?"

Nico shook his head. "She's the one who does things like this more often. I can sew up a surgical wound, but for small wounds like this, she's the expert."

I nodded and watched Laura talk to Joey and Anna. Anna's shoulders were up around her ears. Joey looked a little pale, but he sighed and smiled when Laura said he didn't need stitches.

"I'm going to bandage it up for you, if that's okay," Laura said.

Joey nodded and leaned back in the chair.

"Are you sure he doesn't need to go to the hospital or urgent care or something?" Anna asked. Her voice was pitched and tense.

I got it. He was her kid. One of the most important people in her world. And he was hurting.

It was damn hard to watch, and since I was no longer needed, I told Nico to use the office as long as they wanted and headed back to the kitchen to help Charlie.

He was rocking and rolling when I got in there, orders lined up and ready to be delivered. Jonathan was doing the same behind the bar. Between the two of them, I felt like I wasn't really needed at all. It was kind of a good feeling.

I wandered through the crowd, chatting and laughing with customers. Nico and Laura came back out and joined our group of friends. Nico gave me a thumbs up, so I took that as a good sign.

I made it back to the bar and was about to head into the kitchen when Anna stopped me.

"You didn't think calling me was warranted?"

"Excuse me?"

"Calling me. When you realized my son was injured. Why didn't you call me?"

"I was trying to get a handle on the situation. He told me

what happened, and I did the best I could. I figured getting him checked out by a doctor and nurse was a good idea."

"Of course it was, but he's a minor. As his sole guardian, I should have been informed. I also should have been present. I did not give you permission to get him medical attention."

"Actually, you did. It's in the paperwork you signed when he took this job. Legally speaking, I have permission to get him medical attention when necessary as it relates to his employment."

She huffed, and I took advantage of the moment and went into the kitchen.

"Doing okay?" I asked Charlie.

"All set, boss. How's the kid?"

"Good. Laura patched him up. No stitches."

"I bet he's relieved to know that."

"Yeah."

"You can go out and enjoy the party for a bit. I'll let you know if I need help."

I snorted. "No, you won't. You'll just get shit done like you always do."

He laughed. "Then it means I didn't need help."

I laughed and shook my head, understanding that I was being dismissed.

Without thinking about it, I walked out of the kitchen and found myself face-to-face with a very unhappy Anna Charlotte.

"You're still here?"

"We weren't done talking. You should have called me. You should have let me know my son was hurt. I should have been your first call, not the one you never even made."

"I didn't need to call you. You were already here and let yourself into my office."

She got up in my face. Her big brown eyes got even bigger. Her nostrils flared with her temper. Her oversized breasts rose and fell with each ragged, angry breath.

Fucking hell, she was stunning.

Which meant I had to get the hell away from her before I did something I couldn't take back.

"What do you think you're doing?" she shouted, grabbing my arm when I tried to move past her.

That fire in her eyes made me chuckle. It was definitely the wrong moment for that, but I couldn't help it. She was funny. She came up to my armpit and thought she could intimidate me.

"I'm going to my office," I said over my shoulder, shrugging her off.

I needed a minute. A minute away from her. It was getting bad. She was getting bad. I tolerated her for a while, but I was losing the last bit of my patience with her. I knew she was Finley's friend, but I wasn't going to put up with her shit for anyone, even Finley.

I pushed the door closed behind me and stalked toward my desk. Five minutes. Just five minutes and I'd be able to breathe again.

But the door didn't slam, and I didn't make it to my desk.

"He cut his hand. You told him to clean up glass on the floor and he cut his hand. How could you do that? How could you—"

"Shut up!"

The rest of her sentence stuck in her throat, her mouth open and ready to spew it at me. I'd never raised my voice to her. Hell, I rarely raised my voice to anyone. But this woman. Fucking hell, she had a way about her. She could make a nun swear. I wasn't a nun, but my sex life for the last decade or so was just as exciting.

"I—"

"No. You don't get to barge in here and do this. This is my office. If you have an issue with the way I operate my business, you can leave."

She opened her mouth to interrupt, and I held up a hand to stop her.

"If you're not happy with Joey working here, he can quit. I'm not forcing him to stay here."

She twisted up her lips like she was sucking on a lemon.

I'll give her something to suck on.

The thought sent me stumbling backward. She was off-limits. So far off-limits, she might as well be in another country. I could not... anything with her. I couldn't kiss her, touch her, claim her. It didn't matter how many fantasies I had about her, she was not and never would be mine.

"Joey needs the job," she breathed. "We need the money. And before you start in on what a horrible mother I am—"

"I don't know where the hell you got that idea, but I have never said you're a horrible mother. Not everyone is born with a silver spoon. Most of us have to work our asses off to get what we have."

She nodded, that amber highlighted hair tumbling over her shoulders and falling in gentle waves over her breasts. Breasts I wasn't allowed to notice. Breasts I shouldn't be noticing. Breasts I couldn't help but notice.

"I don't like seeing my kid hurt, and you—"

I took two steps toward her. Her eyes widened as I moved into her space. I didn't give her time to react. I just leaned down and sealed my lips to hers.

Instantly, I knew I'd fucked up. She was definitely going to make Joey quit. And she was probably going to file an assault charge against me. I deserved it, too. I put my hands on her without permission. Without even thinking about asking for permission. I—

Fuck me, she kissed me back. Her lips parted under mine in invitation. One I wasn't going to pass up. I backed her up until she hit the wall, and I closed the door next to us. The last thing I needed was someone walking in on us. Not when I finally got her in my arms.

Hell, no.

4

Her hands slid up my chest. Her fingers closed, gripping my shirt. I leaned in closer, then she shoved me away.

Breath whooshed out of my lungs as I stumbled backward. I looked up at her, red lips and flushed cheeks and anger sparking in her eyes.

Fuck.

"What? Why? This... No. This can't happen. This isn't going to happen. I don't want it to happen."

I straightened and nodded sharply. My body was still on high alert, ready to dive back in and finish what I'd started. Sending the message all around that it wasn't happening was a slow process. One made slower when she clutched a hand to her heaving chest and drew my eyes to her perky nipples pressing against the thin fabric of her costume.

A fucking maid's costume. Jesus fucking Christ. The woman had no idea what she did to me. Hell, I didn't know until I couldn't stop myself from kissing her. But that outfit, with the tight black skirt, the lace-edged top that exposed the very top of perfect globes of skin, and those fuck me heels I wanted very much to listen to, I was out of my damn mind.

All she had to do now was turn around and get the hell out of my office, but she didn't. She stood there, her eyes blazing at me like she couldn't decide if she wanted to kiss me again or punch me.

Probably both.

"You can leave now," I growled, deciding for her. I wasn't interested in being her whipping post. I was far too often, and I needed a break. It was the whole reason I was in my office in the first damn place. She was the one who followed me.

"But..." She drew a deep breath, lifting those breasts my hands itched to mold. She looked at me once more, then turned on one of her heels and let herself out, slamming my office door behind her.

"Fucking hell," I muttered when she was finally gone.

That was not supposed to happen. Nothing was supposed to happen. Not with her. I decided I was ready to start dating, not torturing myself. And spending time with that woman would be pure torture.

But it'd be so damn good.

"Nope." I shook my head, trying to toss the thought out. She worked for Finley, one of my best friends in the world. And her son worked for me. It was too close. Too much.

Plus, we didn't like each other. At all. She never spoke to me unless it was in irritation, and the feeling was mutual. If I was going to get involved with another woman, it was not going to be one who made my skin feel too tight and my body feel like it was on fire. In a bad way.

Nope, Anna Charlotte was not going to be the woman I started dating or kissing or anything else. We were going to go back to hating each other and forget this ever happened.

A knock on the door had my cock jumping. Fucking hell. The lonely bastard was hoping Anna had changed her mind.

"We just talked about this," I grumbled as I moved toward the door.

He didn't listen. I adjusted myself and conjured up pictures of Old Man Bill, one of my regulars who sat at the bar on Monday afternoons and told me stories about his long-lost love. I was going to be him in a few decades.

I opened the door, ready to walk out if it was Anna back for another round of yelling at me. But it wasn't. It was Finley with baby George, my Godson, on her hip.

"What happened to Joey?"

"Really, Fin? Do you think I'd intentionally hurt the kid?"

"Of course not. That's why I asked. Anna came out of here all flushed and furious and dragged the boys out so they could go to the hay maze. She said something about not wanting to be here any longer. Laura said Joey's hand is okay, but obviously there's more to the story."

I shook my head and reached for George. He was quickly becoming my favorite person in the world. He never judged me for not having my shit together, was always happy to see me, and smelled good all the time. He was sort of like a puppy, but I'd never tell Finley that.

"Someone stepped out in front of Joey and he dropped a tray. When he went to clean it up, he got bumped and a piece of glass cut his hand. He washed it, and Laura checked it out, but you know how Anna is about Joey working here. I'm surprised she didn't make him quit right then and there."

"Are you okay?" Finley asked.

Her ability to see past my bullshit was starting to get

on my nerves. I didn't know if it was motherhood that made her more sensitive to the emotions and needs of others or if we'd been spending too much time together, but either way, the last thing I needed was Finley catching wind of anything that happened in the office before she arrived.

I buried my nose in George's neck and smiled when he nuzzled against me. "I'm good. Anna lost it on me, but it's fine. She already hates me, this is just one more reason."

"I don't think she hates you. I think she likes you."

My damn dick jumped again. I swallowed a groan and shook my head. "Nope. Definitely wrong on that one. But it's all good. Joey's a damn good employee, and that's all that really matters to me."

"We both know that isn't true."

I couldn't risk looking at Finley. Not when I was sure she'd see all the things I was feeling about Anna in my eyes. Instead, I focused on George and lifted him over my shoulder. "What do you mean?"

"You don't just care that Joey's a good employee. You want him to do well in school and to work hard and play hard. Same with Matty. I know you care about those boys. You care about everyone in your circle. If you're really honest with yourself, you probably care about Anna, too."

I nuzzled against George in order to avoid Finley again. I nodded, hoping it would appease her. "They're good kids."

"They are. And Anna is a good person. I'm sorry you two don't always get along, but I'm sure eventually you will."

"Doubtful."

"Well, either way, she's gone, and you should come enjoy the party. The place looks amazing, by the way. You always do it right."

I nodded, happy to be on a safer subject than Anna. "I

try. I'll be out in a minute. I need to write up the report on Joey so I have a record."

"Okay, sounds good. And, Hudson?"

"Yeah?"

She waited until I handed over the baby and met her gaze. "I know you'd never hurt anyone on purpose. Not Joey, not Anna, no one. Anna knows that, too. She was just scared tonight. I'm learning that's the default emotion as a parent."

I nodded, offering her a smile and a wink, then encouraging her gently toward the door.

That one hurt. I'd always wanted to be a parent. Hillary and I were talking about it when she died. Not having kids was the only thing in life I regretted. Not that I could have done anything about it when my wife was dead, but I wished I'd had kids. Having Joey and Matty at O'Kelley's was almost like having kids, but not. I knew they weren't mine, but they didn't have a dad and I didn't have kids, so there were times I pretended. Not that I'd ever admit that.

I sat at my desk and tried to breathe. As much as I played it cool when Joey came to me with his hand wrapped in that towel, it scared the hell out of me. He was almost a man, but in that moment, I saw him as a little boy. I wanted to just wrap him up and never let anything else happen to him.

But I was his boss, and that meant making sure he was okay first. The rest of it was his mother's job. And shoving my tongue down her throat did not help any of it. It was best if I just stayed away from the Charlotte family and kept a wall between me and the rest of them.

I filled out the form quickly, a formality more than anything else, and added it to Joey's personnel file, then headed back out to the party to lose myself in the fun.

I'D NEVER BEEN a big drinker. People thought it was strange that I owned a bar and didn't drink a lot, but I bought it for that reason. If I was always around the alcohol, the draw was less. Like a teenager wanting to do something. It was only appealing until it was allowed.

That was why it was almost a surprise to me when the night was winding down and I couldn't make it out the door. I couldn't remember the last time I'd had so much to drink. I stumbled around the party, chatting with customers and laughing with my friends. I was having fun and forgetting about the rest of the day. It was only when the lights came up and the music went down that I realized just how far gone I was.

I shuffled my way through clean-up, telling the few remaining employees how much I appreciated their help, then locked the door behind them and dragged myself to my office. It had been a long time since I slept on the couch in there, but making it home was not an option, so I crashed hard on the couch.

When I was coherent again, the sun was barely shining through the back windows. My office faced the River, which was west, but I could tell the sun was up but not high. Barely daylight.

I checked my phone and groaned. I'd gotten about five hours of sleep. My head was pounding like it held a jackhammer and my mouth felt like I'd forgotten to take the cotton swabs out after dental surgery.

I rolled off the couch and headed for the bathroom first. The medicine cabinet had a large bottle of painkillers. I downed a few and scooped water from the running sink into my mouth. It would take a while for the meds to kick in, but in the meantime, I had work to do.

The place wasn't too bad, which was a nice surprise. I

emptied the trashcans and tossed the bags into the dumpster outside. I wiped down the bar and straightened all the bottles. Bathrooms were good to go, and the kitchen was spotless.

It was too early to open, which was good since I was too exhausted to do it. I thought about going to Cracked for breakfast, but I needed a shower and a change of clothes so I headed home.

The pain killers finally kicked in after my shower and once I got some breakfast in me. My headache lingered, and I knew it was going to be a long day, but it was better than it could have been.

I'd just barely gotten back to the bar when I got a text from Finley.

> I keep asking Anna to come to book club, but she always says no. I know Joey works tonight. Can Matty come with him so Anna can come to book club?

I growled at the phone and tossed it on the bar. I didn't want to deal with Anna. Not with the headache I had.

I ignored the message while I got things set up to open. The entire time, the back of my phone glared at me, encouraging me to flip it over and reply to Finley.

When I couldn't make up any more excuses, I snatched my phone from the bar and thumbed out a quick reply.

> Matty is always welcome here.

Three dots appeared, like Finley had been sitting there waiting for me to reply. She probably was. Which made me feel like shit for ignoring her for so long.

Thanks! I'll let Anna know.

I ignored the twitch in my jeans at the thought of seeing Anna again today. On the weekend, she usually didn't come in when she dropped Joey off or picked him up. But if she was bringing Matty, she would.

I refused to be excited by the idea. I would be lucky to make it through the day with my balls intact if she had anything to say about it.

The bar opened and customers started filtering in. Some looked like I felt, but others showed up with smiles, playing pool and talking and laughing with friends like they hadn't been up drinking half the night. I was getting too old. Damn. I didn't think forty-two was that old, but I was starting to feel like it. I was twice the age of the youngest drinkers, and that realization hit me in the nuts as hard as anything.

I busied myself through the day, trying not to think about Anna coming when it was time for Joey's shift. I absolutely did not watch the door or look up every time it opened. And I sure as hell didn't have to go to the office to adjust myself a few minutes before they were going to arrive.

Absolutely not.

I was in the kitchen with Charlie when Joey walked in to clock in. Everything in me jumped when I realized he was there early and I wasn't out front waiting for Anna.

It was good. It was better that way. I didn't need to see her. There was no reason for it.

"How's the hand?" Charlie asked Joey.

Joey held it up to show him the bandage wrapped around his palm. "It's fine. Ms. Laura said it was good, but my mom's a little crazy. She told me to keep it bandaged up until tomorrow. She's taking me to my family doctor."

"If Ms. Laura said you're good, I'm sure you're good," Charlie said.

"That's what I told her, but she's being nuts. She's always like that."

"I'm almost surprised she let you come back to work," Charlie teased.

"I don't think she wanted to," Joey admitted, flashing a guilty look my way. "I told her it wouldn't be fair of me to quit without notice."

"Is this your notice?" I asked, hating the way my gut clenched at the thought. Shit.

Joey shook his head. "No. She agreed to let me keep working here. I told her no one else is hiring right now, and I need this job to help out at home. I know she hates that, but it's true."

"There's nothing to be ashamed of that your family needs money," Charlie said. "That's how I got started cooking. My parents both worked two jobs and my siblings and I all took on jobs around the house. I was the tallest, so I was the cook. Turned out I was pretty good, and I enjoyed it. Soon as I could, I started working in kitchens to earn some money so my parents could back off a little on their work. They never did, but it was nice to have that spending money. You've got a great work ethic, kid. Don't lose that."

"Thanks," Joey said, his cheeks darkening just a touch under the praise.

"Is your brother here?" I blurted.

Joey looked up at me and nodded. "Ms. Finley said you said it was okay. Is it?"

"Yeah, of course. You just didn't mention him, so I wanted to ask. Did he sit at the bar?"

Joey shrugged. "I'm not sure. My mom walked him in. I came back here to clock-in so I wasn't late."

"You're good. Thanks. I'll go find Matty and make sure he's all set."

"Mmm hmm," Charlie mumbled.

I ignored him and left the kitchen as he asked Joey what he was doing to get ready for the upcoming baseball season.

Matty was not in his usual seat at the bar when I walked out. I scanned the area quickly, wondering if he'd left his seat and found someone to talk to. He was a chatty kid and if he was alone, he usually wandered.

When I didn't see him in the bar, I headed toward the office. I had books for him to read and a handheld video game device he played after he finished his homework. And a workbook for him which he fought me on, but he never had much homework so I bought it to make sure he was getting the best education he could.

I heard her voice before I opened the door to the office. As always, she sounded upset. I sighed and drew a deep breath, then turned the corner into my office.

She was standing over my couch with the blanket I'd slept with the night before in her hands. She'd already folded it in half and was getting ready to fold it again.

"What are you doing?" I asked.

Her head snapped up at me, a guilty look in her eyes. "I was just folding this blanket since it looks like someone slept here last night. I was trying to be nice."

I bit my lip to keep from saying something I'd regret. She was being nice. I'd forgotten about the blanket when I stumbled home that morning and hadn't been back in my office much since I got back.

"Thank you," I managed. "I should have taken care of it earlier."

"It's fine." She avoided my gaze, keeping hers on the blanket. When she was done, she draped it across the back of the couch and smoothed it out. Then she looked around like she needed to do something else.

"Hey, Hudson, can I play a game?" Matty asked, drawing both of our attention.

"A game? What game?"

Matty lifted the handheld device from the bottom left desk drawer, the one I had just for him with all his stuff. There was a pencil case with pens, pencils, colored pencils, glue sticks, and scissors. His workbook, the books I'd bought for him, a few coloring books that he told me were for babies but I saw him using a few times, and the gaming device.

"What is that?"

"It's mine," I blurted. "I like to chill and play sometimes, and I told Matty he could borrow it when he's here, as long as his homework is done. Does he have any homework to finish today?"

"No. He doesn't get homework on the weekends. But that's expensive. He doesn't need to be playing with your game thingy."

"It's fine," I assured her. "It was only a few hundred dollars. I can get another one if I need to."

Clearly, that was the wrong thing to say. She rolled her lips in and nodded. Then she walked over to Matty and kissed the top of his head. "Please be careful. I won't be late. Listen to Hudson and behave. A few hundred dollars might be no big deal to some people, but to me, it's a lot, so don't break that."

Matty nodded, already loading a game.

Anna let go of him and moved toward the door, where I was still standing in the way. She looked up at me, shame and hurt in her gaze.

I opened my mouth to say something, but I didn't know

what to say. I hadn't meant to make her feel bad for not being able to buy a stupid gaming device for her kid. It wasn't a big deal to me to get it, but I shouldn't have made it sound like I was better than her because I had disposable income.

"Thank you for letting him stay here," she finally said through gritted teeth.

"Anytime. I mean that."

She nodded once, then moved around me and left.

Leaving me feeling like I'd just fucked up. Again.

5

ANNA

I BLINKED BACK TEARS ON MY WAY OUT OF THE BAR. GOD, I hated that a little thing could make me feel so worthless. It was a stupid game. Something every kid should be able to have. But mine didn't. Not from me, at least. My kid played games because Hudson bought them for him.

He wasn't fooling me. I knew it wasn't his game thing. He bought it for Matty. It was sweet, but...

No. I couldn't think about Hudson Grant being sweet. It was how I ended up pregnant and how I became a single mom. Nick was sweet when he wanted to be. And then he disappeared. It had only been six months since I'd managed to finally get a divorce, and I was still building my life back. I was not going to fall for sweet and ruin all the work I'd done to get things moving in the right direction.

Besides, I had no interest in Hudson Grant. Or any man. It didn't matter how good that blanket smelled when I picked it up or how my body reacted to his voice when he asked what I was doing. He was nothing except my son's boss.

Without an excuse to not go to book club, I found myself

at the door in a matter of seconds. I pulled out my key and let myself in, since I could, then wondered if that was okay. When Finley came around the corner of a bookshelf and smiled brightly, I figured it was.

"I thought that was you. No one else has keys. I'm glad you showed up." She hugged me and nodded her head toward the back, where they all sat and talked about everything except the book they were supposed to read.

"You didn't give me much of a choice," I confessed.

Finley laughed like she always did and pulled me toward the back, like she knew I'd run if she gave me the chance. "How late does Joey work?"

"Nine. He's not allowed to work later than that yet."

"I turn into a pumpkin before then," Laura said as we turned the corner and the group of them came into view. "Nico and I are at work by seven, which means I'm up a little after five."

"Ouch," Trinity said. "I couldn't handle that."

"Neither could I," Karissa agreed.

Laura shrugged. "I guess I'm used to it, but it means going to sleep early."

I stood there as they all talked about sleeping and who was getting enough and who wasn't. Blake rubbed her extremely pregnant belly and looked like she might fall asleep right there.

"Come sit," Finley said, patting the seat next to her.

I forced a smile and joined her on the couch. I was the odd one out. The one who didn't really know the others. The one who had to be handled since I was alone. The others all knew each other. They'd been friends for years. All I'd done was snap at them and distance myself as much as possible. I was about as good at making friends as I was at holding onto a man.

"Anna joined Book Boyfriends Wanted," Finley told the group.

My cheeks warmed when they all turned to look at me.

"That's exciting. Have you had any good matches yet?" Blake asked.

I shook my head. "Not really. A few were okay, but I don't have a lot of time to sit around and chat or a desire to meet up with a stranger after a few surface conversations. I'm too busy for that kind of crap."

The silence told me that response wasn't the best one. I wasn't sure what I said was wrong, but I'd definitely stuck my foot in something.

"Well," Elise said, "that *crap* is what brought Colin and me together, so it was worth it for me. Same with most of us here."

"I'm sorry, I—"

"It's fine," Finley said. She put a hand on my arm and smiled at me. "We all know what you mean. You have two kids, and you're working full time, and you're doing everything you can to stay above water. Dating and sex aren't a priority for you right now, and that's okay."

I swallowed roughly and nodded. It was best if I just kept quiet the rest of the day. Everything would be better if I did. Then I wouldn't piss off any more of them.

"Sofia, have you met any new matches?" Finley asked a blonde I recognized but didn't know.

Sofia shook her head. "Not lately. I've taken a little bit of a break. It gets to be a lot for me."

"I don't seem to have that problem," Goldie said. We didn't know each other well, but she had a son close to Joey's age and was older like me. I felt like maybe she could be a friend. Maybe.

"What do you mean?" Sofia asked.

"I must have filled out something on my profile wrong because I barely get any matches." Goldie rolled her eyes. "It's like they know I'm not young and cute with perky boobs and a manicured vagina."

"Oh, I feel that to my core right now," Blake said with a groan. "I swear there are times I've debated asking Ian to shave me because I hate that he has to brave that area when we have sex, but I'm not sure I'm willing to risk asking him to go at me with a weed-whacker."

I snorted in spite of myself, drawing the attention of the others.

"What's your verdict, Anna? Clean or not?" Goldie asked.

I looked around the group at the wide open faces and felt every cell inside me start to turn in. I didn't want to share something so personal with a bunch of women I barely knew. I never had. I had so-called friends in high school that ditched me as soon as I wound up pregnant. As the young mom, I never bonded with the other moms when my kids were little. And now, I was the old lady, full of stretch marks and a bush that could have had its own zip code.

But sharing all of that? Not a good idea.

Then I opened my mouth...

"The last man to see me naked was my ex-husband. And the last time we had sex, I got pregnant with my twelve-year-old. My vibrator doesn't care how much hair is down there, which is a damn good thing because if I shaved it all off, I might be able to make a pet for my sons."

The silence after my confession was deafening. For about three seconds. Then they all burst out laughing. Tears rolled down their faces, stomachs were held, and hands were clapped.

"Oh, shit, am I happy to hear that," Goldie said a minute later, still holding her side. "I thought I was the only one. I just turned forty and I swear I pulled something the last time I even thought about shaving, let alone actually getting myself into a position to make any progress."

"I turn forty in a few days, and I'm feeling the same. But I have no one to shave for and no intention of changing that any time soon, so it doesn't matter to me." I lifted my plate in toast to Goldie and knew I'd found a friend.

"A few days?" Finley asked. "When's your birthday?"

"November third. Why?"

"We need to get together. We should all do something."

"O'Kelley's?" Trinity suggested.

"We don't need to do anything," I interrupted. No one heard me.

"Girls' night?" Blake said.

"Isn't that what we're doing right now?" Elise asked.

"Yes, but we can go out and have drinks, you guys can, and dress up and have fun." Blake raised her brows at me as if she was actually asking me to agree.

"I don't need a party," I said.

"It's not a party. It's a night for us to go out and celebrate. We all got together for Goldie's birthday. We do for all of ours." Blake smiled like it was a foregone conclusion that I would want to do something.

Another truth that said none of them knew me. I couldn't remember the last time I celebrated my birthday. Before kids, definitely. Probably when I turned twenty-one and Nick and I went out. He got trashed on my birthday and I ended up having to stop drinking so I could take care of him.

Yeah, I was great at picking winners.

"What did you do for your birthday last year?" Finley asked.

"Um, nothing. I haven't celebrated my birthday in longer than I can remember." I shrugged like it was no big deal. I'd gotten over not being the center of attention a long time ago. My kids were what mattered now.

"Then it's settled," Blake said for everyone. "We're going to start our night at O'Kelley's. We will get all the kids together at someone's house for those that want or need it, and us ladies will go out."

Finley clapped her hands and grinned. "I'm so excited about this. It's going to be so awesome."

I forced a smile. What the hell had I gotten myself into?

WHEN MY BIRTHDAY rolled around two days later, I decided I was going to make the most of the day.

Ha!

No, I didn't. I decided I was going to run away and never come back so no one would ever try to celebrate my birthday again.

I did not want to do something for my birthday. At all. But Finley was so excited, and she was my boss, and the others thought it was a great idea, and I had never figured out how to be friends with other women, so I sucked it up and shoved down all my anxiety and decided if I could survive being married to Nick for fifteen years, I could survive one night out with my boss and her group of friends.

Finley insisted on driving me, claiming she couldn't drink anyway since she was still nursing, so she pushed me until I agreed to let her pick me up. I was waiting outside when she got there, not wanting her to come into my tiny little apartment and see the way we lived.

Yeah, I was embarrassed. She lived in the biggest house in town, and I lived in the smallest apartment in town. To say our worlds were different was an understatement.

I smiled through the stomachache when I got in her car and tried not to sigh at the feel of the expensive leather seats.

Apparently, I failed.

"I know, right?" Finley said. "I told Trent I didn't need a new vehicle since I don't drive far, but he insisted on buying me this shortly after George was born. The only thing he let me talk him out of was something bigger because it would have been a nightmare to park on the street, but these leather seats are to die for."

I ran my hand over the soft camel colored leather and nodded. "They really are. I've never had anything this nice in my life."

"Me neither," Finley said with a laugh.

Okay, so she didn't grow up with money, and before she met a stranger and got pregnant, she was living paycheck to paycheck, but all that changed for her. I wasn't looking for a knight in shining armor to save me from my situation. I could save my damn self.

"I'm sorry Blake sort of forced tonight on you. I really did just want you to enjoy book club. It got a little out of hand."

"It's fine," I assured her.

"You say that now."

"Should I be worried?"

Finley shook her head. "I don't think so. I mean, it's MacKellar Cove. There's only so much we can do."

I laughed with her as the knots in my stomach tightened. Why did I agree to this again?

Finley parked a block down from O'Kelley's. She met me on the sidewalk and looped her arm through mine. She half-dragged me toward the door.

A part of me worried she'd rented out the bar or something and was going to have some huge surprise party for me. When the door opened and it appeared to be business as usual, I breathed a giant sigh of relief.

Some of the women were already camped out at a table in the corner with drinks and food in front of them. When they saw us approach, they cheered and raised their glasses.

"Did you start without us?" Finley asked.

"Nope. We just got here," Elise said. She lifted a glass toward Finley. "Hudson had food ready since he knew we were coming. Had the table reserved and everything and drinks ready to go."

"Sweet," Finley said.

Elise nodded and handed another glass over to me. "Happy birthday."

I smiled. "Thank you."

"Drink that. It'll help." Elise raised one brow, a dare or encouragement. I wasn't sure which.

But I took the drink. I lifted the glass and took a sip, surprised when it was sweet and light and so very dangerous if it actually contained alcohol. "What is this?"

"It's a Hudson specialty. He is a master behind the bar. He made this special for us tonight. What do you think?" Elise watched me closely.

I nodded. "It's delicious. Is there alcohol in it?"

"Yep," Elise said with a chuckled. "A lot. But it's good, isn't it?"

I nodded and eyed the drink again. I took another sip. I

needed to be careful. It was the kind of drink that got me pregnant. Twice.

Laura joined us, then Goldie, and before long, I couldn't see the rest of the bar for all the women crowded around our table, laughing, drinking, and eating.

"How is everything going over here?" Hudson asked. He was across from me, between Blake and Goldie. He smiled at both of them. Goldie smiled back and a burst of red-hot jealousy sliced through me.

"It's wonderful," Finley said. "Thank you for making all of this happen."

"No big deal. Glad I could help." He lifted his gaze to mine. "Happy birthday."

"Thank you," I said automatically. I wanted to say something else, but I didn't know what and before I could think about it, he was gone, turning to go behind the bar again.

"Seriously, what is going on with you two?" Trinity asked.

"What? Nothing. Why would you ask that?" I blurted. My cheeks burned, but that was just from the alcohol. I'd had two of those drinks and was starting to lose it.

"There was some heat there." Trinity raised a brow and looked around the table for confirmation from others. "Seriously? Not one of you picked up on that?"

"He said happy birthday, and she said thank you," Elise recapped. "How is that hot? I've said the same to my parents and Colin's dad, and I can guarantee there's no heat there."

"I'm with Elise," Melody said. "I didn't see it. I mean, I wish Hudson would find someone because he's awesome and he deserves it, but... I mean, so do you, Anna..."

I smiled at her. I knew what she meant. She was friends with Hudson. Everybody loved Hudson. He was a catch. A good, strong, independent man who could do anything.

I was still an outsider. Someone who was always here but never really here. I lived on the outskirts, literally and figuratively. And I always would.

"I need to use the bathroom," I blurted. As soon as I said the words, they became true, but really, it was just a good excuse to get away from the looks they were all giving me.

Poor, pitiful Anna. With no money, no friends, and no man.

Ugh. I was sick of it.

I'd show them, and everyone else.

I locked the bathroom stall and pulled out my phone. All those notifications I'd been ignoring? I was going to answer some of them. Yeah, there was a part of me that knew it was a really bad idea when I'd been drinking, but there was a bigger part of me, the drunk part, that admitted I'd never do it. I was scared out of my damn mind to take a chance and risk it all again.

I wasn't sure I wanted a date, but it would be nice to flirt with someone. To feel like maybe I could be wanted. I spent more than a decade with Nick, and another decade trying to get free of him while he tried to bury me in debt. When we first got together, he made me feel wanted in a world that I never had before. But that was just teenage hormones and kids stuck in the same situation. He made sure I knew that after I got pregnant with Matty and Nick took off for the last time.

I was forty. I might never meet a man who actually wanted me, and I didn't need one to, but for once in my life I wanted to feel like maybe, just maybe I was worth more than the zeros in my bank account told me I was worth.

6

HUDSON

My phone buzzed in my pocket. I didn't think anything of it, but then it buzzed again. And again.

I pulled it out and smiled when I saw I had six messages from Book Boyfriends Wanted. All from one person. And all introducing herself and clearly not intending to all be sent to me.

MYFRIENDSMADEMEDOTHIS

Hi! I saw we were matched and wanted to say hi. I'm a single mom, I'm 40, and I work a lot to take care of my kids. I don't have time for games or bullshit, so if that's why your here, find someone else to fuck with. I also don't really have tim to date. I shouldn't admit that, but who care. You don't know my. If I've scared you of, good. It means we weren't mean to be anyway. If not, maybe you should be. But I kind of hop you aren't.

I snort-laughed at her message. Between all the typos and the fact that she sent it to me six times, the exact same message, my guess was she might not be fully sober at the moment.

I looked around the bar, but half the women there had their noses in their phones. I shook my head and thumbed out a quick response to her.

HEREBYFORCE

Nice to meet you. Definitely not scared off by your first message. Maybe the fifth one. Or the sixth. But it's all good. I like kids but hate games and bullshit, so maybe there's a reason I'm not scared off.

I snickered as I imagined her reading my response and waited for the guilt to come in. After Hillary died, I spent years feeling guilty whenever I would even think about another woman. Eventually, I slept with someone, and I nearly drank myself to death afterward because of the guilt. It took a while for me to stop feeling like I was cheating on my dead wife. There were still times I felt that way, but it had been fading more and more lately. Tonight? Not even a twinge.

A new message popped up from MyFriendsMade-MeDoThis.

MYFRIENDSMADEMEDOTHIS

Clearly I shouldn't be doing the right now. I'm going to go hide and pretend this never happen.

I laughed and sent back a quick response.

HEREBYFORCE

I look forward to talking again. Soon, I hope.

I didn't expect a reply from her, so I stuck my phone back into my pocket and turned my attention to the bar again. I filled drinks and talked to people and ignored the pull to go check on Finley and the rest of the ladies.

Things started to quiet down about an hour later, and I finally gave in to my weakness and looked over at Finley's table. My gaze immediately landed on Anna, a dopey, drunk smile on her face as she laughed at something someone said.

I'd never seen her look like that. Like she wasn't mad at the world. For just a minute, she looked happy and at peace. It was stunning. Which was how I knew I needed to look away.

Jonathan was behind the bar with me and said he could handle things for a few minutes. I needed to take care of some things in the office, so I left him alone and went to clear my head.

Anna Charlotte was not someone I needed to be thinking about. Ever. Hell, I'd already kissed her, and she pushed me away. How many reminders did I need that she wasn't interested?

And neither was I. I didn't like her all that much. She made me crazy. Love wasn't supposed to be like that. Relationships should be easy. The right ones. With Hillary, it was always easy. Not that I made it that way, but she did. I was angry and nasty when we met because my future was being threatened. I was failing two classes and my baseball coach said I needed a tutor or I'd lose my scholarship and get kicked off the team and out of school.

I was pissed. I spent my entire life feeling stupid because I was dyslexic. I couldn't make sense of things, and I was slow. In high school, they pushed me through and gave me extra time because I brought in money for the school. People came to see me play ball.

But in college, I wasn't special. There were guys with twice my talent. I was just another player. Which meant I had to figure out how to pass or leave.

Hillary was the unlucky one assigned to be my tutor. I flat out told her on day one that I didn't need her and that I wasn't going to sit there and have her treat me like I was stupid. She never flinched or pushed back. Just told me she would be there ready to help whenever I was ready to listen.

And she was. She never judged me or made me feel like something was wrong with me. She was the first person who ever accepted me for who I was, learning disability and all.

Once I got over myself, she became my world. She was everything to me. When I blew out my knee and couldn't pay for school, she was still there. Even though I tried again to push her away.

Easy. That's what a relationship was supposed to be.

But Anna? No. Nothing with her was easy. Nothing made sense. Nothing had me feeling like I was whole.

Kissing her was a mistake. It didn't matter that it was a mistake I wanted to make again. It was a mistake. I was only attracted to her because she wasn't someone I'd known forever. Like Finley or Elise or Karissa. Anna was different, but Anna was not my future.

I pulled my mind from Anna and did what I could to focus on the payroll for the week. It needed to be done, and since I didn't have an office manager, I needed to do it myself.

A part of me thought about asking Melody if she could come back to work for me again, but I knew that wasn't the right move. I'd never considered hiring someone to deal with the paperwork before she forced her way into a job at O'Kelley's, but since she left, I thought about it every time I sat down to get things like payroll done.

I checked all the reports against the schedules and time cards for everyone. Everything lined up, thankfully. It was an easy week to deal with, but it was only going to get more complicated the closer I got to the holidays.

I triple checked all the information and was about to submit it when someone knocked on the office door. I looked up and found Finley with Anna hanging off her shoulder.

"What happened?" I blurted, jumping up from my seat and hurrying to them. I helped Finley set Anna on the couch. Anna immediately slumped over.

"She had way too many of your drinks."

"Dammit. I warned Elise the drink had a lot of alcohol in it."

Finley nodded. "Elise told us. Anna said she couldn't taste the alcohol. I don't think she meant to get so wasted."

Anna snorted in her sleep and turned her nose toward the couch. "Yummy."

"I can't get her home by myself. I was thinking about bringing her back to the estate, but—"

"Joey and Matty are home," I finished.

Finley nodded. "I don't know what to do here. I wanted tonight to be a fun night out for her."

"Did something happen?"

"No, not anything bad. But for her to get this drunk tells me she either doesn't let go often or is a lightweight. Maybe both."

"Probably both." I looked at Anna as she smiled in her sleep. Her light brown hair was more red against the dark brown of my couch. She had a few streaks of gray through it. Even with that, she looked younger in sleep. Peaceful. Like she wasn't carrying the weight of the world she usually had on her back.

"By the time I realized how bad she was, everyone else

had left. And I can't really call Trent to come help since George is already asleep."

"I'll help you get her home."

Finley cupped her boobs. "Soon. I need to pump."

"Jesus, I don't need to know that. Or see it."

"Then we either need to leave right now or you need to handle this yourself because I'm about to pop."

"Good God, Finley. Just go. I'll get her home. I'll get in touch with Joey so he knows I'm coming into the apartment."

"Are you sure?"

"Are you really giving me a choice?"

She gave me one of her regretful smiles and shrugged. "It really wasn't my intention to get her this drunk. I just wanted her to have fun. She doesn't relax often. She's worked for me for six months and I've never once heard about her going out or dating or doing anything that's just fun."

"Maybe her version of fun is just different than yours."

"Maybe. But I think she's forgotten how to have fun." Finley winced and grabbed her boobs again. "Ooh, I really need to go. Are you sure you're okay getting her home?"

"Yes, I got it. Just please don't get breastmilk all over the bar."

Finley laughed and rushed forward. She hugged me, not too close, and said, "I won't. Thank you."

"Hey, are you okay to drive?"

She nodded when she got to the door. "No drinks for me. It goes to the breastmilk so I just had water tonight. And food."

"Okay, good. Be careful driving home."

"I will. Thanks, Hud."

Finley was gone, and Anna was sleeping on my couch. What the hell did I agree to?

I drew a breath and knew the only option was to get it over with. I grabbed my phone and pulled up Joey's number to send him a text. He was likely asleep, but I didn't want him to worry when I let myself into his home.

> Your mom is at O'Kelley's and had a bit too much to drink. I'm leaving in a minute to bring her home. You don't have to get up, but I wanted to warn you since I'll be entering your home so you don't worry about who's there.

Before I could tuck my phone away, it buzzed with a thumb's up reply.

"Guess he's not worried," I said aloud.

I looked at the woman who'd been in too many of my fantasies lately. She wasn't smiling anymore. Her mouth had fallen open, and she was drooling on my couch.

"Glad it's leather."

I crouched in front of her and brushed the hair from her face. She was beautiful, and so much easier to be attracted to when she wasn't pissed off and yelling at me about something.

"Anna? Can you wake up for me? I'm going to take you home."

She groaned but didn't wake up.

"If you won't get up, I'm going to have to carry you."

Another groan.

I blew out a breath and did what I told myself I'd never do again. I put my hands on Anna Charlotte.

Her hair was soft when it brushed across my wrist. I pushed down the desire to run my fingers through it and looped my arm under her neck. Halfway there.

She was wearing pants, thank God. I lifted her head slightly, laughing when she snored loudly at the change of position. It was clear she was not going to wake up and walk to my truck, so I slid my other hand under her knees.

She sighed and turned toward me, resting her hand on my chest. It had been a long time since I'd had a woman in my arms like that. The few I'd slept with since Hillary were not women I spent extra time holding. We fucked and fled.

With Anna, I wanted to sit on the couch and hold her for a while. Smell her hair and watch her sleep. The realization punched me in the gut and sliced through me, almost bringing me to my knees.

I gave myself a moment, just one, to indulge in the feel of her pressed against me. I didn't know what it was about her that drew me in, but it was there. Begging me to take more than I was going to take. Not just now, but ever.

I exhaled slowly, then lifted her weight from the couch. She wasn't tiny or light. She was full of plush curves and a sassy mouth. But only one of the two was out tonight.

I stood, adjusting my grip on her so I knew she would be safe while I walked to my truck. Of course, that was when I realized I should have asked Jonathan or Charlie to help clear a path for me to get out of the bar.

The walk through the back hallway was tight since I had to turn sideways so I didn't knock Anna's head against the wall. Charlie came out of the bathroom before I made it into the bar and saw Anna passed out in my arms and jumped into action.

"You sure you want to go out the front, boss? Everyone will see."

"I couldn't make it through the backdoor. Not holding her and pushing it open. This was my only choice."

"I'll help you. Let's go out the back."

"Thanks."

He led the way, holding the door for me to get out onto the River Walk. He knew where I parked my truck and led the way there, opening the passenger door and helping me get Anna situated with a seatbelt on before closing the door.

"Can you get her home okay?" Charlie asked.

I nodded. "All good. I already let Joey know I'd be bringing her home."

"What happened to her friends?"

"They didn't realize how much she had to drink. Finley asked me to help, but she had to go so I said I'd get Anna home."

"You're a good man, boss."

I snorted. "We'll see if she agrees."

Charlie laughed. "Well, I think you are."

"Thanks. And thanks for your help."

He nodded and turned to go back to O'Kelley's. The kitchen was closing soon, but I knew he'd talk to Jonathan and they'd make sure everything was taken care of until I got back.

I'd been to Anna's neighborhood before but not to her apartment. I knew which one it was from Joey's employment paperwork, but it still took me a few minutes to find the right building.

There was a parking space not far from the door, but it was tight, so I passed it for one a little farther away with an open spot next to it. I pocketed my keys and opened Anna's door. She was sleeping soundly, not moving except to breathe.

Thankfully, I realized I needed her keys to get into her apartment. I didn't like going through her things, but it was the only option. Her keys were attached to a keyring that said *Romance readers do it between the covers.* I snorted a laugh. She must have gotten it from Finley.

I unbuckled Anna's seatbelt and lifted her into my arms again. I marched up to the door of the building, relieved and annoyed when I was able to nudge it open with my foot. I took the steps up to her unit and carefully adjusted her so I could unlock the door without having to set her down.

The lights were on inside. I walked into a living room with a couch that was threadbare and lumpy. There was a small TV on a tiny stand across the room. To the left was a kitchen that had definitely seen better days.

"Hey," Joey said, walking out from the hallway that must have led to the bedrooms.

"Hey. Sorry. I didn't mean to wake you."

He shook his head. "I was up. Is she okay?" His gaze was locked on his mom and full of worry.

I nodded. "Yeah, she'll be fine. She had too much to drink, so she'll have a killer headache, of course."

"Is that all? Is she going to be sick or anything? Is she going to die?"

"No. Nothing like that. She's fine. I take it she doesn't drink much?"

He shook his head again. He looked younger than the kid who worked for me. Even though he was only sixteen, I saw him as much older and wiser. Stronger. More mature. But tonight he was just a boy worried about his mom.

"She'll be okay. It happens to everyone. If she was awake, I'd have her drink some water and take a few aspirins or something. It'll be harder on her tomorrow without them, but she'll be fine."

"Does she need a trashcan or something?"

"You can get her something and put it next to her bed. Where does she sleep?"

He pointed to the lumpy couch, and my heart skipped a beat.

Jesus. When Joey started working for me, he said he needed the money, but this was a whole new level. Anna slept on a couch that was probably older than her sons. In the living room. Fucking hell.

"Okay," I said, knowing it wasn't Joey's fault that they were in the situation they were in. It wasn't Anna's either. It was shitty luck and a douchebag ex who left her with a mountain of debt. According to James and Finley, at least.

I set Anna down on the couch, and she moaned softly. Not the good kind of moan, but the kind that said she wasn't okay.

"Are you going to be okay with her?" I asked Joey.

He shrugged. "I don't know. What should I do?"

I sighed and accepted that I was going to be sleeping there, too. "Go grab a trashcan for her. Do you have any water bottles?"

He shook his head.

"Okay, get the trashcan. I'll grab some water. If that's okay."

Joey nodded and went back down the hall.

I filled a plastic cup with water from the sink and set it on the table near the couch. I pulled Anna's shoes off and turned when I heard Joey coming back.

He set the trashcan next to the couch, then looked up at me. "Now what?"

"Now, you go to bed. I'm going to sleep in that chair over there and keep an eye on your mom."

"You are?"

I nodded. "Yep. Get some sleep. You have school tomorrow, right?"

"Yeah." He rubbed the back of his neck. "I have a test."

"Then you need to rest. Do you set an alarm, or do you need me to wake you up in the morning?"

"Nah, I set an alarm. And I'll get Matty up before I leave."

"Okay. I'll fix breakfast when I hear you up."

He nodded sharply. "Thanks. For, um, staying."

"You're welcome. Go sleep, kid."

He nodded and went back into the room he'd come out of earlier.

I locked the front door and checked on Anna once more, then covered her with a blanket and found one for myself. I sat in the chair across the room and accepted I wasn't going to get any sleep. And not because it was the most uncomfortable chair on the planet but because I couldn't take my eyes off the beautiful woman sleeping across the room from me.

And I didn't want to.

7

ANNA

I STRETCHED AS I STARTED TO WAKE UP. MY STOMACH ROLLED. Ooh. That wasn't good. I slowed my movements and evaluated how I felt.

Stomach flipped. Head throbbed. I heard voices, soft ones. The boys must be up.

A door closed quietly, then there was silence. Joey getting in the shower. Good. He was taking care of himself. Which meant I could rest a few more minutes before I had to start making breakfast and let my stomach settle from... whatever.

I drifted back to sleep and prayed the pounding in my head stopped. I was in and out of sleep for a little while. The bathroom door opened again, then the bedroom door closed. I needed to get up soon. It didn't matter how upset my stomach was or why my head was pounding. I had to take care of my boys.

I inhaled deep and...stopped. I smelled...breakfast?

I kept my eyes shut and tried to figure out what was going on. The scratchy, lumpy fabric beneath me was definitely from my couch, aka my bed, but nothing else about what was going on felt normal.

Shit.

My eyes flew open as the last memory from last night rushed back in. Another glass of that drink Hudson made. The one Elise said had more alcohol in it than expected. Dancing. Pool. Flirting with a random guy.

I tried to pull up more memories from after that, but it was a blank. I couldn't remember how I got home. It was a relief to be home, but the in between part bothered me. I shouldn't have had so much to drink. I should have known better. I couldn't remember that last time I had anything to drink. At all. It wasn't something I was willing to spend my limited income on, and seeing my mom drink herself to unconsciousness growing up made me less than a fan of drinking in general. One of the many reasons I didn't like Joey working in a bar, but we definitely needed the money.

"Morning," Joey said, dragging his feet out of his room toward the kitchen.

I followed him with my gaze. I thought he was in the kitchen making breakfast. If he wasn't, then who was?

"Hey, Hudson," Joey said a second later, answering my question.

"Morning, Joey. Eggs good for you? I made pancakes, too. And there's bacon and sausage."

"Really? Awesome."

I pushed myself off the couch on weak knees and knew the way my stomach rolled was no longer because of the excessive amount of alcohol I had to drink last night and all because of the man in my home.

"What are you doing here?" I breathed when I stepped into the kitchen and finally saw him standing at the rickety oven that barely worked on a good day.

He looked up at me and glanced down the length of my body before returning his gaze to the stove. "Morning. I figured you'd be hungry when you got up. I made coffee. And there's toast to go with everything else if you can only handle that."

"Why are you here?"

He glanced my way again, then cast his gaze toward Joey.

Oh, fuck. Did I sleep with him? Did I bring him back to my home with my boys sleeping in the next room, and now he's playing house and making us breakfast?

"No," Hudson said firmly, as if he could read my mind. "Finley didn't realize how much you'd had to drink until everyone had left. She asked me to help get you home."

"And you stayed?"

"I didn't think it was a good idea for you to be alone. I slept on the chair."

I chewed the inside of my lip. Tears stung my eyes. I couldn't remember any of that. I didn't remember everyone leaving. I didn't remember leaving. And I definitely didn't remember Hudson Grant helping me home.

"I wanted to make sure you were okay."

"I'm fine," I snapped.

He nodded, ignoring me and my attitude. "Joey, you want more eggs?"

"Yeah," Joey said, getting up from the table and leaving his phone there. Something he rarely did. "Thanks, Hudson."

"You're welcome. There's plenty more. Enough for your brother, too. You said he'll be out in about twenty minutes?"

"Yeah. Thanks."

Joey carried his plate back to the table and dove in again.

I finally realized the volume of food in my tiny kitchen.

More than I would normally be able to fit in here, let alone could afford to have. "Where did all of this come from?"

"I went to the store an hour ago," Hudson said. He didn't look at me.

"Why?"

"Because I didn't want to use up whatever you had here. In case you had planned to use it for other meals."

"I...This is a lot of food."

"I told Joey I'd fix breakfast this morning. He said he has a test. I figured a good breakfast was best."

My throat was thick, tight. Like I was having an allergic reaction to something. It was hard to breathe.

I mumbled something about being right back and raced down the hall to the tiny bathroom. Tiny bathroom in a tiny apartment with a tiny kitchen. And Hudson Grant looking all big and bad and like none of it bothered him in the least.

I sank onto the toilet seat and sucked in heaving, drugging breaths. The tightness in my throat eased. But everything else stayed. He took me home. He made sure I was safe. He was in my apartment and cooking breakfast for my family.

He was the last person I wanted to rely on for anything. I didn't trust him. I didn't know him, but I didn't trust him. He was like Trent, but beloved instead of just worshipped. Trent MacKellar was always seen as someone bigger than the rest of us. He had money and no worries, as far as anyone was concerned. He was untouchable.

Working for Finley and getting to know Trent, I learned a lot about him. I no longer saw him as untouchable, but he was still the richest person I knew. Times twenty. At least. Which meant he was better than me in every single way.

But where Trent had more money than anyone in town,

Hudson had more fans than anyone in town. Women talked about him in the grocery store. They stared at him at O'Kelley's. They dared each other to flirt with him or go home with him or just get his attention.

And the women weren't the only ones who wanted to be near Hudson Grant. The men did, too. They wanted to be his friend. To get his advice. To be near him.

He wasn't loved because of what he could do for others, like Trent was. Hudson was loved because of who he was. The women who came into Book Boyfriends Unlimited wanted books about men like Hudson. Most eligible bachelors. Wounded in a way that would make them appreciate the women in their lives. Men who would treat a woman like a queen.

I wanted nothing to do with him. I wasn't interested in a relationship, and I definitely didn't want one with a man every other woman wanted. I had enough shit to deal with in my life.

I finally managed to push away the shame I felt at having Hudson Grant see where we lived and got up. I splashed water on my face and decided he needed to go. As soon as possible. If my neighbors saw him leaving my apartment, I'd get shit about it forever. The whole damn town would know.

Nope. Not happening. I needed to go back to my quiet existence, where I was unnoticeable and unimportant.

Matty was at the table when I walked back into the kitchen. Hudson was sitting between my boys, talking and laughing with them. Joey wasn't staring at his phone, and Matty wasn't picking on his brother. They were acting like it was normal for a strange man to be in our home.

"You boys need to get ready for school," I said, interrupting their fun and feeling very little remorse for it.

"Hudson said he'd drop me off," Joey told me.

"The bus will be here in ten minutes."

"I can swing by the school on my way home. It's not a big deal," Hudson said.

I hated when people got in the middle of my decisions. He wasn't a parent. He didn't get it. That didn't make it better. "Joey rides the bus."

"It's just one day, Mom."

I knew my rage was unfounded, but it was there. If I held onto it, it was only going to get worse. I hated the idea of giving in, but if I did, it was a guarantee of Hudson leaving in ten minutes.

"Fine. But if you're late, you're grounded."

"I won't make him late. We'll be there in plenty of time," Hudson said. He took a sip of his coffee and nodded at Joey. Then he turned to Matty. "How's breakfast? Need anything else before I go?"

"This is the best day ever. Can I keep a pancake for tomorrow?"

My heart cracked. Leftovers were a commodity for us. We didn't usually have any, and Matty knew all the extra food Hudson made was valuable. Not just in the sense of money, but in the sense of what it actually meant for him. He didn't have to go through the cafeteria line in the morning and get the free breakfast the school provided for the kids who couldn't afford it. He could eat at home and walk straight to his homeroom when he got to school.

"You can keep all the pancakes," Hudson told him. To his credit, he didn't flinch or hesitate. He acted like it was a perfectly normal question.

"Really?" Matty asked.

Hudson nodded. "Absolutely. I made them for you guys."

"What are you going to eat for breakfast?" Matty asked.

Hudson shrugged. "I don't normally eat breakfast. I work until really late and when I get up, it's almost lunchtime."

"I love breakfast," Matty said. "It's the best meal of the day."

Hudson grinned. "It sounds like you'll appreciate it all a lot more than I will." He stood and looked at me. "I'll put everything away and get Joey to school."

I nodded, unsure of what to say. I didn't want him to do either, but he was being nice to my kids, so I stayed quiet. It meant he would leave.

Joey went to brush his teeth and grabbed his backpack for school. He met Hudson at the door a few minutes later.

"Bye, Mom," Joey said, halfway out the door.

"Get back here," I told him.

He hung his head and walked back to me, letting me hug him and kiss his cheek.

"I love you. Have a good day."

"Love you, too. Bye."

Hudson watched us from the door, a small smile on his face. When I met his gaze, he looked away quickly, like he was ashamed to have been caught watching us.

"Bye, Matty," Hudson said, glancing toward the kitchen where Matty was still eating pancakes.

"Bye!" Matty waved his pancake in the air.

"Bye, Anna. I'll see you soon." Hudson's parting words sent a shiver up my spine. A shiver I definitely could do without.

AFTER MATTY GOT on the bus, I jumped in the shower. My entire body was weak. I stubbornly refused to eat the food

Hudson made for my family, because I'm insane, so I was running on coffee and liquor fumes from my night out.

Happy fucking fortieth.

I got out of the shower and found some comfortable clothes. If I was going to sit around and feel sorry for myself, the least I could do was be comfortable.

I paid a few bills and added up the remaining debt I had left to pay. If it weren't for Ramsey Holland, I'd have a lot more debt in my name, but he worked a miracle and got me out of my marriage and divided up the debt Nick had taken out in my name. Without the money to pay for a lawyer, I was married to him for about a decade longer than I wanted to be. But Ramsey offered a very generous payment plan and got me divorced so I could move on with my life.

I still wasn't anywhere close to paying off all my debts, but every dollar I was able to put toward them felt like a win. Which was why the money Hudson spent on food rubbed me so wrong.

I couldn't afford to feed my boys like Hudson did. They ate breakfast and lunch at school because the state provided it for free to kids from low-income families. They didn't get eggs and pancakes every day. They usually got frozen waffles and school pizza. But it was food I didn't have to buy, so I appreciated it.

One day I would be able to buy my kids lunch. And make them breakfast in the morning. And not worry about every single penny we earned and spent. I wasn't to one day yet, but I was getting closer. Thanks to Finley and the job she gave me.

Finley gave me the day off, but I wanted to thank her for getting me home, even though I wasn't too happy she left Hudson there.

> Sorry I drank so much last night. I hope I wasn't too big of a pain to get home.

> We all have those nights. And no clue. Sorry. Hudson said he'd get you home. I was leaking and needed to go. Sounds like it all worked out, though.

What? Hudson got me home by himself? I thought he helped Finley.

I jumped up and paced my apartment. I couldn't remember anything. His truck, walking inside, anything. How did he get me here? When I thought it was Finley and he helped, I was more okay with it, but just Hudson? He probably had to carry me. And I was not small. Oh, God.

> Oh, okay. Well, thanks for last night. I had fun.

> LOL! You know that sounds dirty, right?

I snorted and shook my head.

> Not what I meant.

> Are you sure? Because you were flirting with someone on your phone. Maybe something dirty happened that you don't remember.

On my phone?

Texting...

Oh, God, who did I message?

I flipped back to my last messages. Huh. Nothing. So, what...

I saw the icon for Book Boyfriends Wanted, and my

stomach turned. Shit. It was coming back. I'd been so sure of myself with the alcohol fueling me.

My hand shook as I reached for the icon and opened the app. No new matches, but a message from someone. I tapped on it and groaned.

Then laughed.

Introducing myself to the same guy six times didn't bother him. He appeared to take it in stride. He didn't even ask for a picture or something creepy when it was clear I'd been drinking.

FINLEY

Are you going to tell me who he was?

I flipped back over to my texts.

I don't know. Someone I was matched with. I made a fool of myself, but he didn't call me on it. Just let it go and said we'd talk again.

Then you should message him today and do some more flirting.

I'm not sure it's such a good idea.

Flirting is always a good idea. It's like fighting, but without the drama.

Fighting is not fun. Ever.

Maybe. But making up can be a lot of fun.

My body flashed with heat. The last time that happened... Nope. I wasn't going to think about how good it felt when Hudson kissed me. He did it because he wanted me to stop yelling at him. We weren't making up. Or anything. He hates me as much as I hate him. And after last night, I didn't think I could face him again, anyway.

I spent the rest of my day cleaning my apartment and figuring out how I was going to avoid my son's boss for the next few years. At least until I got control over my body's reaction to him. He was attractive, and kind, and he'd been a good influence on Joey, but he was not for me. And until my body got the message, I was staying away from him.

8

HUDSON

I nodded at Joey as he walked in and resisted the urge to ask him how his mom was.

I hadn't seen her since I spent the night in her living room and cooked breakfast for their family. She was weird when I left, weirder than normal, and she'd been avoiding me since.

At least, I was convinced she was avoiding me. I couldn't actually prove it, but I hadn't gone a full week without seeing her since Joey started working for me and she barged into my bar and demanded I don't hire him.

Even that first day, I knew she was going to fuck up my life. But back then, I thought it was going to be in a very different way. Not in a consuming my thoughts and wishing I could see her kind of way.

Joey went to work, and I pushed Anna from my mind. I had shit to do, and no time to wonder how a woman who didn't want anything to do with me was doing.

Jonathan was behind the bar and nodded me over when I joined him.

"What's up?" I asked.

He glanced over at the customers sitting a few feet from us. None of them were paying attention to us, but he still leaned in closer. "I didn't get paid this week."

"What?" I blurted.

"Usually my check is in on Wednesday mornings, and it wasn't there today. I normally wouldn't say anything until a few days were passed, but we're looking at buying a house in the next few months and I need to prove I have a consistent income."

"Yeah, of course. Um, let me look into it. I don't know any reason it wouldn't have gone through, but I'll go... Are you good up here?"

"Of course. And I'm sorry to put you on the spot like that, but—"

"No. You don't have to apologize at all. You worked, and you should have gotten paid. Let me see if I can figure out what's going on, and I'll be right back."

Jonathan nodded. He looked a lot less worried than he was a few minutes ago.

I logged into my computer and got into my payment system. Melody set it all up for me when she worked for me a few years ago, but it was an easy enough system and better than the one I was using before. I clicked through to the employee pay section. Everything looked right. All the employees were listed. Hours were in.

I went through to the payments section and stopped. No payments were scheduled for the week.

"What the hell?"

I clicked to a few other screens and stopped. I tossed my hat on the desk and rubbed my head. How in the hell did I not pay my employees? It was supposed to happen automatically. Once I reviewed and approved the time it went through. And I did it every single Tuesday night. I was there last Tuesday. It was Anna's birthday…

"Fuck me," I mumbled as I realized what happened.

I was in the middle of it when Finley brought Anna to me. I planned to finish it up that night, but I spent the night at Anna's house. And forgot all about the paychecks.

Shit.

No one was going to get a paycheck. They had families to take care of and bills to pay, and I fucked it all up for them. Because I couldn't remember to get it done.

I logged into my personal bank account and saw that I had money to cover the payroll in there. Obviously the business account had enough since it was supposed to pay out already, but with money in my personal account, I could write everyone checks and ask them all to pay me back when their paychecks went through. Or I could go to the bank and see what could be done.

The last thing my employees needed was to have to worry about paying me back. The bank was my better option.

I went to Jonathan first to explain to him what happened and ask if he would take care of anything that came up while I was gone. It was close to closing time for the banks already, so I had to go.

Jonathan agreed, but the worried look on his face said he wasn't holding out a lot of hope of me solving the issue.

I jogged to my truck and resisted the urge to tear off down the street. The bank was about ten minutes away, on the outside of town, and would be closing in about twenty minutes. I had to hurry.

The doors were still open when I walked in. People were waiting in line to speak to the one and only teller helping customers. I glanced around, catching the eye of a manager and waving him over.

"How can I help you, sir?"

"Listen, I run a local business and my payroll didn't get processed like planned. Is there anything that can be done?"

"I'm assuming you have your accounts with us?"

I didn't roll my eyes at him. I was proud of myself for that. "Yes."

"Well, we aren't likely the ones who process your payroll, but I can see what we can do. Come with me."

I walked behind him as he turned toward a cubicle on the side with glass walls and absolutely zero privacy. Once he verified my identity, Lucas pulled up my accounts and asked about the payment processing system.

"It looks like we do manage it," he said. "It was set up almost two years ago. Which means it'll be something we can handle for you. Unfortunately, since our system is set up to run your payroll automatically on Monday nights, we have to do this manually and there is a fee associated with it."

"I'll pay it. As long as my employees get paid this week. Some of them would normally get paid today."

Lucas nodded. "I see that. The ones who bank with us usually have their direct deposit the day it's released from your account. The others likely have to wait a day or two for processing."

"How long will this take?"

"We are technically closed for the night, sir. It's not something I can do without getting permission from a manager."

"You're not a manager?"

He shook his head and actually looked sorry for the first time since I walked in. "I'm an assistant manager. But I can do this. Your staff is small, so it won't take me longer than two or three hours to manually process all of this. If you're willing to wait while I speak to my manager about it..."

"Of course. Thank you."

He walked out of the cubicle. I ran my hands over my head again and held my breath. I couldn't believe I did this. The first year I owned O'Kelley's, I almost lost it all. I was drowning in grief and not paying attention to the business. I transposed numbers one night when I was not paying close enough attention and fucked up my accounting for the month. When I thought I was doing well, I was barely hanging on, but my confidence got the better of me and I ordered extra. When my checks started to bounce and brewers stopped signing agreements with me, I had to pull back.

It still churns my gut to think about what I put my employees through back then. Some quit, some stayed but hated me, and some were loyal and never left, like Charlie. But the experience shook me. I told myself I'd never screw up like that again.

Sitting in the bank after hours and begging an assistant manager to work overtime to make sure my people got paid this week was not my finest moment.

Lucas came back a minute later with a smile and another person. She introduced herself as Jane and handed me paperwork to sign.

Jane went through the process with me, outlining what it was going to take and how long it would be. I would have signed away everything left in the account if it meant making sure my employees were okay.

"Your first employees should see a deposit pending tomorrow at the earliest. It might be Friday, though. This is the best we can do." Jane offered no sympathy or better option.

"Thank you. Both of you. I really appreciate your help."

Jane and Lucas nodded.

"Is there anything else we can do for you, Mr. Grant?" Lucas asked.

I shook my head and moved toward the exit where a guard stood, waiting for me to leave. "No. I'm good. Thank you very much."

I hurried toward the door and left them to their work, thanking God for Melody and getting everything set up as easily as possible for me.

When I made it back to O'Kelley's, Jonathan met my gaze with his own weary one. I didn't make him ask. I told him straight out what was going on and when he could expect his paycheck.

"Here's the thing... If you can't wait until Friday, I'll write you a check right now and you can pay me back when you get paid. I'm hoping it'll hit your account tomorrow, but I can't guarantee that. I will cover your check if you need me to."

"I can't ask you to do that," Jonathan said.

"You're not asking. I messed up, and I owe it to you, and everyone else, to make this right. Your checks will be in this week, but obviously, they're late. That's my fault, not yours, but you shouldn't need to pay for it."

Jonathan considered it for a minute, then said, "If it's not in there tomorrow, we'll talk. But hopefully it is."

I nodded. "Let me know. I will write you a check and not think twice about it. Thank you for letting me know it wasn't deposited. I probably wouldn't have caught this until next week."

Jonathan nodded, his face worried again.

I clapped him on the back and went to speak to the others, one by one.

Some of my employees were more concerned than others. A few took me up on the offer to get a personal check immediately, but most of them said they'd wait and see if it cleared the next day.

Joey was the last one I needed to talk to, and I knew I couldn't talk to him alone. I had to talk to Anna, too.

I waited until it was almost the end of Joey's shift, then I approached him. "Is your mom picking you up today?"

"Yeah. She should be here soon. Why?"

"There was an issue with the paychecks for this week. I need to talk to you about it, but I wanted to make sure she's here when I do."

Joey's face fell. He looked at the floor, his hair sliding over his forehead and hiding his face from me. He nodded. "Is it okay if I text her? She's been asking me to meet her outside since it's getting cold."

The words could have been true, but last winter, she always came in. It was an excuse she was telling Joey so she didn't have to admit she was avoiding me. One that was smart, like her. "Of course. When she gets here, we can go to my office."

Joey nodded and pulled out his phone. He walked away while texting.

I was not looking forward to the conversation.

I kept myself busy for the next twenty minutes, waiting for Anna to show up. When the door opened and she entered, I felt like all the air was shoved into my lungs, like they were too full to contain it all.

Then I caught her angry gaze, and it all fled like someone stuck a pin in my chest.

Before she could berate me in front of all of my

customers, I nodded toward the back hallway. She glanced around, still fuming, then followed me. I waved at Jonathan so he knew to cover everything and saw Anna motion for Joey to come with us.

I closed the door behind them and moved around the edge of my desk to sit. My ass had barely hit the seat when Anna started in on me.

"I don't know how you run a business like this. You can't even pay your employees on time? How can you expect my son, or anyone, to continue working here when you're not going to be reliable with your paychecks?" Her anger was palpable, like I could reach out and touch it right there in between us.

"You're right, and I apologize. It was an error that's entirely my own. I've already spoken to the bank and they are in the process of correcting it. But I know that doesn't help anyone's situation right now."

"You're damn right it doesn't," she muttered.

Joey shot her a look, but she ignored him.

"If you aren't going to pay him, why should he stay here?"

"I am going to pay him. This was not intentional. None of my employees were paid today. But, as I said, I've already spoken to the bank. Deposits will be processed tonight and paychecks should be pending in all accounts tomorrow or Friday, at the latest."

"What if that isn't good enough?" Anna barked. Her lower lip trembled. Her knuckles were white on the arm of the chair. Everything about her screamed fear.

"I've offered every single employee a personal check from me right now. Since Joey is a minor, I wanted you here for this conversation. The check could be made out to either of you. If you can't wait until the bank processes the deposits tomorrow or Friday, I'm happy to pay him right now, and when the deposit clears, you can pay me back."

"Are you kidding me?" she asked, her voice softer.

I shook my head. "Not in the least. I messed up. And I don't want any of my employees to end up paying late fees or having checks bounce or any other issues because of my error. Same for Joey. Some employees have taken my offer, some have said they'll wait, but each person was given the same offer because I value every single one of my employees. What happened was a rare occurrence and not something I foresee happening ever again."

Anna stared at me. Glared, really. She was trying to decide if I was being honest or if I was trying to trick her.

I stayed still and let her evaluate me. I didn't know her world, but a late check could mean the difference between having a roof and being homeless. It could mean the difference between buying groceries and starving. It could mean paying for heat or freezing.

I didn't want anyone to have to deal with those things, but especially not her. The desire to help her was strong. Stronger than it had been with my other employees. And seeing her there, acting strong but looking scared, I wanted to make all her worries go away.

"Did the person who made the error take you up on your offer?" she asked.

I drew a breath. "I made the error."

"You don't have a business manager?"

"No."

"You really should. This might not be a big deal to someone like you, but to most people, missing a paycheck is not easy."

"I understand. Again, I apologize. I am doing everything I can to make it less painful for everyone."

She chewed the inside of her lip and looked away. I missed looking into her eyes the second she took them away from me. I almost felt like I could tell what she was thinking when she looked at me, but now, I had no idea.

"We have to pay the electric bill today. It's the last day. Joey's check covers it for this week."

I nodded and flipped open the checkbook I already had on my desk. I logged into my computer so I knew how much Joey's pay would be and scribbled it on the check. I tore it off and handed it to Anna.

"I..."

"I am sorry for causing you stress. It was not intentional. I will make every effort to avoid this happening again in the future, but I respect your decision if you and Joey feel the best thing is for him not to return to work here."

"Mom," Joey pleaded.

"No," Anna said. "He can continue to work here. He enjoys the job, and he doesn't want to give it up. And this... It's above and beyond."

"It's the least I could do after the error I made," I admitted. I was not going to tell her I made the error because I was too worried about her. She didn't need to know that.

"Well, thank you. I really appreciate it."

"You're welcome. I'll see you tomorrow, Joey."

We all stood, and they nodded at me, then moved to the door. Anna glanced back, then let them out and disappeared.

I took a breath and closed my eyes. That went better than I expected. All except the part where I wanted to give them a check for triple the amount I owed Joey just so I could see Anna smile. That part was not good.

9

____

"How do you forget to do something like pay your staff?" James asked Thursday at guys' night. Besides being one of my closest friends and a local cop, he was kind of an ass. But he was the kind that made you laugh because he only acted that way with the people he was close to. He was also compassionate and understanding. He caught Joey stealing two years ago and instead of hauling him off to jail, James gave Joey a second chance and a year later, helped me hire him.

I rolled my eyes. "It wasn't on purpose."

"You're lucky no one quit," Nico said. As a fellow business owner, I knew he got it. Nico owned the cancer clinic in town and employed almost twenty people.

"I know. I really expected someone to. Anna threatened to have Joey quit, but she didn't force him to."

"She said she knows how much he likes working here. But she's always worried about money." Trent knew Anna better than the rest of us combined. Even though Finley said Anna didn't engage much, Trent had a way of pulling people out of their shell, whether they liked it or not.

"Why don't you have a business manager that handles all of that for you? When Melody was doing it, you said it made your life easier, but you never replaced her when she started her business." Ramsey hated it when his wife worked for me, but he got over it when he realized she only came to me because she thought she needed a job before he divorced her. Thankfully, they worked it out, and she created a business that made her happy, but he was right. My life was harder without her working at O'Kelley's.

"Hiring people isn't easy," I said.

"You hire people all the time," James interjected. "You have a new server every other week."

"Yeah, but that's different. They're not handling my entire business. They're bringing food and drinks to people. If I hire someone who ends up skimming money off the top, I'll never figure it out. Not until they disappear and I lose the bar." It was my worst fear. To lose everything I'd worked my ass off to create.

"Why would you think that would happen?" James asked.

"Because it happens all the time to people. When Melody marched in here and said she was going to work for me, I wasn't worried about her running off with my money because I know her. But hiring someone off the street to do all of this... I can't even imagine that."

They all looked at me like I was insane. They didn't get it. Maybe I was being overly cautious, but it took me twice as long to make sense of numbers as someone with a normal brain. I flipped them around constantly and still made mistakes after double and triple checking my work. My accountant reviewed my business transactions every quarter before I paid my taxes so I knew everything was done correctly. I didn't trust myself, but even less than that, I didn't trust a stranger who could take advantage of my dyslexia and steal from me.

"You could promote someone who already works for you," Nico suggested. "My business manager started out at as a receptionist. She was good at it and got promoted to business manager. When she came to me, she had experience that matched what I was looking for. If I'd had someone already in my office who could do the work, I would have pulled them up first, though."

I glanced out at the bar and my servers hurrying around. They smiled at customers and chatted with them. They made suggestions and upsold lots of food and drinks over the course of the night. But Nico was right. A few of them had the potential to do more. If they wanted.

"I might have to think about that," I admitted.

"Good. And while you are, you can tell us who you've met on the app so far," James said.

"How the fuck...? You know what, never mind."

James smirked, the shithead. "I knew you would meet someone. Who is it?"

I shrugged. "I don't know. The whole point is not to use names."

"Okay, well, how long have you been talking to her?"

"A little over a week. She messaged me one night when she'd clearly been drinking. She sent me the same thing six times, introducing herself. She thought it was going to different people."

James's brows shot up. "And you still talked to her?"

"Sure. We've all done dumb things when we were drinking. And the whole point of the app is to meet people. Why am I going to get upset that she's talking to people when I am, too?"

"Who else are you talking to?" Nico asked.

"No one as regularly. The one woman is funny and smart, but she's busy with kids and a job and life. The others all feel young to me. Some of them are pretty shallow, from what I can tell. I feel like a dirty old man."

The others chuckled. "Well, you are kind of old," James said.

"Fuck you. I'm not even a full year older than you are."

"Still older." James lifted his glass and finished his beer. He was smart enough not to ask for a second one.

"I'm going to ask Laura to marry me," Nico blurted.

"Yeah, we know," James said. "Congrats, man. Marriage is pretty damn great."

"How the hell do you know?" Nico asked, turning to glare at James.

"You've been with her for a year and a half. I'm kind of surprised you haven't already gotten married." James wasn't entirely wrong.

"Did she say something? Is she pissed?" Nico sounded worried.

"Not to me, but I doubt she'd say something to me."

"Has Trinity said Laura's mad?"

"Nico, don't stress," Trent said. "Laura worked for you for years before you got together, right?"

Nico nodded.

"And she has a lot of patience. And she loves you. Don't let anyone else make you feel bad for when you ask the woman you love to marry you."

Nico nodded thoughtfully. "You're right. It's no one's business."

"It's not. When I asked Finley, people thought I was crazy. We barely know each other, but I know everything I need to know about her. And I love her. The rest is easy."

Ramsey snorted. I had to admit, I did, too.

"What?" Trent barked, glaring at both of us.

Ramsey raised his brows at me, but I shook my head so he could speak instead.

"Marriage is tough. It's conflict and trust and joy and pain all rolled up together. Love isn't always enough. But it's the best place to start. I hope you and Finley stay together, and I hope you and Laura stay together. But if anything happens to your marriages and things start to fall apart, the only advice I can give you is to go back to right now. Think about how much you love them when things are good, easy. And find your way back together."

"What he said," I agreed.

"You never had any challenges in your marriage," James said to me.

"Sure I did. But we dealt with them. Hillary was low on conflict. She was always agreeable. I let too many things go when I knew it wasn't what she really wanted. I regret that now, but it's too late."

"Do you think your next marriage will be different?" Nico asked.

"I'm nowhere near thinking about marriage. I've only barely started being willing to talk to women."

"Yeah, and we all know how that went," James said with a laugh.

I flipped him off.

James snickered.

"Every relationship is different. And every relationship has its challenges. Nico, if you need anything, let me know. As the most recently married one here, I'm trying to be helpful." Trent rolled his eyes at James, Ramsey, and me.

"We're trying to be helpful," Ramsey said. "We're just trying to be real."

"That's not always helpful," Trent said.

"I think Hudson should tell us more about the woman he's talking to," James said, drawing everyone's attention back to me. "I want to see him all twisted up."

I groaned and walked away. The perks of owning the place.

I SPENT the weekend working and trading occasional messages with MyFriendsMadeMeDoThis. She was funny and self-deprecating, but in a way that made her relatable. A part of me wanted to meet her in person, but I wasn't quite ready for that yet.

Every shift through the weekend, I considered which employees might be able to shift to business manager. The job was one that would have to come with benefits and a salary, so it would be a bump in pay for whoever took the job. In my head, I made my list, and in person, I triple checked everything I was doing so I didn't risk messing anything else up.

By Monday, I was completely on board with hiring someone. When Finley came in with George for lunch, I decided to talk to her about it. Maybe she'd have some advice.

"Hold your Godson," she said, handing him over while she unloaded everything and parked the stroller he'd been in.

The baby looked up at me with big brown eyes. Something deep within me stirred. I tucked him against my body and smiled at him. He reached up for my beard and tugged on it. His gummy grin always made me feel like I did something right, even though I was sure it was just his way of saying he recognized me.

Finley and Trent welcomed me into their family like I was a part of it. It wasn't easy to get to know Trent, but we were making it work. Finley loved him in spite of the way he treated her at first, and George was the most perfect baby ever.

He made it hard to let go of the dream I'd always had of having my own kids.

"How are you?" Finley asked, finally sitting down. She didn't reach for George, just let me hold him.

"Good."

"Yeah?"

"Yeah, why? What do you think is going on?"

"Nothing. Anna told me about the paychecks last week. Sounds like she gave you some shit about it."

"I deserved it. I messed things up for everyone. People had every right to be mad."

"Yeah, but you fixed it. And you paid everyone out of pocket. Most employers wouldn't do that."

"It was the right thing to do," I grumbled. I didn't want her thinking I was going above and beyond. If I'd done everything right in the first place, I wouldn't have needed to fix it.

"You're an amazing boss, Hudson."

"With a messed up mind. I need to hire a business manager."

Finley shrugged. "Not a bad idea. Got anyone in mind?"

I looked around the bar. "Nico suggested promoting a server."

Finley followed my gaze. "Too bad Piper no longer works here and has her own business to run. But yeah, promoting someone isn't a bad idea. What if no one wants the job?"

I hadn't thought about that. Why wouldn't someone

want to make more money? Have benefits? "You really think that?"

"Yeah. It's possible someone will say yes, but it's also possible no one will. What are you going to do then?"

"Shit. I was trying to decide who to talk to first because I didn't want to piss anyone off."

"Maybe you should talk to them as a group. Tell them what you're looking for and ask people to speak to you if they're interested."

"How do I decide who to hire?"

Finley laughed. "You hire the best candidate."

George gurgled and tugged on my beard again. I looked down at him. Life seemed so much easier from his perspective. Eat, sleep, poop. It was a damn good life. He was loved and taken care of and never needed anything. He had amazing parents and a good home. Something too many kids grew up without.

"I'll start talking to people today. This is complicated."

"No, it isn't. You just don't like pissing people off. You're a softie. You just don't show it."

I rolled my eyes and handed back the baby. "Lunch?"

"Yes, please."

"Burger and fries?"

"Yes, please."

"Anything to drink?"

"Yes, please."

I chuckled. "Are you going to eat whatever I bring you?"

"Yes, please."

I laughed. Finley had a way of making me feel better. She eased all the tightness inside me. It was funny because I'd never been attracted to her, but damn, I wish I could have been.

In contrast, her employee was haunting my dreams and always wound me up tighter than a rubber band.

One day, she was going to make me snap.

WEDNESDAY AFTERNOON, I was in my office when someone knocked on the door. It was open, but when I looked up, I was surprised to see Anna there. And not looking like she was going to murder me.

"Hi," she said. "Can I come in?"

"Yeah, of course. What can I do for you?" Being civil felt awkward.

She walked in and took a seat across from me in a visitor's chair. She slid an envelope toward me. "I wanted to thank you."

"For what?"

She looked up, her gaze colliding with mine. There was vulnerability there, a look I didn't see from her often. "For paying Joey. I know I was...a bitch to you about it. And I am sorry for that."

"You don't need to apologize. I messed up the checks and paying was the right thing to do."

"Yeah, but—"

"Anna, it was my fault. I appreciate you paying me back. But all I did was correct an error I made."

She closed her mouth and nodded. Her hands were in her lap. She twisted them together, fiddling with the strap on her purse.

I waited. I wanted to ask what else she wanted to say, but I had to tread carefully with her. Having her there and not yelling at me was a nice change. Almost as nice as pressing her against my wall and kissing the hell out of her.

No, that wasn't true. Kissing the hell out of her was definitely better.

She finally looked up at me. The vulnerability was more obvious now. I adjusted my position, preparing for whatever she was going to say.

"Thank you for giving Joey this job. And for letting Matty stay here after school. I know you didn't have to do either, but I'm not sure how we would have gotten through the last year without your help."

Something inside me shifted at her words. Joey was a great employee and hiring him was a good business decision. And Matty was no problem at all. For her to be so appreciative told me just how many people in her life had been kind to her. And why she was always on edge with me. From the day I hired Joey, she was looking for something she could use to get him away from me, but she wasn't going to find anything. I think she was finally seeing it.

"They're amazing kids. And that's all because of you. I know their lives, and yours, haven't been easy, but neither of them have allowed that to make them bitter or angry. They are smart boys who work hard and smile often. You're an amazing mother."

To complete and utter shock, she burst into tears.

After a second of not knowing what to do, I got up and closed the office door. Then I grabbed tissues from the bathroom and offered them to her. She took the box, and I sat in the chair next to her.

"Thank you. I'm sorry. I shouldn't be sitting here crying."

"It's okay," I said, even as every inch of me said it wasn't. I hated when people cried. It pulled hard on me to fix whatever was causing that much emotion to bubble out of a person. And with Anna, that pull was even stronger than normal.

"It's not okay, but thank you. No one's ever said I'm a good mom."

"I didn't say that, Anna. I said you're amazing. You are. You don't see it because you're in the middle of it, but your sons are great people. You're the only one who had anything to do with that."

She sniffed and nodded. "Thank you."

"You're welcome."

She looked up at me. We were leaning toward each other and so close it wouldn't have taken much to kiss her again. Her eyes widened, then dropped to my lips. She licked hers, readying them.

Everything slowed down, like time was standing still so I could enjoy the moment. She leaned closer, her body stretching toward mine.

I reached for her, my hand going up to cup the side of her face. She nuzzled against it, just enough to let me know she was on board with whatever was happening.

Then she closed the last bit of distance between us.

Our lips touched, and she gasped. I froze, not knowing if that gasp was for more or to stop.

She grabbed the front of my shirt and tugged me closer, and it snapped something in me.

I hauled her out of her chair and into mine. Her thighs parted so she could settle on my lap. I was hard in an instant, thumping against her warm center as our lips parted and our tongues tangled together.

I groaned, or maybe she did. My hand went into her hair to twist her head where I wanted it to go. She sighed happily, sinking against me and knocking off my baseball hat to run her fingers over my shaved head.

My other hand went to her thigh, then slid to her hip, drawing her body closer. I couldn't remember the last time I felt so out of control. But I wasn't. I knew exactly what I was doing. I just needed it all to happen now.

She gasped again and sat back. She looked beyond me, then scrambled off my body.

My brain took a little longer to realize someone was at the door. Knocking.

"Hudson? Are you in there?"

Joey. Of all people.

"Oh, my God," Anna hissed. She wiped her lips and dragged her fingers through her hair. Her cheeks were flushed and her eyes shiny with pleasure.

I wanted to give her more of that.

"Hudson?"

"That was a mistake," Anna hissed.

"Don't you dare say that," I snarled.

She looked at me, her eyes wide with defiance and desire. She turned away, grabbing her purse and taking hurried steps toward the door. She opened it just as Joey was starting to walk away.

"Mom?"

"I was giving Hudson the money we owed him. We were talking."

Joey looked around her to where I was standing, arms crossed, in front of my desk. I prayed the kid couldn't see the erection I was sporting thanks to his mom.

"Um, hey. I was just going to let you know I was heading out."

I nodded. "Thanks."

He looked between us again and settled on his mom. "Are you ready to go?"

"Yes. I'm ready," she said. She glanced back at me, her gaze unreadable. Then she left.

Fucking hell. What was that?

10

—————

I did my best to push that kiss with Anna, and her insistence it was a mistake, out of my mind the rest of the week. Instead, I focused on O'Kelley's and finding a business manager.

Unfortunately, that was a lot harder than I expected it to be.

I spoke to Jonathan first. As a bartender, I'd worked most closely with him. He was intelligent and capable. And not even a little interested.

"Thanks, boss, but honestly, I love that I don't have to think about this place when I leave. Harry works odd hours just like I do, and we're buying a house, and changing my job just doesn't feel like the right move for us right now. Maybe when we have kids, but we're not there yet."

"I get it," I told him. Family was important. And having time to spend with the people you love was more important than a job, even one that paid better and had what most people would say were better hours. The hours definitely wouldn't be better for Jonathan.

"Are we okay?" he asked after the conversation.

I nodded. "Of course. I would never hold anything like that against you. Being there for your family and spending time with your husband is the best choice you can make. I didn't realize his hours were as crazy as ours."

Jonathan laughed. "Maybe not as crazy, but they're definitely not regular. He and I both like working afternoons and evenings and having our days off."

"If you were interested in the job, we could work out something like that," I said, feeling a little hopeful.

Jonathan shook his head. "I know we would try, but I'm not sure how. You talk to suppliers and receive orders early in the morning. If that was part of my job, and I would imagine it would be, it would mean being here day shift."

I sighed. He was right. I couldn't force him to fit into the job that wasn't quite suited for him. "I know. Thanks for at least considering it. Obviously, you gave it some thought."

"I did. And I'm sorry."

"No need for that. You've saved my ass many times behind the bar. I appreciate it."

Jonathan nodded and got back to work.

The next day, I spoke to Danielle, who had a similar answer. Then Charlie, Pat, Neve, and Rodney. None of them were interested in the hours or the responsibility.

Which meant I was stuck. Sure, I could keep going down my list, but the other servers, bartenders, and cooks I had were people who'd been with me for less time and not people I thought were ready for a job like that.

I was back to zero.

And Anna was avoiding me again.

I tried hard not to let that get to me, but when a solid week passed without seeing her even once, it was hard not to take it personally. Again.

But I was getting more regular messages from

MyFriendsMadeMeDoThis on Book Boyfriends Wanted. She was funny and sarcastic and made the days go by faster when we chatted.

MYFRIENDSMADEMEDOTHIS

Why do men always think they're right?

HEREBYFORCE

Because we are.

MYFRIENDSMADEMEDOTHIS

Really? That's your answer? I guess that is the answer. Men are cocky, overbearing jerks who have no sense of boundaries.

HEREBYFORCE

How do you really feel?

MYFRIENDSMADEMEDOTHIS

LOL! Sorry! No, not really.

HEREBYFORCE

Who made you feel that way?

MYFRIENDSMADEMEDOTHIS

Someone I have to deal with far too often.

HEREBYFORCE

Is he creating a problem for you?

I couldn't explain the protective instinct I had for this woman. I'd never met her and I didn't know much about her, but over the last few weeks, we'd developed a friendship of sorts. One that told me she was just as scared of getting hurt again as I was, but for different reasons. And she had kids to worry about.

MYFRIENDSMADEMEDOTHIS

No, he's just one of those people I can't figure out. Most of the time he makes me crazy, but then he'll do something out of character and I think he's a good person.

HEREBYFORCE

If you're not sure, you should keep your distance.

MYFRIENDSMADEMEDOTHIS

I know. And I am.

HEREBYFORCE

Good plan.

MYFRIENDSMADEMEDOTHIS

So, what drives you crazy about women? We're not easy to deal with.

I barked a laugh and thought about Anna. She definitely wasn't easy to deal with.

HEREBYFORCE

Hot and cold.

MYFRIENDSMADEMEDOTHIS

You mean changing her mind?

HEREBYFORCE

No. Never. But getting wrapped up in the moment, then getting pissed off. Or letting your guard down, then retreating. It can really mess with a person's mind.

MYFRIENDSMADEMEDOTHIS

I agree with that one. Completely. Be consistent. Be who you are. Don't change because you think it's what someone wants to see.

HEREBYFORCE

Exactly. It's hard to let people in, but it's better that way. I'm dyslexic, and when people find out, they think I'm stupid, but it just means my brain works differently. Sometimes it means I need more help with things or take longer to do something, but a lot of people aren't willing to hear that.

MYFRIENDSMADEMEDOTHIS

I get that. I've seen it with others. Thank you for telling me.

HEREBYFORCE

Thank you for not running.

It had been a long time since I admitted I struggled to anyone. It was easier with her since I didn't know her name and wasn't seeing her reaction live, but I definitely felt better being honest with her.

ANOTHER WEEK WENT by without seeing Anna. Joey would come to work and leave on time and acted like nothing weird was going on, but Anna was no longer walking into O'Kelley's, and she hadn't been to book club all month from what I could tell.

"What are you doing for thanksgiving?" Finley asked a few days before the holiday.

She hadn't been sending Anna over to pick up lunches either. She was coming herself or not ordering from me. It was starting to piss me off.

"Where's Anna?" I asked her.

"Working. Why? Did something happen?"

Finley watched me closely while I tried to figure out how

to answer the question. If I told her the truth, she'd never let go of the idea of us together. If I lied, she'd probably see right through me. Either way, just asking about Anna tipped my hand, and I was screwed.

"I haven't seen her in a few weeks. Joey's coming to work, and Matty comes after school, but Anna's been absent. Just wondering if she's okay."

Finley snorted. "I thought you hated her."

"I never said that."

"No, you just act like you can't wait for her to leave when she's here and you're short with her."

"Did she tell you that?"

"Hud, I've seen it. I adore you, but she thinks you're an ass."

"Fuck," I groaned. I was an ass to Anna. For a long time. Old habits and all that. But damn if there hadn't been a shift inside me. One that I wasn't sure I wanted to happen, but one that happened anyway.

I fucking missed sparring with her. And kissing her. And seeing her.

My dick was getting sore from the number of times I'd taken myself in hand thinking about Anna in the last few months. And I was running out of memories to draw from.

"You like her, don't you?" Finley asked. Her voice held more amazement than anything else. Her eyes sparkled with excitement. The edges of her lips curled up.

"I didn't say that."

"You didn't say you didn't, either. I thought you two hated each other."

I shook my head. "I'm pretty sure that's a one-sided thing."

"Wow. You really like her. What did you do that she won't step foot in here anymore?"

"Did she say that?"

"Not in so many words, but when I ask where she wants to order food from, she never wants to order from here. She says last time you didn't have our order and it cost her extra time to go to a second place."

"Maybe it's better if things stay that way. I'm not used to anything like this."

"Are you talking about Hillary?"

I wiped down the counter and leaned on the edge. "Yes and no. Things between us were easy. Once I got over my anger at needing a tutor and accepted that she was just trying to help, Hillary and I just clicked. We were insepa-rable after that. We didn't fight or disagree or have issues. Not very often. But with Anna? That's all we do."

"All relationships are different," Finley said. She sipped her water and shrugged. "I never thought I'd end up married to someone like Trent. There are times he intimi-dates me because of his money. I know that sounds bad, but I'm used to scraping by and working hard for everything. Living without worry is new, and it's an adjustment. I'm trying to balance Trent's life and mine to give George an upbringing that doesn't allow him to think he owns the world, even though he sort of does."

"George is not going to end up a spoiled ass like Trent was," I growled. Trent used to show up at O'Kelley's and act like he was a tourist. I knew who he was, and the night he and Finley hooked up, I didn't say anything to her. I regretted it once she found out she was pregnant and he refused to step up and help. He came around eventually, but it took him far longer than it should have.

"I know. And Trent's getting better."

I snorted. Finley knew the score on her husband.

"All I'm saying is your relationship with Hillary is

different from any other relationship you're going to have. And that's okay."

I nodded slowly. "I guess."

Finley was quiet for a minute. "So, thanksgiving? Do you have plans?"

"Working. You know how it is."

"I do. We were thinking of having lunch at the estate. Xavier's going to open the theater that night, so he won't be around late either. Want to join us?"

Alone for holidays had been my norm for years. It was time for family to be together, and since I didn't have any, it was time for me to be alone. My parents died years ago, and without siblings and no extended family around, I was used to spending the day alone and working at night and giving the locals a place to relax after a long day of family time.

But alone didn't sound as appealing as it usually did. Time with Fin, George, and Trent would be good.

"Yeah, I would. Thanks," I told her, smiling back when she beamed at me. "What can I bring?"

"Nothing. You know how Trent is. He'll have everything taken care of. Come at eleven?"

"I'll be there. Thanks, Fin."

"You're welcome. I'm glad you're going to come. It'll be a full house, but it'll be fun."

"Yes, it will be."

THE LITTLE SNAKED TRICKED ME. As soon as I walked in, I knew it. The first person I saw was Matty, and the second one was George, who was shoved into my arms by Finley with a whispered, "You can't get mad when there's a baby in your arms."

"You're cruel," I hissed at her, then hauled the baby over my shoulder and refused to give him back.

"I want you two to get along. And neither of you had anywhere to go for thanksgiving, so I invited both of you here. There's nothing wrong with that."

I scowled at her, even though I knew she was right. There was nothing I could say about Finley inviting whoever the hell she wanted to her own damn house for her own damn holiday celebration.

But I sure as hell wasn't going to be happy about it.

Finley walked away, knowing she needed to before I actually did say something. A few minutes later, Karissa joined me.

"You look good with a baby," she said with a smile and a wistful look in her eyes.

"You would, too."

She shook her head, still staring at George. "My chance for that has passed. I've made my peace with it."

"There are always kids who need to be loved, Rissa. You and Xavier should consider adopting or fostering."

She shrugged. "Maybe when McJenna is in college. Right now, she has to be the focus."

"I get that."

"But you should think about it."

I laughed. "Not with my lifestyle. I work too many nights and weekends to even think about bringing a kid into it. A baby. And not having a partner would make it impossible."

"Anna made it work," Karissa said without the slightest hint of irony.

"She's unique."

"You make that sound like it's a bad thing."

I shook my head. "Not even a little. Just saying not

everyone would be strong enough to do something like that."

"True." George babbled at her, drawing her attention for a minute. "Finley said you're looking at hiring a business manager."

"Yeah. I'm finally admitting I need to. Melody spoiled me."

"Melody worked for you years ago."

"Yeah, and I fought against replacing her ever since."

"You didn't want to hire her," Karissa said with a laugh.

"Nope, I didn't. But she made a good case for herself. And I've struggled since she quit. Don't tell anyone, but it's made me resent Ramsey just a little."

Karissa zipped her lips and twisted the key, then tossed it away and winked.

"Thanks. Happen to know anyone looking for a job?"

Karissa shook her head. "No, but Goldie might."

"Really?"

Karissa nodded. "Yeah. She has a lot of connections with all the work she's been doing. I think you should ask her."

"Okay, I will. Thanks."

"You're welcome. Now, your payment for that advice is to hand over our Godson."

"Not fair," I growled at her.

She reached for him, and he cooed happily at her. "See? He wants to come with me. You have to stop hiding in the corner and scowling at everyone who comes near you."

I scowled at her for good measure. She laughed and whisked the baby away, leaving me alone to fight for myself.

Trent nodded to me as I moved into the house. I headed toward him and accepted a bottle of water he offered.

"I figured if you're working tonight, water is your drink of choice," he said.

"It is. Thanks. You guys created quite the gathering."

He laughed. His gaze scanned the room and lit up when it landed on Finley talking to Anna on the far side of the room. "You know this was all her. My holidays usually involved a high priced dinner and an expensive drink. Xavier and McJenna would be the only people I celebrated with. It was nice, but I've never been someone who collects people like Finley does."

"She definitely does that," I agreed.

"She said if we've got all this space and all this money, we should spend it on the people we love. Her mom has been here all morning cooking, which made me feel endlessly guilty, but she insisted she wouldn't have it any other way."

"I can see that. You just wanted to write a check and have it all handled, didn't you?"

He nodded, sipping his drink and looking at the counter. "That would have been easier. No one would have to stress. The food would have been done. We could all enjoy the day."

"Look at Kim? Do you think she's not enjoying this?"

Trent looked at where I indicated and found his mother-in-law. Kim was surrounded by family, smiling proudly with George in her arms and a very pregnant Blake next to her in a chair. Kim was beaming from ear-to-ear and laughing at something Ian said.

Sure, she looked tired, but it was the kind of tired that was refreshing. The kind of tired I was after a long night at O'Kelley's where people had fun and no one fought. Kim wasn't worn out, she was overjoyed.

"She looks happy," Trent admitted.

"Yeah, she does. It might have been hard to make all of this work, but that doesn't mean she didn't enjoy it. Watch her face when everyone sits down to eat and praises her for how good it is."

"You sound like you have some experience with that."

I nodded. "I do. There are always times when it's better to do something yourself than to pay someone to do it. I've rarely had the money to write a check and move on, but when I have, it doesn't give me the same sense of satisfaction."

"Are you saying I'm missing out on life because I have money?" Trent asked.

"Sometimes, yeah. But I think Finley is good for you. She's going to help you see the joy you can get from getting a little dirty once in a while."

He smirked.

"Not like that." I chuckled with him.

"You're right," he said. "She is helping me see that. I only saw Kim as tired and working too hard, not as loving to provide for her family in this way. Thanks. No wonder Finley's so set on finding you a woman."

"Oh, shit. She is?"

He smirked again. "I guess you hadn't figured that one out, huh? Yeah, you're screwed, my friend."

"Fuck me."

Trent laughed. "Yep."

11

ANNA

My cheeks hurt from the effort it took to keep my smile firmly in place. I was not going to let anyone know how... I didn't even know what emotion I was, but it was not happy.

I should have known Finley would invite Hudson to her thanksgiving party. She said it was going to be family and a few friends, and insisted I come with the boys. I tried to say no, but we both knew I had no other plans and she was my boss. I couldn't say no to my boss without a good reason.

So, we went. My boys were excited to see the inside of MacKellar Estate. I was, too, but it held a lot less appeal for me than it did for my boys. I knew how quickly something could be ripped away from a person, and financial security was definitely one of those things.

Not that I thought it was going to happen to Finley. God, I really hoped it didn't because as much as I was not happy with her, I did like her. A lot. She deserved happiness.

"Mom, Trent said we can go play in his game room. Is that okay?" Matty asked.

I looked up at where Trent was waiting for the boys. He smiled at me, and I nodded.

"Yes, but behave," I told them as they rushed away, forgetting I even existed.

It was supposed to be a fun day. A day to be thankful. It was also the first traditional thanksgiving my boys had had in years. They likely didn't remember the one and only thanksgiving they both had with their father and his family. It was the year Matty was born, before Nick took off and never came back.

My parents were long gone by then. They never even met my boys. Holidays and family weren't important to them. They were truly awful people, and my boys were better without them around, but I felt bad that they only had me and not a huge group like George would grow up with.

"How are you doing, Anna?" Kim, Finley's mom, asked as she joined me on the end of the couch.

The living room was massive. The furniture was comfortable and likely cost more than my rent for an entire year. All thirty people Finley invited for lunch fit easily in the room without a thought of it being crowded.

"I'm good," I said, scooting over to give her space to sit. There was plenty, but she sat right next to me with her leg pressed against mine.

"That's so good to hear. You've been such a blessing for Finley this year. I know everyone will say George is what she's most thankful for, but I hope you know that we're all very thankful for you, too."

My throat tightened at her words. Not many people had ever said they were thankful for me, in any capacity. "Thank you."

She patted my hand as though she understood just how much her words meant. "I know you've given Finley a lot of advice about raising sons, and I know you've become so much more to her than an employee. She's leaned on you a lot, and my daughter has always been fiercely independent. You didn't know her before she was pregnant, but letting go of things the way she has and trusting you to take over the store were huge for her. You made her maternity leave possible."

I smiled. Finley told me the same thing, but she said it when she was paying me a bonus that she said was to show her appreciation. I used that money to pay off one of Nick's debts, and to get a little breathing room for myself and my sons. I never thought of that as more than a tool. It didn't dawn on me that I gave Finley something she needed.

"I'm sorry if I upset you," Kim said. "I just wanted you to know that I'm happy you're here, and I'm happy you're in my daughter's life."

"Thank you."

Kim patted my arm again, then left me to sit in my astonishment. The people around me faded away as the weight of Kim's words sank in.

I excused myself to absolutely no one and hurried to the ground floor half-bath. It was ridiculous that Kim thanking me should have such an impact on me, but it did. All the jobs I'd had, the people I'd worked for and with, the people who'd been a part of my life, none of them had ever said they appreciated me the way Kim said she did. The way she said Finley did. It was nicer to hear than I thought it would be. It wasn't empty or meaningless. Her words had weight to them. Weight that settled in my heart and made me feel like being there wasn't about Finley feeling bad for the poor woman she employed out of pity.

It was stupid, but it made me feel like she actually liked me.

I didn't like needing that validation, but I'd never had it

before. My high school friends were just like me and smoked and drank and acted stupid. My coworkers after high school were mostly the same people. Once I got pregnant, those friends lost interest in me since I couldn't smoke or drink anymore. And I never made any mom friends. I'd been on my own, alone in the world, for years. Until I inserted myself into Finley's conversation and took a chance on her hiring me.

And found something I told myself I didn't need.

When I finally got myself together, I washed my hands and patted my cheeks and told myself no one would notice I'd been crying. I turned the knob to open the door, finding it hard to turn.

Because someone was turning it from the other side.

"What the... Oh," I gasped.

Hudson.

I didn't want to talk to him at all, but I definitely didn't want to be cornered by him in the hallway away from everyone else, where I could lose my damn mind again and give in to the intoxicating scent of him.

"Hi," he said, stepping back. He plastered himself against the opposite wall, giving me plenty of space to get around him.

"Hi." I couldn't move. My feet were stuck to the floor, my eyes glued to the man in front of me.

"Were you... I mean, are you okay?"

I ducked my chin and let my hair fall in front of my eyes. I nodded.

His fingertip brushed my chin, lifting my gaze to his. He narrowed his eyes and studied me carefully, assessing for himself if I was okay.

Whatever he saw must have been enough because he

released his hold on me. He stepped closer. Close enough that I could smell his cologne.

"Hudson."

"What happened a few weeks ago was not a mistake, Anna. I need you to know that."

I sucked in a sharp breath, my breasts lifting with my inhale.

His gaze dropped to them. He licked his lips. He moved closer. "Tell me not to kiss you again, Anna."

I stared at him, the words inside my brain. I knew I needed to say it. He wouldn't do it if I told him not to. But there was a look in his eyes that I couldn't resist. A look that said he didn't want to resist.

No man had ever looked at me that way. Like he couldn't wait to get his hands on me. It sent chills down my spine that settled between my thighs and made my core tingle.

This man, who stole spaghetti and meatball cups and gave teenagers jobs and took care of pregnant women when they weren't his responsibility, he made me crazy. I didn't want to want him, but God, I did.

"Anna," he said again, his whisper harsh, pleading, begging.

"No."

"You said this was a mistake, Anna."

"And you said it wasn't," I taunted him.

"Fucking hell," he growled as he closed the gap between us.

He pressed me backward into the tiny half-bathroom. The door closed behind him, locking us in the too tight space. My back hit the wall opposite the door and his front pushed me tighter against the flat surface.

His lips still hadn't touched mine. His breath fanned

across my face, his eyes lit with desire and demands. I wasn't sure which made me shiver, but I did.

I wanted all of it.

"Anna," he growled.

"Hudson."

His name on my lips broke something inside him, and he finally sealed his mouth to mine. He pried my willing lips open and thrust his tongue deep into my mouth. His hands captured mine, linking our fingers together as he drew our hands up the wall and pinned them above my head.

It was a full body assault. The kind I'd only seen in movies. The kind that made you painfully aware of every inch of the other person while forgetting what parts belonged to you and which to them.

I shook as he kissed me, his tongue and lips pushing me to my limit and then over. It was insane to think I could orgasm from a kiss, but I was close. One brush against my clit and I'd be gone.

He thrust his thigh between my legs as if he knew how close I was. He held both my hands in one of his and dropped the other to my hip, guiding me over his leg.

"Anna," he groaned. His fingertips dug into my thick backside, and he thrust against me again.

Maybe I wasn't the only one losing my fucking mind.

"Oh, God," I whispered. My body shook, spiraling and falling before I had a chance to think about it.

He didn't say anything else, just held me as I fell apart. I'd never come that easily in my life. I wasn't sure whether to feel foolish or powerful when I caught the look in his eyes.

Lust.

"That was sexy as fuck," he growled.

My cheeks warmed, and he leaned down to kiss me

again. His tongue fucked my mouth. His hands roamed my body. Everything inside me begged for another orgasm.

He pulled back enough to meet my gaze. His was pained, anxious. "Don't say this was a mistake again. Please, Anna. Just don't."

I nodded, and he stepped back. He opened the door, peeking out, then glanced back at me with a smile and left.

I sank to the toilet and ran a hand through my hair. I couldn't stop the smile that lifted my lips, or the brightness in my eyes. I did my best to smooth my hair down. I splashed water on my cheeks. Then I left the bathroom.

"Come sit with me," Kim said when I joined the group in the living room again. "We're getting ready to eat."

Everyone took their seats, Hudson and I separated by five people. I told myself that wasn't intentional, but when he didn't look at me through the entire meal, I started to wonder if it was.

Before everyone finished, Kim stood and tapped her knife on the edge of her glass. "I am so grateful for every single person here. Even though this isn't my home, I wanted to take a moment to thank everyone for coming. Thank you to Finley and Trent for hosting all of us. And to all of you for being such amazing parts of our lives. I'd ask that everyone please say something you're grateful for today. Maybe it's cheesy, but it's always good to remember our blessings. Today, one of my blessings is Anna and the support she's given to Finley this year. Anna? Would you go next, please?"

My body was still wobbly, and my emotions were a little cloudy, but I smiled at her and lifted my glass. "I'm grateful to be here today. To let my boys experience a big family holiday and be welcomed so completely into your home and your lives. Thank you."

"Very sweet," Kim said. "Hudson? You're next."

His gaze collided with mine for half a second before he yanked it away. He smiled at Kim and said, "I'm grateful for the opportunities I've had in my life and the ones yet to come."

"That sounds like you have big things planned," Kim teased. "Blake? How about you?"

The rest of the table was called on one-by-one. It was nice to hear what others were grateful for. Everything from family to friends to a home. Matty was grateful Hudson let him play games. Joey was grateful for the chances he'd taken and the lessons he'd learned from going after what he wanted.

My brain stopped on that one. I was happy to hear him say that, but there was something in the way he said it that made me wonder what he was talking about.

I smiled my way through lunch and chatted with every-one. It was nice to not be alone for the holiday. The boys had fun, and I had to admit, I enjoyed myself, too.

When others started to leave, we made our way toward the door. We thanked Finley and Trent for having us, and I begged off staying later since I was working the early shift the next day. Finley wasn't doing any Black Friday sales, but she wanted the store open early for people who were out and shopping around town.

"Hey, Mom, can I go meet Tierney?" Joey asked about an hour after we'd been home.

Tierney was Joey's new girlfriend. I wasn't entirely sure when they started dating, but I'd been hearing her name more and more lately. Her parents seemed nice, and Tierney was always polite when I saw her. She played volleyball for the school and was a good student. She had a younger brother and an older sister, and they lived in a very nice house in the middle of town.

"What were you talking about when you said you're grateful for the chances you'd taken and the lessons you'd learned?"

"What?" he asked, looking up from his phone. He'd been staring at it, likely planning something even before he had permission. God, how I hated that I was the same at his age. But where I snuck out if my parents said no, Joey never had. To my knowledge.

"At lunch. You said you were going after what you want. What were you talking about?"

My first clue that I wasn't going to like his answer was when he avoided my gaze. He shoved his phone into his pocket and hooked his thumbs into his belt loops. He rocked back on his heels and drew a deep breath.

"Joey?"

My heart was in my throat. Was Tierney pregnant? Was Joey kicked out of school? Was he dropping out? My brain immediately ran to all the worst-case scenarios I could imagine. I knew he was safe, but only so far as I could see. Maybe—

"I registered for the SATs."

"You did what?" I barked.

It wasn't my finest moment. Not even a little. I hated that I jumped to angry when he said it, but I was. No, that wasn't true. I was scared. Terrified. I'd been working my ass off to pay off the debts his father left in my name, to the point that my savings account didn't even exist and my checking account never had a comma in it.

I told Joey college wasn't an option. That I didn't have the money and scholarships were hard to come by. It was a tough conversation because his teachers and guidance counselor were pushing hard for them to start thinking about college. He didn't have the grades for a scholarship thanks to his learning disabilities, and sports scholarships were even harder to get.

"I want to go to college, Mom. I know we can't afford it, but I'll take out loans, and I'll work and I'll do whatever I need to do."

"Is Tierney talking you into this?" I sneered. Again, not my finest moment. She'd mentioned her older sister was at Columbia.

"Tierney wants me to be happy, but no, she's not. You're the only one who isn't on board with me doing this. You didn't go to college, so you don't see it as an option."

"College debt is debilitating for most people. You end up owing tens of thousands of dollars, if you're lucky. Some people owe hundreds of thousands. Do you know how long that would take you to pay back? Even if you get a job that pays well, it's decades. That affects your ability to do other things in the future."

"Hudson did it."

"Hudson?" There was no more air. He was the one who started this. Who put the idea in Joey's head that college was possible.

"Yeah. He got a baseball scholarship and went to college until he got hurt. His wife was his tutor, and she had loans, but he said it wasn't that bad."

I paced the living room and fought back the tears in my eyes. I wanted to give my kids the world. I wanted them to have unlimited opportunities. I would have done anything for them.

But saddling them with debt that would follow them their entire lives, encouraging them to do something that would affect their futures, I couldn't go along with it.

I knew all the statistics. College grads earned more than people who never went to college, but no one talked about the college grads who sold their soul to pay off their debt. The ones who were paying more than my rent every single month for twenty years in order to pay back the money they borrowed.

It wasn't smart or reasonable. But Hudson made him think it was.

"Stay here with your brother," I said, not looking at my son.

"But I was going to meet Tierney."

"No. I'll be back in an hour. We can talk then."

Joey sighed, but he nodded.

I had a bar owner's ass to kick.

12

———

I was fuming. There had to be steam coming out of my ears. My face was flushed and my body burned. I couldn't believe Hudson convinced my son college was an option. I was barely hanging on, and even if he could get loans, saddling him with the kind of debt I'd been trying to pay off for years was not how I intended to have my son start adulthood.

Fucking Hudson.

By the time I got to O'Kelley's, I'd calmed down a tiny bit. A parking spot was open right up front, which made me smile at my good fortune, and I let myself into the packed bar.

What the hell?

I was more than a little surprised how busy it was for thanksgiving night, but I quickly brushed that aside and went in search of the man I was there to see.

I stomped toward the bar, my gaze catching on Hudson. My body flushed for an entirely different reason, but I couldn't let my stupid hormones and teenage desires get the better of me. Not when my son's future was on the line.

He looked up and saw me before I made it to the bar. His lips started to turn up into a smile, then he caught my expression and frowned. He nodded toward the hallway. Smart man. He didn't want this to be a public conversation.

He made it to the office before I did and was waiting just inside the door. He closed it behind me and crossed his arms, blocking my one and only escape like he thought I was going to run out without telling him what was going on after driving all the fucking way across town to yell at him.

God, I was so mad!

He stood there, watching me and not speaking. I wanted him to ask what was wrong, but he didn't. He just stood there.

"Why did you tell Joey to register for the SATs?" I finally blurted.

"What?" he asked.

I spun on him. He'd dropped his arms to his sides. His head was tilted. His gaze was far off, like he couldn't remember talking to my son about his future.

"Joey said you encouraged him to register for the SATs. Why did you do that?"

Hudson shook his head like he was coming out of a fog. His brows tugged together. He focused on me. "That's what you're so angry about? Why is that an issue?"

"Are you fucking kidding me?"

The lightness in him fled. His arms crossed again. His muscles drew tight. "In order to get into college, he needs that test. Every school requires it. Unless he's planning to go somewhere that needs the ACT, but usually it's—"

"He's not going to college," I snapped.

"Wh—" He stopped the question before it was out there.

I couldn't look at him. I knew how people felt about college. It was a requirement to get most jobs. Especially good ones. It was what most people did. There were ways to pay for it. But not great ones.

"He's been talking all year about college. I assumed—"

"Like you assumed he had my permission to work here last year?" I spat.

It was a low blow, one I shouldn't have tossed out, but I was angry and scared and this man was the one creating all the turmoil in my world at the moment.

He descended on me, closing the distance between us before I had a chance to realize he was even moving. "You agreed to let him work here after that. I had no way of knowing, and I thought we put that behind us."

I mustered up all my anger and defense and glared up at him. I hated that being so close to him made all my good parts shiver. I wanted to not find him the least bit attractive. I wanted to be able to resist the pull I felt when I was so close to him.

"Yeah, well, that was before you decided to interfere in our lives. Again."

"What's so wrong with him going to college?" Hudson asked. His voice was harsh, confused but also not backing down. He thought he was right.

"How in the hell is he going to pay for it? I sure can't. And student loans are creating a crisis in this country. He's going to carry loans the rest of his life, and I'm not going to put that on him."

"Shouldn't that be his choice?"

I scoffed. "He's a teenage boy. Do you really think he makes smart decisions right now?"

"He's not a typical teenage boy. He has a job, and he works hard in school. He takes care of his brother. He wants this. Why are you fighting it so hard?"

"Because not all of us can drop a few hundred on a video

game thingy without a second thought! I can't. My kids can't. I'm barely scraping by, and I live in a hellhole that shouldn't be legal for people to live in. But debt has nearly destroyed me. I can't get out of there because I can't afford anything better. And I'm not going to allow my kids to suffer the way I have."

"Did you go to college?"

"What does that matter?"

"Did you?"

"No." I crossed my arms and straightened my spine. "And I've done just fine without a college degree."

"I agree," he said. "But there are a lot of opportunities for people in college. Especially someone like Joey, who wants to be an engineer."

"He what?" I gasped. He never told me that. He didn't tell me anything.

"Didn't he talk to you about this?"

"No," I snapped. "But clearly he talked to you. So, my kid is making plans for his future without letting me know, but he's involving you. Is that supposed to make me feel better?"

Hudson scowled. "You're a real piece of work, you know that? Why can't you just be okay with him making choices for himself?"

"And why can't you stay the hell away from my family?"

We were both breathing heavy. Our chests rose and fell together. Our breath mingled. Our bodies were tense and tight.

And then we snapped.

I don't know which of us moved first, but the next thing I knew, he was backing me against the door and pressing his body to mine. His lips were on mine, his tongue prying my mouth open.

I scratched my nails down his back, earning a hiss. He

withdrew from our kiss and dragged his teeth across my collarbone before clamping down on my earlobe.

I growled at him.

He hitched my leg up and settled himself between my thighs. He was hard, and I was wet, and fuck me, I knew where this was going.

A whisper in the back of my mind said I needed to stop, but all the adrenaline in me was pumping in time with my desire and I knew I'd have better luck stopping a runaway train, because that was exactly how I felt.

His beard scraped down my throat as his fingers pulled my shirt up. His warm palm burned my skin. Branding me. Marking me. Claiming me.

I pushed him back and yanked my shirt off. His gaze dropped to my nipples, tight against my cotton bra. The cheap kind from a big box store. It wasn't fancy or lacy or pretty. It was simple and white, because that was cheap.

But with his gaze on me, it felt like lingerie.

His breath pushed out of his nose like a bull ready to charge. He reached back and tugged his shirt off, then he stalked toward me like a man on a mission.

I got wetter just knowing I was that mission.

He lifted my thigh again and thrust against me. My body tightened at the movement, readying itself for him.

He did it again, and again. He stared at my breasts the whole time, his gaze locked on the fleshy mounds and the way they bounced between us. Then he dropped my leg and cupped my breasts and pinched my nipples.

I cried out, my head slamming against the door. He shoved the cotton aside and replaced one hand with his mouth. I hated myself for how easily he made me come apart. First in the bathroom at Finley's, and now in his office. He hadn't gotten into my pants either time, but I came like he'd been buried inside me.

"Fuck," he growled, licking my nipple and nibbling his way to the other side. "Again."

He licked and sucked my other nipple until my body went flying a second time. I was pissed. I didn't want him to have that kind of control over me. To be the only one who was weak with desire.

I pushed him away and spun us, pressing his back to the door. I dropped to my knees and unbuttoned his jeans. He groaned, helping me shove his jeans and boxer briefs down his legs, exposing his thick, hard cock.

It had been a long time since I was on my knees in front of a man. I couldn't even remember the last time. But I knew I wasn't very good at giving blow jobs. Nick told me time and again that I needed work and encouraged me to practice, but he always said I wasn't very good. After he came, of course.

"Anna," Hudson said softly.

I didn't want him to be nice to me. Or to pity me. I didn't want him to see the uncertainty in my gaze or know I wanted to please him. I just wanted to make him lose control.

I leaned forward and wrapped my lips around his cock. He thrust deeper into my mouth, then immediately withdrew.

"Fuck," he hissed.

I closed my eyes and focused on the way he felt. His thighs clenched tight beneath my fingertips. His cock pulsed between my lips. His fingers went into my hair, tightening when I withdrew and encouraging me deeper when I took him in my mouth.

The longer I sucked him without instruction, the bolder

I grew. I cupped his balls. I dragged my nails down his thighs. I sucked harder.

His panting grew desperate. His pumping sped up. The hold he had on my hair tightened. I prepared myself for him to spill down my throat. I didn't want to choke on him, but it was possible. I relaxed my throat and breathed through my nose.

Then he grunted and yanked me back.

He squeezed the edge of his cock and growled. "On the couch. Now."

"What?" I asked, still dazed from being pulled off him.

"I need to be inside you when I come."

I stared at him, wondering if I heard him correctly.

"Anna," he growled.

My body responded to that. Fucking asshole. But I did what he said.

He pulled the rest of my clothes off, swearing when my boots kept my pants from coming off easily. He took a breath and untied them, tossing them over his shoulder when they finally came free.

Then he disappeared into the bathroom, back a minute later with a condom and a dangerous look in his eyes.

Fucking hell, the man was hot.

Come leaked from me, pooling between my legs. I couldn't remember the last time I was so wet. Maybe never. And all he'd done was play with my nipples.

He looked at me, and I resisted the urge to cover my body. Fuck him. If he didn't like my curves, I didn't care. I wasn't there because I wanted a relationship with him. Or because we were meant to be. I was there because I was mad at him. And because I didn't like him. And because...

"You're so fucking beautiful," he whispered.

My body tingled at his words. I didn't want them to mean so much, but they did.

He moved between my legs and positioned himself at my entrance. He caught my gaze and held it. His hands pressed my thighs wide. He watched me as he worked his way inside my body.

I couldn't look away from him, feeling like I was trapped inside his gaze. Emotion welled up in my throat. I didn't want to feel anything. It was sex. Two people who couldn't do anything except fight and fuck. And we were finally doing the second one.

When he notched fully inside me, we both groaned. Hudson closed his eyes for a minute, and I took the time to stare at him. He looked different without a hat on, but the shaved head and full beard made him that much more of a badass. His lips were full and plump and perfect for kissing. His body was strong from lifting liquor boxes and chairs and kicking ass when he needed to. There was a thick coating of hair on his chest and down his abs. I reached up to touch it, loving the softness of it against my palm.

His eyes opened, and he looked down at where we were joined. His hands moved there, spreading me wider. His thumbs tugged my flesh apart as he started to move, exposing my clit.

He took turns stroking my clit with each thumb. Gentle strokes at first, just enough to light sparks inside me. As his hips thrust harder, his thumbs stroked faster, and I couldn't stop the racing train of orgasms barreling down on me.

"Fuck," I groaned.

"Yes."

I gritted my teeth and stopped fighting it. He felt too good. Too right. Too everything. Buried deep inside me, I'd never felt better during sex. Nick wasn't big on making sure I came when he did. He wasn't big, period. But Hudson filled me up and stretched me out and rubbed against all the parts inside me that needed a good rubbing. My clit pulsed and throbbed. Deep inside me twitched and clenched.

"Please. Yes. Oh, yes!" I grunted, vaguely aware of the fact that we were in a public place and anyone outside the door could hear us.

Hudson grunted and fucked me harder. His hips took everything I had, and his thumbs grabbed hold of the rest. My body hung on to the last thread of reality, then snapped as I came.

I lost myself in the orgasm. My body shook, bucking and thrusting and demanding as my orgasm took over. I was sure I screamed, but I couldn't care. Hudson kept pounding into me, my orgasm triggering his. He roared and slammed home, stilling deep inside, where I could feel him pulsing and releasing.

After a second, he collapsed onto me. His hands were trapped between us, our bodies wet and sticky.

My brain tried to tell me I made a mistake, but I was too blissful to care. I'd never had sex like that in my life. I wasn't going to think about who it was with or how bad of an idea it was just yet. Those thoughts would come, but for a minute, I needed to enjoy the weight of a man on top of me and the pure joy of an orgasm that rung me out and made me want to cry.

It could have been hours or only seconds, but way too soon, Hudson rolled off me. He went straight to the bathroom. He left the door cracked. That was intimate. A kind of intimate that went beyond sex and reminded me this was a bad idea.

All of a sudden, I couldn't get out of there fast enough.

I grabbed my jeans and panties, yanking them on. My

thighs were wet, but I needed to go. I didn't have time to use the bathroom or clean up. I just had to go.

I pulled on my bra and was looking for my shirt when I heard him behind me.

"It's by the chair," he said. No emotion.

"Thanks," I whispered. I grabbed my shirt, then tugged it over my head and yanked my boots on. I didn't bother tying them up before I shoved my arms into my coat and draped my purse over my shoulder.

"You're leaving?"

"Yeah. I only came here to tell you..." I stopped. It didn't seem as important anymore.

"To stay out of Joey's future," Hudson finished for me. His voice was flat.

I nodded. I could see him out of the corner of my eye, but I couldn't look at him. He made me lose my damn mind. All the time. I never yelled at people. Until him. I never fucked men in offices. Until him. I never thought about a better future. Until him.

I couldn't afford any of it. I needed to stay away from Hudson Grant. He was too dangerous for me to be around because he made me want things I'd never have.

"Happy thanksgiving," he said quietly.

I looked up at him. Big mistake. He was still naked. Beautiful. Tempting.

But it was the look in his eyes that got to me. The one that said he didn't want me to go. The one that said he wasn't going to ask me to stay. The one that I desperately wanted to answer.

I nodded once, then left his office. And didn't look back.

13

Really good sex was supposed to alleviate tension. It was supposed to make you feel like you could do anything. I was supposed to... not be with my son's boss.

I couldn't face him. Ever. If I could, I would just freaking move. But I had two boys in school, debts to pay, and a job that I actually enjoyed.

Hudson Grant wasn't going to ruin my life. He wasn't in my life. And he wasn't ever going to be.

I hid out the rest of thanksgiving weekend. I worked, and I spent time with my kids and I tried to figure out how I was going to afford to buy them things for Christmas.

Joey and I had a tentative truce, but it was very tentative. He didn't say anything else about college or SATs or anything. He went to school, went to work, and helped out at home.

Matty could sense things weren't normal and asked me why I was mad at Joey one night at dinner.

"I'm not mad at him," I assured both boys.

"It sure seems like it." Matty was the one who was never

afraid to speak his mind. He got that from his father. Thankfully, he didn't get much else from Nick.

I didn't know how to answer Matty, but Joey did.

"I told Mom I want to go to college, but college is expensive and Mom doesn't want me to end up broke when I'm older."

"Like us?" Matty asked.

"Pretty much, yeah," Joey said. "We all work together to make our family the best we can be, but Dad fucked us—"

"Joey!" I shouted.

"What?" he glared at me, daring me to contradict him. "It's true. I know it's true. Dad didn't want us. Hell, you probably didn't either, but you're not like him."

"Never say that," I told my son. Tears filled my eyes. "Never say that. I love you both more than anything in the world. You weren't a part of my plan when I got pregnant with either of you, but that doesn't mean I'd change a thing about you. You two have saved me more times than you'll ever know. I love you."

"I love you," they said together.

"As for your father, he..." I couldn't come up with words to excuse what he did. Or explain it.

"Mom," Joey said softly.

I looked up at him and saw a boy who was closer to a man than he was to a boy.

"Dad was always a jerk. When he was here, he was mean to you and he ignored us. I know Matty doesn't remember him, but I do. He wasn't abusive, but he wasn't a father. He never cared about any of us, and we're better off without him."

I nodded, unable to squeeze any words past the lump in my throat.

"I know you're worried I'll end up in debt like you are. I

know you're only in debt because of Dad. It isn't fair. But debt isn't all bad."

"It can be life-changing."

"So can college," Joey countered.

I sucked in a breath. That one stung. Not because he was wrong, but because he saw the world so differently than I did.

"I know you're mad at Hudson and think he's to blame for this, but it's not his fault. I asked him about college because I knew you wouldn't want to hear it."

"And what did he tell you?"

"That there are scholarships available and student loans and that if I'm smart and pick a school that's affordable, it can be reasonable to pay for. He said his wife worked through college tutoring other kids and some other people he knew worked for their colleges doing other things. They have programs to help."

"It's still expensive," I said.

Joey nodded, his hair sliding down his face. He brushed it back and met my gaze with an even brown one that matched mine. "I can't become an engineer without a degree. That's what I want to do, Mom. I love math and science, and it's not easy for me, but I want to do it. I really think I can do it."

Fuck. There it was. The mom guilt. Having a kid who struggled in school meant having a kid who always doubted how damn smart he was. If he had any idea, he wouldn't look at me with that self-doubt or that fear that I was protecting him from something bigger. Something worse.

I wasn't. My reluctance to talk about college stemmed from my fears about debt and money and never having enough. I didn't want to put it on my boys, but it was our reality, and Joey was painfully aware of it. It had been two years since he was caught stealing a purse to try to get money to buy food for Matty. Two years since how bad our situation was slapped me in the face and I knew I had to make changes. I worked harder to spend smart, and Ramsey managed to stop the bleeding as far as Nick being able to add more debt in my name, but Joey was the one who had to open my eyes to how bad things were.

And now he thought I was saying I didn't want him to go to college because he wasn't smart enough.

"Joey, you listen to me," I said firmly. Tears rolled down my cheeks, but I ignored them. "You can do anything. Anything. You are one of the hardest working and smartest people I know. I hate that I ever made you think you couldn't go to college and dominate. You can. You are an amazing young man, and I couldn't be more proud to be your mother."

"I'm not that smart, Mom. I know that."

I shook my head. "Oh, sweetie, you have no idea. Being smart has nothing to do with being normal. Your brain works in its own way. It's not the way mine works or Matty's works, but that doesn't mean it's wrong. We are all different. But you are smart and capable. Much smarter than me. I'm sorry for making you feel like college was out of reach because you aren't smart enough. That never crossed my mind."

"Are you sure?"

I cupped his cheeks and lifted his head until his gaze met mine. "Absolutely. I wanted to go to college, but it wasn't an option for me. Your dad never considered it, and I told myself that was good enough. I told myself that a lot with him."

"He was never good enough for you, Mom."

I smiled. "He was good enough to give me the two greatest parts of my life."

"Well, one. You got the practice kid out of the way, then made perfection," Matty said.

I snorted and shook my head.

Joey scowled at his brother. "I think Mom was just pushing her luck, trying to get perfect twice. It failed. The original is always better."

"Why would you try for perfection twice? If something is perfect, you don't have to duplicate it or improve it. They knew you were a dud."

"Matty!" I shouted.

He chuckled. Joey jumped out of his chair and wrapped Matty in a headlock. The two of them fell to the floor and wrestled.

I didn't need any other man in my life. I had the two best ones in town right there in my living room.

As it always did, December flew by. One minute I was sleeping with Hudson in his office, and the next the boys were almost done with school and going to be home for winter break in a few days.

And I had zero Christmas shopping done.

Christmas was always lean for us. When the boys were little, they got things like food and diapers so they had something to open, even though it wasn't anything fun. I always tried to buy them something fun, but as they grew up, it got harder and harder to find things they liked that were in my budget.

The Friday before Christmas, the last day of school before break, I was off work so I decided to cruise through the local shops and find something for the boys. I was walking down an aisle of Cove Consignments when Goldie turned the corner.

"Hey," she said, looking just as surprised as I was.

"Hi. How are you?"

"Good. Crazy. Are you shopping for your boys?"

I nodded. "Nothing like waiting until the last minute."

She laughed. "I'm with you. I think they get harder to shop for as they get older. Paul only wants to play video games and talk to his friends."

"Joey's the same."

Goldie laughed again. "I'm glad I'm not the only one. I've missed you at book club."

My stomach twisted. I kind of felt guilty for not going back, but I also felt awkward hanging out with Finley and her friends. It was sweet of her to invite me, but like everything else she included me in, I knew it was just because she was so nice.

"I don't know any of them very well," Goldie confessed. "Laura pushed me to come at first. She works with my little sister. Ally and I are not close at all. We have the same dad, but she's nine years younger than me. Laura and I clicked, but everyone else I'm still trying to get to know. Slowly. And I'm spewing all of this all over you like a crazy person who has no social skills."

I laughed with her and shook my head. "I am always that way. The curse of being the oldest one in the room."

"Right? Oh, my God, so true. I always feel like I'm so old when I'm with all of them. But then I look at their healthy relationships and balanced lives and I know I could take a few notes on how to do better in this decade."

I snorted. "I haven't had a good decade in the last few, so I'm all for advice."

Goldie chuckled. "Okay, so, I'm going to be the weird one with no social skills again and ask if we can shop together. I'm guessing you're off today?"

"I am. And that would be fun."

"Phew. I was worried I was going to need to slink away and pretend I wasn't horribly embarrassed by getting brushed off."

I shook my head. "Not a chance. I could use a friend."

"Me, too."

We smiled and continued shopping. When one of us found something, we showed the other. We were laughing and having fun, and I felt like myself for the first time in far too long.

"What are you guys doing over break?" Goldie asked as we moved from one store to another, coats pulled tight and noses buried in our scarves.

"I'm working. I think Joey is, too. We don't do much."

"Does that mean you're in town? Because you and I should get together. If you think the boys will get along, I'm good with that, too, but we should hang out. Dinner or a drink or something."

"I'm not sure," I said, hating that I was going to turn her down because of money.

"Paul goes to his dad's for some of break. I'll have my house to myself. How about you come over and we can have dinner? Save me from my loneliness?"

The pleading look on her face was enough to make me think she was being honest and really just wanted to spend time together. We were having fun. And I could go out one night. It would be my Christmas present to myself.

"Okay, sounds good."

"Oh, yay. I was so worried you thought I was a crazy person."

"Well, sort of, but in the best way."

Goldie laughed. "I will definitely take that."

We spent the rest of the afternoon shopping and I finally found a few small things I thought the boys would enjoy. When we parted ways, I was smiling and happy. It was going to be a good break.

CHRISTMAS DAWNED four days later with very little fanfare in our tiny apartment. I got up early and made pancakes for the boys, a tradition I started when they were in elementary school. I made my coffee and started our movie marathon. We added and removed movies over the years that we liked, but I always started with sappy romantic movies that gave me hope that maybe one day I'd choose a man who didn't make me want to cry and wish we'd never met.

Hudson popped into my mind, but I pushed that thought away just as soon as it appeared. Hudson was not ever going to be mine.

The boys came out of their room together. Both were wearing sweats and tees with bare feet and bed head. They walked right over to me and curled up on the couch next to me, hugging either side of me.

"Merry Christmas," they both said.

"Merry Christmas. I love you boys."

"Love you, Mom," they said.

We sat there for a while, both of them wrapped around me while the sappy movie played on the screen that was barely big enough to see from across the room. When the movie ended, they shifted, then crawled off the couch and went to the kitchen.

Their muffled voices while they got breakfast made me

wonder what they were talking about. Usually it was bickering that made me yell, but they were quiet and not fighting, which was suspicious.

They came back to the couch and curled their feet under them as they sat and watched the movie. By the time that one was over, we were laughing and talking about our favorite Christmas memories.

"I remember when we got those little green men the one year. I loved those," Joey said.

"I was so mad when you wouldn't let me play with them," Matty admitted.

"Yeah, I haven't always been the best brother."

Matty shrugged.

"Sorry. I'm trying to get better. We only have each other. Right, Mom?"

I nodded. My boys were good kids. Hudson was right. I'd done a pretty good job.

"I wish I could give you guys more presents, but I hope you like what you got," I told them when we finally moved toward the pathetic tabletop tree I found in the garbage one year. The lights didn't work when we got it, and you couldn't fit more than a gift or two around it, but it was more than we had when we rescued it from the trash.

"You didn't have to get us anything," Joey said.

I ruffled his hair and smiled. "Of course I did."

He opened his gift first and gasped when he saw the SAT Study Guide. I wasn't sure he would actually like it, but the look in his eyes said he knew it wasn't just about the book. It was about me accepting his dream and supporting him in whatever he wanted to do.

"Thank you, Mom. I never thought I'd be excited about a test, but thank you."

I laughed with him. He flipped the book open and

scanned a few pages. He scowled at it, then nodded and closed the book.

"This is going to help a lot. Thank you."

"You're welcome."

Matty opened his next. His eyes went wide when he realized it was a game for the device Hudson kept in his desk drawer. "Whoa, really? This is awesome, Mom. Thanks!"

"You're welcome. I wish I could be home more so you could be here, but as long as you're at O'Kelley's and Hudson lets you play the games, I figured it would be good for you to have your own."

"Hudson doesn't care. He doesn't use it. He just got it for me." Joey elbowed Matty, and he cleared his throat. "I mean, yeah, you're right. Thanks, Mom."

I smiled at him and shook my head.

They went through the few things I put in their stockings, then they told me to stay on the couch and that they'd be right back.

Whispers in their bedroom worried me. I wasn't sure what to expect. When they came back out, they were smiling widely and holding something behind their backs.

"What did you two do?" I asked.

"It's Christmas. We got you a present," Joey said.

They stepped apart and brought forward a purple Christmas tree. I laughed. It was adorable. "Where in the world did you find that? It's beautiful."

"Hudson helped us. I asked him if he knew where we could get one like this. I saw you looking at it one day at that store you like to walk through by Cove Bakery," Joey said.

I walked forward and touched the purple pine needles. It sparkled, just like the tree in the window of Island Designs. Maybe it was tacky, but I thought it was gorgeous.

"It even lights up, Mom," Matty said proudly. "We made sure."

"Thank you, boys, but you didn't have to do this. Where did you get the money?"

"Hudson gave everyone bonuses. He said it's extra money to say thank you for all the hard work we've done this year. I used a little bit to buy you this tree because we knew it would make you happy. The rest you can use to pay off more debt."

"You didn't have to spend your money on me," I said.

Joey laughed. "Yeah, Mom, I did. Because I love you. We both do. We'd do anything for each other because that's what family does."

I nodded and hugged my boys. "Yes, it is. And I have the best family around."

"Yep, you do," Matty said.

I laughed. And kissed their cheeks. Then we all went back to the couch and watched another movie while I watched my beautiful purple sparkly tree.

It was a perfect day.

14

———

I SMILED AT THE MESSAGE. I COULDN'T REMEMBER THE LAST time I had so much hope for my future. Between my new friendship with Goldie and dipping my toe back into a world that involved the opposite sex, I was feeling good.

MYFRIENDSMADEMEDOTHIS

> Work is how we pay the bills. Do you enjoy your job?

I was starting to like him. After almost two months of talking online, we'd definitely built a friendship. Most men would have wanted sex by this point, but this guy hadn't even asked if we could meet. It was like he understood how hard it was to start something new.

HEREBYFORCE

> I love my job. And the people I work with. The hours aren't always great, but I really can't complain. How about you?

MYFRIENDSMADEMEDOTHIS

> My hours are good, and I enjoy what I do. I'm not sure how long it'll last, though.

I hadn't told anyone else that truth. Finley said she wasn't planning to let me go, but I understood how business worked. If she didn't make money, she had to cut costs. And winters in MacKellar Cove were tough. She reduced store hours since there wasn't as much foot traffic, which reduced my income, but even the hours we were open felt too much at times.

HEREBYFORCE

> What makes you say that?

MYFRIENDSMADEMEDOTHIS

> You know how it is around here. It's quiet. I'm not sure my boss will be able to afford to pay for me year round after this year.

HEREBYFORCE

> Hopefully that doesn't happen.

MYFRIENDSMADEMEDOTHIS

I agree.

HEREBYFORCE

Do you think we know each other?

A tease tickled the back of my neck. I'd asked myself that question many times. When I walked down the street, I wondered if the men I passed could be HereByForce. I found myself smiling at random people, just in case one of them was him.

But in all our conversations, I hadn't figured out who he was. Which meant if we did know each other, we didn't know each other well.

MYFRIENDSMADEMEDOTHIS

I don't know. I don't have any guesses as to who you are. Do you think you know who I am?

HEREBYFORCE

No. And I'm afraid to ask. What if you already hate me?

MYFRIENDSMADEMEDOTHIS

If I already hate you, maybe this will change my mind. What if you hate me?

HEREBYFORCE

I can't think of any woman I hate.

MYFRIENDSMADEMEDOTHIS

Hopefully that means we're good.

HEREBYFORCE

Does that mean you want to meet?

All the air whooshed out of me. I knew it would happen. Eventually, one of us had to say it. It had been weeks of regular chats. I was curious. And it would be nice to have someone other than Hudson to think about.

I'd only seen Hudson in passing over the last few weeks. I stayed out of O'Kelleys. I would text Joey when I got there to come outside to the car. I suggested other places to eat when Finley wanted to order lunch. I avoided every possible contact with him.

But meeting up with another man instantly made me think of Hudson. What would he think if I went on a date? Why did I want to know? Did I want to date someone else? Did I want to date him?

HEREBYFORCE

Never mind. I don't want you to feel pressured.

MYFRIENDSMADEMEDOTHIS

It's been a long time since I went on a date.

HEREBYFORCE

Then how about a drink?

I took a breath and closed my eyes. I could do this.

MYFRIENDSMADEMEDOTHIS

Tomorrow night. Eight pm. O'Kelley's. Do you know where that is?

HEREBYFORCE

I've been there a time or two, yeah.

MYFRIENDSMADEMEDOTHIS

I'll sit at the bar. I'll be wearing a purple sweater.

HEREBYFORCE

See you then.

Butterflies lifted off in my stomach. I smiled.

Then I imagined Hudson's face when he saw me with another man.

My thighs tingled. My pulse quickened. My lips parted.

I didn't want to be turned on thinking about Hudson getting jealous, but I was. Maybe he wouldn't care. But maybe he would.

I hoped he would.

I SENT GOLDIE A TEXT, knowing I needed encouragement from a friend. She was excited for me and made me promise to spill all the details when we had dinner in two nights.

Matty was sleeping over at a friend's house, and Joey was going out with Tierney and a few other friends to the movies. I dropped both my boys off, then went to O'Kelley's.

The pit in the center of my stomach tightened when I walked in the door. It was busy. Not the busiest I'd ever seen it, but definitely busier than I expected. That many people witnessing what was sure to be a failure on my end was not something I was looking forward to.

Neither was feeling pressure to go home with a stranger. Sure, I made the date when I knew I was free, but that didn't mean I wanted anything more than a drink with the guy.

What the hell was I thinking?

I was about to turn and go when I saw Hudson watching me from behind the bar. His arms were crossed over his chest and he was glaring at me.

Why did I choose his bar for this?

I swallowed my uneasiness and admitted to myself it was the same reason Finley said she met Trent there. She knew, just like I knew, Hudson would never let anything bad happen.

But for me, he might be the bad thing happening.

My knees wobbled as I moved across the bar toward him. I slid onto a stool at the end, where I could see the door and disappear down the hallway to the bathrooms if I needed a break.

Hudson's gaze didn't stray for one second. When I finally looked up, his eyes were so dilated they were nearly black.

"Can I get a drink?" I asked him.

He nodded sharply. He didn't say anything as he grabbed a glass and filled it with ice. I turned away from him, not wanting to watch as he crafted me something I was sure to like a little too much. When the thunk of the glass hit the bar in front of me, I spun back around and found him still holding the glass and watching me.

I stared up at him, hoping the quiver deep inside me didn't show on my face.

"I haven't seen you in almost a month," he said. His voice was quiet in the loud bar, bordering on harsh, like he was holding something back.

"I've been busy."

"Not too busy tonight?"

I shook my head. "Matty's at a sleepover, and Joey's out with friends."

"And you're…?"

"Meeting someone."

He blew a breath out of his nose. "Anyone I know?"

"I doubt it."

"What makes you say that? I know a lot of people."

I considered what he was saying and wondered if Hudson knew HereByForce. If he did, would that make it better or worse?

"What's his name?"

I almost said his screen name but decided not to share

that information with Hudson. He would mock me for using an online dating site. "Why?"

"Wondering if I know him. I didn't realize you were dating someone."

"Who said I was?"

"I asked what his name was. You didn't correct me."

Shit. He was right. "Is that a problem?"

"Nope. Nice sweater."

I sipped my drink. "Thanks."

"I guess you're a fan of purple."

"Why do you say that?"

He shrugged. "Purple tree. Purple sweater. Seems like that's a favorite."

"How did... Oh, I forgot you helped Joey with that. Thank you. It was a wonderful surprise. I love it."

Hudson nodded again. He seemed stiff. Uncomfortable. Like how I felt.

I ignored him another moment and scanned the bar. I knew telling HereByForce what I was wearing meant giving him the power to decide if he wanted to meet me or not. If he didn't show, I had no choice but to assume he wasn't interested.

My phone buzzed in my bag, and I dug it out. A new message.

HEREBYFORCE

Purple looks damn good on you.

I gasped. He was here. And he was watching me.

MYFRIENDSMADEMEDOTHIS

I'm definitely a fan. Since you know who I am, are you going to come say hi?

I waited, my heart in my throat. I looked around to see if

I could spot anyone on their phones. People were talking and laughing with friends. Some had phones out, but most were engaged in conversation. I didn't spot anyone who could have been HereByForce.

HEREBYFORCE

I already did.

I tilted my head to the side and tried to figure out what he was talking about. The only one I'd spoken to since I got there was...

No.

It was not possible.

I lifted my gaze to his. He was staring at me. His phone was in his hand. He lifted one dark brow. A challenge or a question. It didn't matter which. I had to go.

I scrambled off the stool I was on and shoved my way through the crowd. Hudson Grant could not be HereByForce. Just no. He wasn't the kind, considerate man who'd spent two months getting to know me. He wasn't the guy I was enjoying talking to.

My car was too far away, so I rushed down the snow-covered sidewalk and prayed he didn't make it to me before I made it to my car. I don't know why I was worried, though. When I got in my car and cranked it up, I didn't see anyone on the sidewalk.

He wasn't chasing after me.

I pushed down my disappointment and pulled away from the curb. It wasn't fair. Hudson drove me crazy in every way possible. He never showed that side of himself. The side that was kind and thoughtful and impossible to resist. As much as I debated meeting HereByForce tonight, there was a pull to him I felt since our first talk.

On my birthday. When I messaged him six times.

I groaned and shook my head. I was so stupid. Why did I think dating was a good idea? Even online dating. Eventually, it moved to real life, and real life was messy.

I berated myself the entire drive, and when I got home, I'd decided I was done dating. It wasn't worth the humiliation of someone like Hudson learning all the private details I'd shared with him. I felt like such an idiot.

I was almost to my door when a vehicle door closed behind me. It was dark, and my neighborhood wasn't the best, so I hurried to the safety of my building. Then he called out to me.

"Anna. Wait. Please."

I sighed heavily. Hudson. A part of me was happy he'd come after me, and a part of me was completely shut down. He knew things. He knew about feeling like a failure as a parent. He knew about Nick and some of what he put me through. He knew I didn't feel desirable. He knew so many things. Was he toying with me the entire time? Did he know who I was and wanted me to feel stupid when I figured out who he was?

"Why?" I asked.

"Because we need to talk. Let's go inside." He'd already caught up to me and was standing a step below me on the cracked concrete. Snow was piled up on either side of the walkway. It had mostly melted where salt had been liberally applied, but the temperatures were dropping and more snow was coming.

I told myself the shiver that raced through me was from the cold and not from the man standing a foot away. I spun and walked inside, feeling his silent strength behind me as I walked.

Inside my apartment, I wanted out. I had no interest in hearing how Hudson tricked me for months and was just trying to get a laugh. Or how he figured it out and wanted to let me know so we could end this. Or anything. Why? Why did this happen to me?

"I had no idea who you were until you walked into O'Kelley's tonight," he said. His voice scraped on every nerve in my body. "A part of me hoped maybe it was you, but I never let myself completely form that thought because it was unfair to the woman I was talking to."

"Why?"

"Why what?"

"Why did you hope it was me?"

He laughed and ran a hand over his face. "You make me fucking nuts, Anna. You challenge me in a way no one ever has. You dominate my thoughts, and when I get close to you, I lose my fucking mind."

My breath fled from my chest, making me weak. I sank to my couch and leaned forward, putting my elbows on my knees.

"You don't feel the same," he said, dropping to the chair in the corner. It wasn't a question. He was interpreting my actions. But he was wrong.

"When we're together, we're either fighting or fucking. How does that work?"

He breath a laugh and shrugged. "I don't know, but there's no one I'd rather do either with."

My gaze snapped to his, and I knew he was being honest. I tried to put him in the box I'd shoved him in a year ago. The asshole box. Like Nick. A man who thought he knew what was best for everyone. But the more I tried to put him in there, the harder it was for him to fit. Hudson wasn't who I thought he was. He'd shown me that, but I didn't want to believe it. He was kind and generous. He was sexy and passionate. He was smart and strong.

And for some reason, he was looking at me like I was everything he wanted.

"Anna," he groaned. His fingers gripped the arms of the chair. The same chair he'd slept in when he brought me home on my birthday.

"I don't want to fight with you right now."

A slow, sexy grin lifted his lips as he took my words and understood what I was telling him. He prowled toward me, his movements unhurried as he walked across the small room. He leaned over me, forcing me to tilt my head back. His face was an inch from mine, his hands on the back of my couch. He smelled like beer and man. My heart pounded hard, my breath easing from me. I felt like we had all the time in the world.

And we were going to use every second of it.

I reached up and grabbed the gaping edge of his shirt. His warm skin was just beneath it, begging for my fingers. He hissed at the contact but didn't move away. I slid my hand up, lifting his shirt as I went until his upper body was exposed.

I held his gaze as I leaned forward. He watched me until the angle stopped the connection and I licked his nipple.

He groaned. "Anna."

I flicked my tongue over his nipple, loving the soft groans that came from him. I moved to the other one and gave that one a little bite. His groans got louder.

Another second and he grabbed my hips and flipped us. I came down on top of him, my thighs spread wide for him to settle between them. I moaned at the feel of his thickness against me and rocked over him.

"Take what you need from me," he whispered. His hands shifted my hips, encouraging me to move.

"I need you," I admitted.

Sure, an orgasm would be good, but it would be better if it was one he offered willingly. I could get myself off whenever I wanted, but having a partner do it was not usual for me.

"Me, too," he whispered. Then he claimed my lips and pulled my body flush to his.

We kissed like teenagers on the couch, neither of us hurrying things along. My hips shifted, and his thrust, but we kept it to kissing and a few roaming hands while we settled into the idea of what was happening between us.

Hudson Grant, the man I spent the better part of the last year hating, was driving me out of my damn mind without even getting me naked.

"Hudson," I whispered.

"Yeah?"

"Do we need to start fighting?"

He chuckled. "I'd prefer option two."

"Good."

15

HUDSON

WHEN ANNA WALKED INTO O'KELLEY'S IN THAT PURPLE sweater, I almost swallowed my fucking tongue. She was stunning. It highlighted her wide hips and her full figure. And she was wearing it for me.

Not that she knew that, but she was.

I almost told her the minute she sat down, but I wanted to be sure it was her. When she took off, I almost didn't follow her, but Jonathan told me I was an idiot if I didn't.

I needed to buy that man a drink. Or a car. If he hadn't said he'd handle closing, I wouldn't have my hands full of the woman who'd starred in all my fantasies over the last few months.

"Matty's gone all night?" I asked, needing to know if we would be interrupted.

She nodded.

"And Joey's out with friends? Until when?"

"His curfew is eleven. His friend's mom is bringing him home."

"So, we have almost three hours alone?" I asked.

She sighed and shifted her hips. My cock was throbbing

and painfully hard, but I'd deal with the mess it made if she kept going and I came in my pants.

"Are you going to let me fuck you right here on this couch?" I asked her.

She shivered at my words and bit her lip. "Better than fighting."

I chuckled and eased my hands up her sides, lifting the soft sweater up and away from her body. She wore a tight tank top beneath it, one that cupped and molded to her curves. Her bra strap twisted with the thin straps of the tank top and begged me to tug them down and feast on her breasts.

She didn't resist the move, helping to unhook her bra while I lifted one breast to my lips in offering. She gasped when I bit down on the tight little bud, then shifted her hips again.

Fucking hell. I saw stars. It took everything in me to hold back from thrusting up against her and losing myself in her, but I wanted to be inside her when I came. I only had one condom in my wallet, a wishful thinking condom I never thought I'd get to use after she tore out of my office the last time I was lucky enough to stop fighting with her long enough to fuck her.

I switched to the other nipple, leaving a wet trail between them. She moaned and rocked and eased herself to where she wanted to go. I intended to take my time. Last time, it was quick and angry and amazing, but this time I wanted to drive her right to the edge and let her dangle there before she fell over. I wanted to taste her on my tongue and feel her on my fingers. I wanted her wrung out and wet and so ready for me that there was no resistance when I pressed into her.

"Hudson," she whispered.

She was already close. Fuck, the woman could come in a second. I loved how easily she fell apart, but I wanted to feel it.

I tugged at the stretchy fabric that covered her center and managed to get my hand inside. I brushed damp curls on my way down. She bucked against me, her core seeking my fingers as I twisted my hand to find her center.

When I did, I groaned right along with her. She was soaked, dripping wet and pulsing. I ignored her clit and slid two fingers inside her, biting down on her nipple as I did.

She tightened around my fingers and came with a near silent scream that had me aching to get her somewhere she could make all the noise she wanted.

"Fucking hell," I growled. "I need more of that."

She did, too, if the way her hips rode my hand was any indication. I pressed my thumb against her clit and swore when she fell apart just that fast a second time.

I pulled my hand out, loving the pained cry she gave me when I did. "On your back, Anna. Now."

She didn't hesitate to do as I asked. I eased her leggings and panties over her thighs and shoved a pillow beneath her hips. I pressed her thighs wide and blew air gently on her skin. She quivered and come leaked from her center. I leaned in and licked it away, groaning at the flavor of her on my tongue.

"Please," she whispered.

I had no intention of stopping anytime soon, but she didn't know that. I licked her again, then added my fingers to her channel once more. Three this time. She moaned and clenched around them, lifting her hips to meet my strokes.

"So good."

I hummed in agreement and dragged my tongue around her tender, soft flesh. My fingers pumped in and out of her in a slow rhythm, not enough to take her higher yet. Just getting her used to it so when I pushed, she would jump.

She mewed and whimpered, begging for more without saying a word. I ached to sink into her and lose myself, but more than that, I ached to watch her lose her damn mind. It was one thing to make a woman as responsive as Anna come. It was another to tease her on the edge and leave her gasping for breath. I wanted the second one.

My movements were slow and lazy. I explored every inch of space between her thighs. I kissed her thighs and nipped at her flesh. I licked the seam between her leg and entrance and sucked on her clit. Everything I did was pure bliss for me, and hopefully for her.

Her noises turned from out-of-her-mind desire to frustration. A grunt followed by a shift of her hips. She was ready for more, and I was more than happy to give it to her.

I speared my fingers deeper, surprising her and getting a gasp and a moan for it. I pressed my tongue to her skin more firmly. I sped up the rhythm I used to pump in and out of her, thrusting deeper and faster. She tightened around me, her breathing speeding up with the way I fucked her with my hand.

"Please," she whispered, the word barely audible above the blood rushing through my ears and pumping hard into my cock.

I broke on that word. A woman who never asked for anything was asking me to make her feel good. It wasn't easy for her. She waited until she was hanging on the edge, desperate to fall but unable to do it alone.

I put everything I had into taking her higher than she'd ever been before, higher than she knew she could go. I lashed her with my tongue and fucked her hard with my fingers. I rubbed her G-spot and sucked on her clit. She started to fall, and I changed my movements and pushed her higher, and higher, and higher. Until she was gasping for breath and her movements were jerky.

Then I let her fall.

The sounds she made, quiet in volume but intense, were a blend of surprise and delight. She growled and hummed and moaned. Her body vibrated with energy, her orgasm forcing her erratic movements and demanding the orgasm continue.

I wasn't ready to let up. I stayed with her, sucking her clit and teasing her channel as she fell and coasted down to earth once more. I watched her face as tears streamed down her cheeks and a peaceful smile tilted her lips.

She opened her eyes and found me. She reached for me, her hand cupping my jaw. I nuzzled against her and she curled her fingers for me to come to her.

I wiped my beard and face on my shirt and rose up to kiss her. It was a tender kiss, one shared between lovers. Her hands caressed my back and shoulders, drawing me closer until my weight was on top of her.

"What are you doing to me?" she asked, our faces a breath apart.

I smiled. "Hopefully, the same thing you're doing to me."

She grinned back and shifted her hips. Her eyelids fell, and she moaned at the feel of us lined up.

"Anna?"

"Please, Hudson."

I stood and hurriedly removed the rest of my clothes. I rolled the one condom I had down my length and looked at her.

She was staring at my cock. She licked her lips.

I stroked it, needing the pressure to calm down before I sank into her and lost my mind instantly.

Her eyes widened, and she leaned toward me.

"Not now," I said. "I'll lose it. And this is my only condom, so if we trash it, we're done."

"Then we better not waste it," she said.

My cock agreed completely.

Anna shifted to lie flat on the couch. I positioned myself between her thighs, a spring from the couch hitting my bad knee. I moved to a better position and focused on her again.

She was stretched out before me like a gift. Her entire body was on display, ready and waiting for me to make her feel good. I knew I was one of the few who'd ever been blessed with this view, seeing her like this. And I considered myself very lucky.

I lined us up and rubbed my cock through the wetness between her thighs. She moaned and wiggled. When I pressed inside her, she relaxed and let me in. After a few strokes, I sank all the way into her. We both sighed.

"So good," she whispered.

"Yeah," I said. I cupped her face, and she lifted her gaze to mine. "Thank you."

She smiled. She knew I wasn't just thanking her for sex. It was more than that. Bigger than that. It was a chance for more. For both of us. A chance I don't think either of us thought we'd ever get again.

I started to move, retreating just enough to stroke back in. I didn't want to separate us. I wanted to stay inside her, buried deep and connected, forever.

The thought shocked me, but as it rolled around in my head, I didn't fight it. Anna challenged me. She pushed me. It was different than being with Hillary, but just as good. Just as right.

With that new knowledge and acceptance, I lost myself in Anna. She met my thrusts with her own. She moaned and writhed with me. Her hands ran up and down my arms, circling my waist and encouraging me to take what I needed from her. What we both needed from each other.

I felt her tightening around me. Her eyes slipped closed. Her body flushed. I was right there with her, but I didn't know if I could hold out for her to come first. I changed my angle, and she moaned.

"Anna," I grunted.

"I'm close," she whispered.

Harder, deeper, more, so much more. Sweat dripped down my face. My balls tightened up and demanded I let go. My throat clenched. My muscles screamed. My entire body needed the release.

Then she let go. Her channel locked around me, making it almost impossible to keep up my rhythm. She dragged me in, pulling at me like we were holding hands when she jumped and I had no choice but to follow her. So, I did.

I slammed into her, spilling myself deep inside. My body emptied, everything shaking from my toes to my fingertips. The colors behind my eyes were like a dream, like nothing I'd seen before. I wanted to take her some place new, and she took me there with her. To a bliss I didn't know could exist.

My arms gave out, and I fell onto her. I propped myself on my elbows to keep some of my weight from her, but she just held on. Our hearts pounded together, the same rapid pulse traveling through the rest of our bodies.

We laid there until my cock softened and started to slip from her. I kissed the side of her face and pushed myself up. In the bathroom, I tied off the condom and rolled it up in toilet paper. I buried in under other trash and hoped Matty and Joey didn't dig through and find it.

Anna was still stretched out on the couch when I got

back to the living room. I smiled and moved toward her, then saw she was chewing on her bottom lip.

"Are you okay?"

She looked up at me, her gaze drifting down my naked body. It stalled on my cock, and he jumped. She quickly looked away. She sat up and reached for her clothes.

"Anna, what's going on?"

"I need to get dressed."

"Okay, but why?"

"Because we need to talk."

Three years of marriage was long enough to know those words were never good. I stifled my groan and grabbed my clothes, reluctantly pulling them on. She shoved her hair back and fiddled with her hands, then sat on the couch.

I sat in the chair across the room, needing space if she was going to tell me we were a mistake. Again.

"What are we doing, Hudson?"

"I thought it was pretty obvious."

She glared at me. "Spell it out for me."

I sighed. "Okay. I like you. A lot. Talking on the app showed me a different side of you, but I like the side I knew in person, too. You push me and you make me think about the things I do. You make me want to be a better person."

She sucked in a breath and nibbled her lip. "That was a damn good answer."

I chuckled. "Does that mean you're not going to tell me this was a mistake, too?"

"Do you think it was?"

"Fuck no. I think it was some of the best sex of my life. I didn't come here for this, but I'm not disappointed it's where we ended up. We haven't always been on the same page, but I like this page."

She laughed. "Me, too."

"Good, so we're going to get to know each other and go on dates and tell people we're together."

"We're going to take all of that slowly," she said carefully.

"I'm okay with that."

She twisted her hands together and looked up at me. Her eyes shined with unshed tears and worry. "I'm not very good at being in a relationship. Nick—"

"Was a fucking idiot. Anything he ever told you was wrong."

"We were together a long time."

"And he gave you two amazing sons, that he gets no credit for, and a shit ton of debt. He doesn't get to make you feel anything." I paused as I realized something. "Unless you're still in love with him."

She scoffed. "No. I don't think I was in love with him, even when I told myself I was. We were kids when we got together. He was dangerous and exciting and he pissed my parents off. When we had Joey, I thought he would start to settle down, but he didn't. And after Matty, well, Nick said he wasn't interested in domestic bliss with any of us. He said he never wanted to be tied to me."

"Again, he's a fucking idiot."

She smiled. "Thanks."

"The last relationship I was in was with my wife. It was good. I loved her. And since she died, I haven't been involved with anyone. I'm not saying I've been celibate, but I haven't gotten to know anyone."

"So, you're saying we're both going into this with a lot of baggage and very little experience."

I laughed. "Yeah, I guess I am. We're going to have to figure it out together. You okay with that?"

"Yeah, I guess I am."

"Good. Now, can I kiss you again?"

"You only had one condom."

"True, but I can get really creative without a condom."

Her mouth parted in an O, and her eyes widened. She licked her lips, something I noticed she did when she was turned on and when she wasn't sure what to say.

"We still have an hour before Joey's curfew. Does he usually come home early?"

"Nope. But I don't think it's a good idea for him to find you here."

"I understand that. You never answered my question."

"What question was that?"

"Can I kiss you again?"

She smiled. "I think it's either that or we start fighting."

I laughed and stood. I moved slowly, loving the way her gaze traveled my body as I grew closer to her. "We are pretty good at making up after a fight."

"We're also pretty good at skipping right to the making up part."

I nodded and sat next to her on the couch. I lifted her onto my lap, my hands resting on her hips. "Hell yes we are."

She leaned forward and pressed her body to mine. We were nose to nose, hips to hips. I breathed her in, still smelling us in the air. "Don't hurt me, okay?"

I nodded and kissed her gently. "I promise."

She smiled, a little wobbly, but she smiled. Then she closed the distance between us and kissed me like we had all the time in the world.

With any luck, we did.

16

———

Anna and I spent as much time together as possible over the next few days... which was not much at all. With Joey and Matty home for the school break, she was working fewer hours and with them all the time. I did everything to ensure her I didn't mind at all. Her sons had to come first. Always.

I did ask if she had plans for New Year's Eve. Joey wasn't on the schedule and hadn't said anything about it. But Anna said it was a family night for them. A night they always spent together, celebrating the year that ended and looking forward to the one to come.

Maybe next year I could celebrate with them.

How quickly and completely I pictured myself as a part of their family scared me just a little. I hadn't imagined having a family since Hillary died, but being with Anna, Joey, and Matty felt right to me. It made me feel like the piece of myself I'd been missing for years was finally back in place.

"Do we have more vodka in the back?" Jonathan asked,

catching me daydreaming while I was supposed to be working.

I nodded. "Yeah. We should have two cases back there."

"You good up here while I go check?" he smirked as though he knew my thoughts had drifted to my secret relationship with Anna.

Yes, it was a secret. She asked if we could keep it between us for now. Until she had a chance to talk to Joey and Matty. I agreed, even though I wanted to tell everyone we were together.

"Boss?" Jonathan prompted again.

I waved him off. "Yeah, I'm good. Go."

Jonathan snickered and clapped me on the back as he walked by.

I went back to serving customers and watching out for people who'd had a few too many drinks. Of all nights, New Year's Eve was the one that worried me the most. It was a night that made people feel invincible and bulletproof. And stupid. So very, very stupid.

Jonathan came back with two bottles and jumped right back into serving with me. We were hopping. An hour later, we were out of vodka again, and another hour after that, we ran out of rum up front. Thankfully, I'd ordered enough extra of both to make it through the night since I'd learned over the years how much people drank when the year was ending.

We finally hit a lull in the evening, and Jonathan took his break. No one was trying to catch my attention, so I pulled out my phone and sent Anna a quick text.

> Busy here tonight. I miss your smiling face. Hope you're having fun with the boys.

She replied almost immediately.

We're being silly and talking about the future. It's been a long time since I felt like we could. I know you're a big part of the reason a good future is possible for my boys.

You get all the credit for what you've done. I haven't done anything.

You hired Joey, even though I yelled at you. You gave him direction he didn't have. And you encouraged him to dream bigger than I was willing to let him. Same with Matty. Thank you.

He showed up here the man he is. And all of that is because of you. You might have been scared to let him dream, but you didn't stop him from dreaming. You are amazing.

Thank you.

Someone down the bar called for a refill, so I slid my phone away and went back to work.

Jonathan returned just as it was starting to get busy again. It stayed that way until almost eleven. I knew the rest of the night was going to be slammed and made a quick decision.

"You good here for a few minutes? I need to run out. I won't be long."

Jonathan nodded. "No problem. Go see whoever it is that put that smile on your face this week."

I smirked and nodded, not bothering to give him the satisfaction of knowing he was right, even though it was obvious he did know.

I jogged to my truck and cranked it up. The streets were quiet even though houses were lit up all over. I parked near Anna's building and started to get out of the truck before I realized I couldn't just walk up and knock on her door.

She didn't want to tell Joey and Matty about us yet, which meant showing up on New Year's Eve was not a good idea. But I really wanted to see her.

I grabbed my phone and sent her a quick text, asking if she could come outside for a minute. I drummed my fingers on the steering wheel, staring at my phone until I heard a door slam. I looked up, and she was there.

The crappy lighting cast a yellow glow around her, high-lighting the amber strands of her hair. She had a thick sweater wrapped around her shoulders and untied boots on her feet. Loose pants flowed around her legs as her hair lifted with the gentle night breeze. Her gaze scanned the parking lot, looking for my truck.

I opened the door, and she smiled immediately.

We met at the edge of the sidewalk, far enough from the building that we weren't blocking the door, but close enough that she wasn't too exposed to the cold.

"Hey," she said. She shivered and tugged her sweater tighter around her shoulders.

"Hey," I said, running my hands up her sides to try to warm her up.

"I thought you were working."

I nodded. "I am. I just wanted to see you. To say Happy New Year."

Her lips lifted in a brilliant smile she tried to hide with a nibble on her lower lip. "I was disappointed I wasn't going to see you tonight."

I tugged her in closer, wrapping my body around hers. She shivered again, but it was a different kind of shiver. The same kind I felt to my core whenever she was close. "You smell good."

She laughed. "We baked cookies. It's a tradition we have. We bake a batch of cookies and have to eat them all before midnight. Then we bake more for tomorrow."

"I like traditions like that. What other ones do you have?" I nuzzled against her neck and kissed her jaw.

"We watch movies and talk about school and work and we laugh and forget that we live in such a shitty place."

I hummed against her throat, loving the way she melted into me. "That sounds like an amazing night."

"You're not even listening to me," she said with a laugh.

"I am. I heard everything you said. It's always good to forget your surroundings when they don't inspire you to dream bigger. And talking and laughing and spending time together is the best way to spend an evening. I wish I could be in there with you."

She squeezed my waist. "I'm sorry I asked to take this slow."

I pulled back. "No. Don't apologize. This has to work for both of us, and you have a lot more considerations than I do. Joey and Matty are your world, and you know the best way to tell them. You have nothing to apologize for. Or feel guilty about."

She nodded after a minute. "You're nothing like I told myself you were."

"What did you tell yourself I was like?" I went back to kissing her neck.

"I thought you were rude and selfish and a jerk. That you were the worst thing that happened to Joey."

"And now?"

She moaned softly when I licked her throat. "And now I wish you could keep doing that all night."

I suckled harder and nibbled on her collarbone. She tipped her head back to give me more access, and I took advantage of it. I held her close and drove her crazy with one hand on her breast and the other supporting her, my tongue and teeth sliding up and down her neck.

"I want you," she whispered.

"You'll have to touch yourself later and think of me. God knows I'll be doing that."

"I'm sorry," she said.

"No apologizing. It makes the time we do have together that much better, Anna. I don't regret this. Any of it."

She nodded and pulled me in close. I held her, kissing the top of her head while my cock accepted the fact it wasn't getting inside of her tonight.

"I promise I'll tell them."

"And I promise, I'm not mad. You will know when it's the right time. Right now, I want to make out like teenagers for a minute. It's like you have a curfew and we're almost up against it."

She smiled and tilted her chin up. I took my time leaning down to meet her in the middle, savoring every second of anticipation until our lips met. Cold skin parted to make way for warm tongues, and I groaned. My hands dipped to cup her ass and haul her body even closer to mine. I let myself get lost in her, taking as much as I gave and wishing I could skip ahead to when she was mine and everyone knew so we didn't have to hide.

A car door slammed a few buildings over, and we pulled apart. Her cheeks were flushed, and her lips were wet. She looked beautiful.

"I should go back in."

I nodded because I knew if I opened my mouth, I'd argue with her and ask her to stay.

"I don't want to."

I breathed a laugh. "I don't want you to either."

Without waiting for either of us to say anything else, I stepped into her again and yanked her to me, bending her back to kiss her like I couldn't get enough. Because I couldn't. She gasped and moaned and hiked her thigh over my hip, rubbing herself against me.

I grew harder again, wondering if I had time to fuck her in the back of my truck at the same time I knew I'd never do that. We were in our forties, not our teens. She deserved better than that.

When we finally pulled apart again, our breath pulsed out of us in pants that mingled in the air before fading to nothing.

"I need to go in."

"I know. Think about me."

She bit her lip. "I will." That breathy little admission nearly had me begging for her to call me later.

"I'm going to take you on a real date sometime, Anna."

She smiled. "I don't need fancy."

"That's good because I don't do fancy. But you deserve to be spoiled a little. When you're ready, we're going out."

She nodded.

"Have a good night. Happy New Year."

"Happy New Year."

She smiled and waved and hurried back to her building. I waited until she was inside, then turned and went back to my truck.

Smiling.

"I saw you," Joey said to me two days later. "On New Year's Eve. Kissing my mom."

Oh, fuck. It was like that old song about mommy and

Santa Claus, but different. Worse. Not funny at all because Joey was not only a teenager who understood the difference but also my employee.

"Joey, look—"

"My dad was an asshole. Still is, I guess, but I don't know. She's been through enough. You can't hurt her." His fists were clenched, but his eyes said he was about to cry.

"I don't intend to."

"Then why is she keeping you a secret?" he bellowed.

"That's something you're going to have to ask her."

He shook his head. "I'm asking you. Because she'll just deny everything. That's what she always does. She thinks I'm still a kid and doesn't want to tell me things. I'm not a kid. I'm a man. I'm the man of our family. I'm taking care of things. It's what I do."

I gently steered Joey toward the hallway and into my office. He was about to fall apart, and I didn't think he'd want to do it in front of all of his coworkers.

He sank onto the couch and stared straight ahead. I debated calling Anna, but she was working. I knew she would come, but if he thought she wasn't going to tell him what was going on, then calling her wouldn't help.

It was up to me.

"Your mom and I have been seeing each other. Not long. A few weeks. We've been talking longer, but we didn't know we were talking to each other."

"Is that the app thing?"

I nodded. "We decided to meet and when we realized who each other was, we decided to give a relationship a chance. But she doesn't want to put you and Matty in the middle. I know both of you already, and I think she knew it could get messy in a hurry. She needs to make her own decision about being with me or not. You and your brother might not make that easy for her."

"Why? We like you. You're not like our loser dad or the other losers she's dated."

"That's what I'm talking about. You see me as a good option, but she might not. She has to decide."

"So, what am I supposed to do?" He sounded a lot younger than he was. And having a conversation beyond his years.

"You let her make her own choice."

"I keep quiet. I don't tell her I saw the two of you together. I pretend I don't know anything?"

I ran a hand over my head. It was asking a lot of him. And deceiving his mom. It felt like the right answer, but I wasn't sure if it was. She had reasons for not wanting him to know about us. I assumed it was so she could make her own decision about us, but what if it wasn't? What if I was fucking it all up by not telling him to talk to her?

"Yeah," I said, making a decision. "That's what you do. Your mom has to decide when she wants you to know. She has to decide if she wants you to know. If you push her, she'll feel pressured."

"I don't lie to her very well."

"That's a good thing." Just made it more complicated. "Do you think you should tell her?"

"I don't know. I think the way you were kissing her means you need to be warned not to hurt her."

A smirk started to lift my mouth, but I locked it down. He was a good kid, and protecting his mom was the right move. "I understand. And I have no intention of hurting your mom."

"You two haven't always gotten along really well."

I chuckled. That was an understatement. "True, but

we're trying now. I really like your mom. She challenges me. And she's smart and funny and she has two amazing kids."

"She's been hurt a lot. Mostly by my dad and her parents."

"I know. What she's been through isn't right. I wish I could take all that pain away for her. But I think she's ready to move past it."

Joey nodded. "She's been happier the last two months."

I couldn't stop my smile. "Good."

"That's been because of you." It wasn't a question.

"I hope so."

"Then it sounds like you might be good for her."

"I hope so."

Joey glared at me for a long moment. I didn't back down, just let him get it out. If he was going to continue working for me, he had to trust me, and the only way for that to happen was if he knew he could be honest with me.

"I wish she'd told me."

I understood that, but it wasn't my place to push for that.

"I won't tell her I know. And I won't tell my brother. But if you hurt her, you have to answer to me."

"And Ms. Finley and Mr. Trent, I assume," I told him.

"Yeah, them, too."

"Understood."

Joey turned to leave my office.

"Hey, Joey?"

"Yeah?"

"Thank you for not telling me I can't see her."

He smiled. "You're welcome."

That went about as well as could be expected. Now all I had to do was convince Anna to tell him so there weren't any secrets.

TWO DAYS LATER, Anna and Goldie came in for lunch. The kids were all back in school and it was a Friday. The first of the New Year.

"Hi," Anna said when I walked over to take their orders.

"Hi. What can I get you two?"

Anna's gaze locked on me and scanned down my body.

Well, damn. I was definitely on board with that.

Goldie cleared her throat. "I'll have a chicken sandwich and a really big glass of ice water after that look."

My cheeks warmed, and I was thankful my beard hid any chance of a flush. Anna wasn't so lucky and looked like she'd forgotten sunscreen.

"Goldie," she hissed.

I chuckled.

"Fries?"

"Sweet potato," Goldie said. "Don't forget the ice water."

I smiled at her. "Got it. Anna?"

"I'll have whatever's under the table because I'm going to hide now."

Goldie and I both laughed. "She'll have the same as me since seeing you turned her brain to mush."

"Goldie," Anna hissed again.

"What? It's not like we all don't know you two are sneaking around like teenagers and bumping uglies whenever you can. Which is not nearly often enough if you're looking at him like you want him to be your lunch."

"Oh, my God. Kill me now," Anna said. "Why did I agree to come here for lunch?"

"Because the food is as good as the scenery," Goldie said without missing a beat.

I chuckled and shook my head. "I'm going to go put your orders in. I'll be back in a few with those ice waters."

"Dump mine over my head, please," Anna said.

I shook my head and laughed.

I brought their waters back and heard Goldie talking about her assistant flirting with her.

"You can fire him for that," I told her.

She shook her head. "He's just a flirtatious guy. I think he likes to get a rise out of me. But he's harmless. His brother is the same way. Seeing the two of them together is really funny."

"If he crosses a line, make sure you do something about it. That can get dangerous."

"Thanks. I will. He's never done anything. Just tells me I'm beautiful and I shouldn't date losers and stuff like that."

"Well, I can agree with him there."

She beamed at me. "Thanks. You're too sweet."

"That's what I keep telling this one. I'm not sure she believes me yet."

Anna laughed and shook her head. "You have your moments."

"Two chicken sandwiches," Charlie said, delivering the plates himself. "Did you put in that order yet?"

I shook my head. "You need something?"

"More buns. We're starting to get low."

I nodded. "I'll put it on the list. Thanks."

He clapped me on the back and waved to Anna and Goldie.

"Know anyone who needs a job?" I asked them, teasing.

"Why? Are you looking to hire someone?" Goldie asked.

I ran a hand over my head and nodded. "Yeah. I need a business manager."

"I actually might. Are you open to me putting out some feelers?"

"Really? Yeah. That would be great. I've asked everyone here, and no one wants it. Finley told me to talk to you about it, but with the holidays, I completely forgot."

"I already have a few people in mind. I'll reach out to them and get them your information. Does that work?"

"Yes, hell yes. Thank you."

She smiled. "You're making my friend smile. It's the least I can do."

"She makes me smile, too," I said, staring at a blushing Anna.

"Ew," Goldie said. "Okay, enough of that. I don't need a front-row seat to your mating."

I snorted and shook my head. "Just be glad she hasn't told people yet, or I'd bend her over this chair and kiss the hell out of her."

Anna gasped, her lips parting.

Goldie grinned. "I need a man like that."

"That one's mine," Anna growled.

"Fuck yeah, I am," I said. I winked at her, then walked away before I did something stupid, like tossing her over my shoulder, carrying her to my office, and claiming her as mine with the entire bar around to witness it.

Damn, did I want to do exactly that.

17

ANNA

I watched as Hudson walked away. My heart thudded, both from being close to him and from how much I wanted to fulfill every promise in those hazel eyes of his.

"Damn. I mean, when you told me you two were together, I didn't expect to get burned just from being so close to you. Wow." Goldie's gaze flickered from me to Hudson, then back to me.

"I think I've just gone too long without sex. I feel like I can't control myself around him."

Goldie shook her head and picked up her sandwich. "It's not that at all. He radiates *fuck me* vibes. I know it's code not to go after a friend's ex, but if you cut him loose, I might not be able to resist the temptation."

I chuckled as my gut burned at the thought. If things ended with Hudson, and I hated that I was already expecting it, it would hurt to watch him with someone else. I'd never tell a friend they couldn't date him, but if he and Goldie got together, I'd have a really hard time with it.

"I'm kidding, you know," Goldie said softly, putting her hand on my arm.

I forced a smile. "I know."

"I really am, Anna. I mean, the way he looks at you is enough to melt me, but he doesn't do it for me. Even if he did, I'd never go after a friend's ex. And I hate to admit it, but I like the clean-cut type."

"I can see that for you. You're a little polished, especially compared to me."

Goldie shook her head, her neatly pinned blonde hair not moving an inch. She held a perfectly cut, bite-size piece of her chicken sandwich that didn't dare drip down her arm like my full sandwich was doing. "I'm not polished. I just have to look the part at work."

"I had dinner at your house last week. You're polished. And I'm not saying that's bad. Just that I understand wanting a guy like that. I think I've always had a thing for guys that leaned toward the rough edge."

"Hudson doesn't strike me as rough. He's more like a grumpy teddy bear."

I snorted. "Okay, yeah, that totally fits him."

Goldie laughed with me.

We ate our lunch and chatted about the boys and back to school. We agreed our next dinner together we'd bring the boys and let them all get to know each other.

"When are you going to tell Joey and Matty about you and Hudson?" Goldie asked as we waited for our check.

"I don't know. I'm scared," I confessed.

"Do you think they won't be okay with it?"

I shook my head. "I haven't dated much. Until less than a year ago, I was married to their dad. Not that he was around, but I wasn't willing to get involved with anyone in case he tried to say I was having an affair and that he should be compensated. And I didn't really want to get involved with anyone."

"It'll be an adjustment for them, but they like Hudson."

"That's part of it. If things don't work out, it'll crush them."

"But what if they do?"

I looked up and saw Hudson coming toward us. Goldie's question echoed in my mind.

The idea of it working out with Hudson was one I hadn't let myself ask. The last time I got serious with someone, I married him, had two kids, and he ran off and left me with a ton of debt.

I couldn't picture Hudson doing the same, but everyone had flaws. What were his? When would they come out? Would I be able to handle them?

"Anything else I can get you two?" Hudson asked a few seconds later. His hand rested on the back of my chair, his thumb stroking my back. It was the only contact we could risk in public. And it wasn't enough.

I looked up at him and tried to imagine a future. With all of us living together, my boys calling him dad. A white picket fence, a wedding ring on my finger. Waking up to him every morning and going to sleep with him every night.

It was a kind of domestic bliss I'd never known. It was counter to everything I'd experienced before. And my brain immediately shut it down.

I leaned forward, separating myself from his thumb on my back. I grabbed my water and let Goldie answer for us. Both of them looked at me, trying to figure out what was wrong, but neither pushed me for an answer.

"Can you bring the checks?" Goldie asked.

"Already taken care of," Hudson said.

"Did you pay for our lunches?" she asked.

"You're going to help me find a business manager, and

Joey never eats the free food he's allowed to have working here. I owe both of you at least a few meals."

"I can pay," I protested.

"I know you can," Hudson argued. "I never said you couldn't. I am trying to be nice."

"She means thank you," Goldie said for me. "We both really appreciate it, Hudson. We'll see you soon."

Goldie ushered me up and out of my seat and out the door, barely giving me time to get my coat on before we were stepping onto the snow littered sidewalk.

"What are you doing?" I asked her.

"I'm not letting you mess this up. Not yet."

"I'm not—"

She raised one brow at me and dared me to be honest.

I sighed. "Fine, I was about to mess this up. Because it's not going to work out. He's suburbs and cottages. He's security and stability. He's paid lunches and video game devices. I'm none of those things. I'm a single mom up to my eyeballs in debt. Why in the world would be want to be saddled with me?"

"You've obviously forgotten the way you two were looking at each other when we first got there. You don't need a reason to love someone."

"Love? No. I don't love him. Lust, maybe. For both of us. He was married, and his wife died. He's been out of dating about as long as I have. He doesn't love me, and I don't love him. We're just getting to know each other. And it's going to end anyway, so don't even go there. I'm not getting the white picket fence with Hudson Grant. Or anyone, but especially not with him. He's way too good for me."

"Anna..."

"No, Goldie, don't. I just... I'm going to enjoy whatever is happening between us, but I can't focus on long term. That's why I'm not telling the boys. They'll start to think of him differently, and when it ends, they'll be hurt. I can't put them through that. I just can't."

"I think you're wrong. About all of it. But you're not ready to hear it yet, so I'll let it go. But one day, you're going to understand that you're going to need to take a chance if you're going to get anything better than what you have right now."

"What I have is good enough. I don't need better." I don't deserve better.

"I disagree," Goldie said. "But we can agree to disagree. Are you going to come to book club on Sunday?"

"I'm not sure."

"You should. I'd really like to have a friend there. Is Joey working Sunday?"

I shook my head. "Not this week."

"Good, then you have to come. I'll pick you up so you don't chicken out."

I laughed. "Sometimes I don't like you."

"I'm okay with that. I get it a lot."

I hugged Goldie and tried to hold in all the emotions trying to break free. She hugged me a little tighter, like she knew I needed the extra squeeze to get them back in. When she released me, she smiled.

"I'll see you Sunday. For now, I need to get back to work."

"Say hi to Patrick," I teased.

She rolled her eyes. "If only he was twenty years older, maybe I wouldn't feel like such a creep for thinking he's cute. Oh, well."

"You're not a creep. And I think you should take a chance."

She snorted. "I will if you do."

I glared at her. "Touché."

"See you Sunday."

I waved as she wrapped her coat tighter and turn to go to her car. I was not looking forward to book club.

"No freaking way. You got married?" Willow shouted.

Goldie and I had just walked into Book Boyfriends Unlimited. We didn't know who Willow was talking to, but Goldie tugged me forward to find out.

"I did," Elise said as we turned the corner. "We eloped on New Year's Eve. Just the two of us. It was really nice."

"I knew," Finley said, smirking at everyone.

"How did you know?" Willow asked.

"Trent helped them set everything up," Finley said.

"Thank you for not telling everyone. And for making it so nice. We need to thank Trent, too. It was really amazing of him to do everything he did," Elise said.

"Tell us everything. I'm up to my eyeballs in diapers and formula," Blake said. "I need to live vicariously through people who have the energy and the vagina to have sex."

"My nephew will give you a break, eventually. Once you're cleared for fun again, maybe Maddox can spend the night with George so the boys can play," Finley offered.

"I don't think I'm going to let Ian touch me ever again. Not if I'm going to be this exhausted every time we have a baby."

"It gets easier," I said.

They all turned to look at me.

"Sorry. I didn't mean to interrupt."

Blake shook her head. "Please, interrupt and tell me all about when it gets easier. Right now I feel like I'm floating because I'm existing on such little sleep."

"It's like that. When they start sleeping through the night, it's easier. Then again when they eat solid food and sleep even longer. And again when they can get themselves in and out of bed and fix their own breakfast. Not that it's easy with teenagers, but it's a different kind of challenging. More mentally exhausting than physically."

"Ooh, you almost had me," Blake teased. "Okay, I have hope again. And Elise hasn't told us a thing because I was complaining. Elise, tell us everything. How was the hotel?"

"The hotel was gorgeous," Elise said. Her smile was dreamy and faraway, like she was seeing it all again. "Trent set us up in this amazing suite. It was far too expensive and lavish, but it was amazing. And he wouldn't let us pay for anything."

"That's a nice perk," Trinity said.

"Very nice. And unexpected. I think Colin asked Trent because he figured he'd know of a good place to stay, but neither of us expected he would pay for everything. He even got us dinner reservations the evening of our wedding and paid for that. We had breakfast delivered to the room every morning, and it was everything a destination elopement should be." Elise grinned widely and clapped her hands together. She was sporting a simple band with a solitaire diamond engagement ring. It suited her.

"You look happy," Blake said.

Elise nodded. "I am. I never thought I'd get married. Hell, I never thought I'd have a relationship again. But Colin is amazing. He's never once rushed me or made me feel like I was being ridiculous for how slowly I wanted to take things. Most guys would have been impatient, but not him."

"He's perfect for you," Willow said.

Elise smiled. "He really is. I know I'm lucky."

"I'm happy for you," Finley said. "We all are. You deserve

a man who lights you up and makes you feel like you're worth the wait in every possible way."

"We all deserve that," Elise said.

"From your lips to God's ears," Sofia teased.

"Any prospects?" Trinity asked her.

Sofia shook her head. "Nope. I took a break from dating. I never dated much anyway, and being on all the time was exhausting."

"I feel that so much," Goldie said. "I have to be on for work, and when I leave for the day, all I want to do is chill out. Of course, I'd love a guy who melts my panties like Anna has, but—"

"Melts your panties? What?" Finley barked. She looked between Goldie and I as I tried to hide behind my hand. "What are you talking about? Who are you talking about?"

"I'm so sorry," Goldie whispered. "It just came out."

"Start talking," Finley demanded. "Or Goldie will."

I gave Goldie a wide-eyed look that I hoped would get her to not say anything. She rolled her lips in and shook her head.

"Who is she talking about?" Finley demanded.

I was a little afraid of my boss at that moment. She was glaring at me and singularly focused on making me answer. I wasn't ready to tell my sons, but telling a room full of Hudson's friends was only slightly less appealing. When things ended, I'd lose people. Or at least my relationships with them would change. I was not looking forward to it.

"I have a guess," Elise said.

"Who is it?" Finley demanded.

"I thought Anna and Hudson would get together," Trinity said. "I told Karissa months ago."

"You're good," Goldie said before I could formulate a response.

"Hudson?" Finley shouted. "From next door?"

"I like it. He needs someone like you. Someone who won't put up with shit but who's going to be everything he's ever wanted," Elise said.

"That's true," Finley said. "He always wanted kids. He told me he and Hillary were talking about it when she died."

"And he adores Anna's kids. Have you seen him with them?" Willow asked.

"Guys, she's melting down in a very different way," Blake said.

They all turned to look at me. Panic was in full swing. Hudson only wanted me because I had kids?

"When James and I got together, all we did was fight. But it was hot. I didn't want to be around him unless we were having sex. And all the fighting you and Hudson did reminded me of James and me," Trinity explained like it made all the sense in the world.

"So, he hates me and wants my kids?" I squeaked.

"Anna, he doesn't hate you," Finley said. "He likes you. He told me he does. He's a good guy. And he would never be with you because of anything other than he likes you."

"Can we go back to the whole melting panties thing? Because if he has that effect on you, why are you even worried about anything?" Elise asked.

"Because she hasn't been in a relationship since her ex and she thinks things with Hudson are going to end. She hasn't told Joey and Matty she's seeing Hudson," Goldie provided.

"Listen, I get that more than anyone else," Elise said. "I really do. When I met Colin, I had zero interest in a relationship. I wanted to run from him. But we kept getting thrown together. And like I said, he never pushed me. He let me be comfortable with how our relationship progressed and how we did everything. I know other guys I tried to date or hooked up with never would have been that patient. Things with Hudson might end—"

"Elise!" Finley hissed.

"She needs to know that. It's true. We can't tell the future. It might end. They might not last. What Anna's really afraid of is if they do. That's the scary part for someone like her and me. A relationship ending is comfortable. She didn't want us to know because we're friends with Hudson and if things end, she thinks we're going to choose his side. Same with her sons, I'm guessing. You probably took on more than your fair share of shit from your ex, from the debt you mentioned and full responsibility for your kids, but also explaining his absence and convincing them he's not the worthless garbage he is. You have said very little about him, and my guess is you try hard to protect his image for the sake of your kids. You'd do the same with Hudson. He could cheat on you and you'd still say it just didn't work out. Not that Hudson would, but you know what I mean. Anna's doing the heavy lifting. And having hope and giving up a piece of your protection to someone else is terrifying."

Everyone stared at Elise while she spoke. I felt her words to my very core. Everything she said was the absolute truth. It wasn't easy to admit, but it was what I'd been thinking.

"What she said," I whispered.

They turned back to me, and I saw the pity on their faces. That was worse than the misunderstanding.

"Nope," Elise said. "You can't pity her. Life sucks for all of us. We all have our struggles. We all handle them differently. Sometimes life kicks the shit out of you, and you have a harder time getting back up again. But she's up. She's dating. She's trying. That's more than a lot of people would do."

"But—" Finley said.

"Anna, Hudson should consider himself lucky to have a shot with you. I love Hudson, and I don't say that lightly, but you're stronger than you give yourself credit for. Don't sell yourself short. And talk to your sons. Give them the chance to show you how strong they are, too, because with a mom like you, I have no doubt they're stronger than any of you know."

My throat tightened at Elise's encouragement. I nodded, unable to force words out.

Finley reached over and grabbed my hand. Blake smiled at me. Trinity winked. Goldie mouthed *sorry*. Everyone else went back to their cake and conversation, letting me absorb everything.

"I'm really happy for you," Finley said after a minute. "And if things don't work out, I'm still going to love both of you. I don't want you to ever think I wouldn't."

"Thank you," I whispered.

I let the emotions run through me and made a decision I should have made a long time ago. I was going to tell my boys about Hudson. And I was going to try to let him into more than just my body.

If I was honest with myself, he was already working his way into my heart, but I wasn't sure my heart was strong enough. But with these amazing, courageous women around me, maybe one day I would be.

18

─────

I filtered out of Book Boyfriends Unlimited with everyone else. Since I arrived with Goldie, she was my ride home, but I wasn't completely ready to leave yet.

"Are you okay?" Goldie asked.

I stood on the sidewalk and looked at O'Kelley's. I was still scared. There were still a lot of unknowns. But I wanted to be brave and give us a chance.

"I think so," I said after a minute.

"Do you want me to wait for you? I don't mind. But if he's going to give you a ride home, that's okay, too."

"I don't even know if he's here."

"He's always there. And if he wasn't, I think he'd show up if you asked him to."

"Am I crazy?" I asked her. I felt crazy. I felt like I hadn't felt since I was half my age and was with Nick. When I was young and free and thought I had the whole world in front of me. I'd changed in twenty years. I had two kids to think about, and a lifetime of hurt and betrayal to overcome. Was it really a good idea to get involved with someone? Especially someone who really was a good man and deserved so much better than me?

"I think at our ages, we get used to stability. We don't like to shake things up. If nothing changes, nothing changes. There's nothing wrong with that, but if you aren't willing to step outside your comfort zone and see if there's something better out there for you, you'll never know if you can be happier."

"Is it really that simple? What if what's outside my comfort zone makes me less happy?"

"It might. But then you go back to your comfort zone and don't try again until you think there's a chance it'll be better."

"I'm scared."

"We're all scared. He is, too."

I drew a deep, cold breath and let it out slowly, the icy air hovering in front of me before dissipating and disappearing. I wanted better. It was easy to go after it for my sons, but for myself, it was a bigger challenge. For myself, I spent years saying I didn't deserve it.

What if I was right?

"I'll go in with you. If he's there, you can talk to him. If he's not, I'll drive you home."

"Don't leave me," I begged, grabbing her arm.

"I promise."

I held on to Goldie's confidence and let her lead me inside. It was dark inside and not very crowded. A group of people were playing pool and having a lot of fun. More people were scattered around the tables and a few sat at the bar.

I barely saw any of them because the moment we walked in, my gaze landed on Hudson. He was smiling at something a man said to him. His smile transformed his face, taking the harsh edges off him and making him look more approachable and friendly.

He lifted his gaze and saw me, a slow smile curling his lips as desire sank into his eyes.

Goldie shoved me forward, her solid strength by my side.

Hudson never once looked away from me. He said something to the man he'd been speaking to, then met me at the end of the bar. "Hey."

I just stared at him. I was so sure an hour ago, then so completely terrified just a few minutes ago, and now all I wanted was for him to wrap his arms around me and say all the words for me.

"Anna wanted to talk to you. Can you two go to your office?" Goldie said for me.

Hudson nodded. "Of course."

Goldie slid onto a stool and flagged down the other bartender. Hudson held his hand out for me to go ahead of him down the hallway to his office.

He closed the door behind us and moved to the far side. He crossed his arms and stood there, waiting for me to speak.

"Iwanttotelltheboysaboutus," I blurted. All the words ran together, barely intelligible.

"What?"

I took a breath and tried again. "I want to tell the boys about us. I want them to know we're dating."

"Seriously?" He breathed a laugh and shook his head.

"Yeah. It's time. I don't like lying to them, and everyone else I know, and I want to tell them."

"Shit, I thought you were here to end things."

"Why did you think that?"

"Because you looked like you were going to throw up. I figured you didn't want to be the one to say we're done."

I shook my head. "I don't want that. But if you do—"

"No," he blurted. He moved across the room toward me. "Not a chance." He stopped just before he touched me. His body was close enough I could feel his heat all over me, surrounding me but not touching. "I'm in this, Anna. I want us to have a real shot."

"So do I."

He nodded and leaned down, stopping again before we touched. "Can I kiss you now?"

"Yes, please."

He smiled and closed the last bit of distance between us. It was a kiss of relief and desire and demand. It was a kiss that rearranged parts of me and filled in with parts of him. Admitting to him that I wanted us to have a chance was scary, but he didn't laugh at me or reject me. He wanted the same thing. And that was good.

His hands stayed in neutral zones, even though the kiss wandered into the obscene. If we were anywhere else, we would have been naked and sealing our agreement in another way. But he was working, and I had to get home.

He pulled back after not nearly long enough. He licked his lips and breathed deeply, his warm breath fanning over my cheeks as he forced himself to calm down.

"I'm really happy you're going to keep seeing me. I have one request."

"What's that?"

"Let me take you on a date. A real date. With dinner and whatever else you want. Dancing, a movie, bowling, I don't care as long as we get to go out and I can show everyone that

I'm the lucky son-of-a-bitch who gets to hold you and touch you and kiss you."

My lips lifted higher and higher with his words until I felt like my cheeks would split open. I nodded, and he kissed me again, the kind of kiss that stole my breath and my brain and a piece of my heart and gave them all to him.

When he pulled back this time, he just grinned. "Thank you."

"I should be thanking you. You're the one who asked me out."

"Trust me, I'm the lucky one here."

I just shook my head.

"Unfortunately, I need to get back out there now, though. Jonathan has to leave early tonight."

"Oh, I'm sorry."

"Nothing for you to be sorry about. I wish I could spend more time with you. Let me know when you want to go out. Any night. I'll make it work."

"I need Joey to be home with Matty."

"I understand."

"Weekends are usually tough for me."

"I don't care what night it is."

"I think Thursday will work. Is that okay with you?"

"Absolutely. Double check and let me know. I'm free whenever you are. I'll make sure of it."

"You have a business to run. You can't just take off anytime."

"For you, I will."

"Hudson."

"My employees are amazing, and I'm always here. They can handle things for a few hours. They do it all the time."

I nodded. "Okay. If you're sure."

"Definitely. Check your schedule and Joey's and let me know." He kissed me again quickly, then pulled back and moved toward the door.

I followed him back into the bar. He didn't touch me or anything when we were in view of others, but I felt his gaze on me like a caress. Goldie was sitting at the end of the bar with a pink drink that looked good. I grabbed her glass and took a sip.

"That's club soda," I said, making a face.

"Um, yeah. I'm driving. Jonathan added a splash of grenadine so it's pretty."

I chuckled. "As long as it's pretty."

Goldie winked at me. "All set?"

I nodded. "We're going on a date Thursday night."

"Good for you."

"As long as my boys are okay with all of this, then yes."

"They will be. I'm sure of it."

"I hope so."

BOTH BOYS WERE on the couch watching a movie when I got home. They barely looked up at me when I walked in. I put my purse down and set my boots in the closet, then sat in the chair Hudson slept in more than two months earlier.

I was so embarrassed that day, waking up and realizing he was there. I lashed out at him, but he kept coming back. He always came back. Something Nick never did.

"You okay, Mom?" Joey asked when a commercial came on.

"Yeah. I wanted to talk to you boys about something."

Joey and Matty exchanged a look and shifted in their

seats. The commercial played in the background, muddling my thoughts.

"I'm dating someone. We've been seeing each other for a few weeks, but we started talking before that. He's really kind and smart and funny. I like spending time with him."

"Do we get to meet him?" Matty asked.

I nodded. This was the hard part. Admitting who it was. "You already know him, actually. I've been dating Hudson."

"Oh, cool. Hudson's awesome," Matty said.

I glanced at Joey. He hadn't said anything. He didn't look happy, but he didn't look angry either. I wasn't sure what he was thinking.

"We're taking things very slowly right now. Nothing here is going to change. But I wanted you guys to know."

"I like Hudson," Matty said. "Are you going to kiss him?"

"She already has," Joey said.

"Yes, I have, but how do you know that?"

"I saw you two on New Year's Eve," Joey admitted. "When you went outside, I went to see what was taking you so long and I saw you two. I asked him about it—"

"You asked Hudson?" Why didn't he tell me?

"Yeah. Man to man. He needed to explain what his intentions toward you were."

My heart melted for my little boy. He wanted to protect me. To make sure I was okay. Instead of talking to me, he went to the man who kissed me.

"What did Hudson say?"

"He said he really likes you and that he's not going to hurt you."

I exhaled a laugh, not willing to admit to myself how much of a relief that was.

"Are you okay with me dating him?" I asked Joey directly. He had more contact with Hudson than Matty and knew him in a different way. I didn't want it to be awkward for Joey at work.

Joey thought about it for a minute, then nodded. "I wasn't sure at first. I thought maybe he would be weird around me. He's been the same so far. If anyone at work says something, I don't think he'll brush it off."

"What do you mean?"

"I don't know. If another busboy says I'm getting extra shifts because Hudson is dating you or if a server says I get more tips or something."

"Have you had issues with anyone saying anything?"

"No, Mom, I'm just... I know how this town works, okay? I know what people say. It's not always easy being the son of the guy who skipped town or the grandson of the people who took your money and ran. People have talked about us my whole life. It's all dying down, but you dating the owner of the local bar is going to start these assholes talking again."

"Language," I growled.

Joey sighed. "Sorry."

I took a breath and looked at my son. He reminded me so much of his father at times that it hurt, but Nick never had the compassion or care for others that Joey has. Joey got all the good parts of both of us, and he turned them into a boy who was becoming a man with a good mind and a solid strength. He was someone I was proud to call my son.

"I didn't know you heard all those things people said," I admitted. "Living here was never easy for me growing up. People didn't expect much from me, and I lived up to their expectations. My parents didn't have money for me to go to college, so they told me I was too stupid to even think about it. When I started working, they made fun of me wanting more for myself than minimum wage jobs. I gave them money because I thought they would see that I was working hard and I wanted to help them. They could barely afford to stay here because they drank and smoked and wasted their money on stupid things. I wanted them to be proud of me and how much money I was earning, but they were just horrible people who hated everyone and everything. They took the money I gave them, and the money I hadn't given them, and they left town while I was at work one day. Just vanished. I couldn't afford to pay for this place by myself, so I moved in with your dad."

"We all know what a peach he was," Joey said sarcastically.

"I know. But he's your father, and for all his faults—"

"All he has are faults," Joey said.

"He's still your father, Joey. He wasn't good to me, but he was never abusive. He was just not interested in being a father. But he's the one who missed out on not being a part of your lives. And all those people out there who like to talk like they know anything, they have no idea what really happened in either situation."

"Why don't you tell them?" Matty asked.

I shook my head. "It's not worth it. They're not worth it. Do you know Jeremy's dad?"

Matty nodded at the mention of his best friend.

"Do you know what he does for a living?"

Matty shook his head.

"Because it doesn't matter. If he's a good father to Jeremy, it doesn't matter what his job is. Because you know a person is about a lot more than how much money they earn."

"Not everyone thinks that," Joey said.

"I know. And you're always going to encounter people who will think less of you because you grew up here. I wanted to get out of here when I was a teenager, and if I'd taken the money I was making and saved it instead of giving it to my parents, I would have. The only way I did was moving in with your father. When he left, I couldn't afford where we were and had to move back here. I never believed in myself, and I am so happy you fought through my fears and believed in yourself and want to go to college. It scares me, but I want you to have everything you desire in life. And if that means getting away from here and finding your own path, I want you to do that. But do it for you, not because of them. I've spent a lot of years trying to outrun my past and trying to live up to or live down the things others said about me. It's not a good life."

"Is that why you like Hudson? Because he doesn't treat people that way?" Joey asked.

I thought about it for a minute and nodded. "I guess that's part of it. I made assumptions about him when you started working there, and I've treated him poorly because of who I thought he was, but I've gotten to know him and I know he's a good man."

"He bought me video games," Matty said.

Joey and I laughed at the awe in Matty's voice.

"Yes, he did. He's kind and generous, and he treats people with compassion. I like all those things."

"You deserve someone like that, Mom. No matter what your crappy parents or our crappy father ever said or did to you," Joey insisted.

"Thank you. Both of you. I'm sorry life hasn't been easy for you boys, but I think we're getting better. I think this is going to be a good year for us."

"Definitely," Joey said.

"Yeah, it is. Maybe Hudson will buy me another video game if you keep dating," Matty said.

"Matty! I'm not going to date him so you can get presents," I said.

He shrugged. "It was worth a try."

Joey and I laughed.

"You are too much, kid," I told my youngest.

"Nah. I think I'm just enough." Matty smirked.

He was right. We were all just enough.

19

HUDSON

Nine candidates. Damn. I owed Goldie a few drinks. I had no idea where to start, and in a few weeks she delivered me more than enough options, all of them qualified.

I spent a few days reaching out to them all and setting up interviews for the following week. I knew I'd put it off if I didn't do it right away, and I knew the business would be much better off if someone else was in charge of the things that involved numbers.

Plus, I knew I needed to have all distractions aside so I could enjoy my date with Anna that night.

We'd talked a few times during the week. She said things went well with her boys and that Joey confessed he saw us kissing and asked me about it. She asked that I come to her in the future with anything regarding her sons, and I assured her I would. I had to learn where the lines were, and I would.

I took the afternoon off so I could shower and change and be presentable when I picked Anna up for our date. She told me she was up for a surprise so I had an entire evening planned. I didn't know what she liked to do, but I was hopeful she would enjoy the night I had in mind.

I knew if I didn't show up for guys' night, I'd get harassed about it, so once I was ready for my date, I headed back to O'Kelley's to see my friends and accept whatever shit they were going to dish out.

James whistled. "Look at you. I didn't even know you had a head under that hat. Although I'm not surprised it's shiny."

I flipped him off.

"Nice shirt," Ian said. "You're looking a little extra fancy tonight."

"What's the occasion?" Sebastian asked.

"He has a date," Knox provided.

"You can sit with James," I told him.

Knox laughed. "You know the old men who come into my hardware store have nothing to do except talk about everyone else. I swear they know more about this town than the rest of us combined."

"Except you, I guess," Rowan said. "Who are you going on a date with?"

"Anna Charlotte," I told him.

"Really?" Rowan asked.

I nodded. "That okay with you, Officer?"

Rowan smirked at me. "Of course. I like Anna. She's had a hard run, but she's always smiling and friendly. She doesn't back down."

"You sure you can handle her?" Sebastian asked.

"I'm sure," I told him.

"You better be good to her," James said, all traces of humor gone.

I met his gaze evenly and nodded. "I intend to be. I'm not

playing games with her. We've been talking for months and dating for a few weeks. This isn't a fling."

James held my gaze. When he extended his hand to me, I knew that was as good as him giving me his blessing. James and Trinity were friends with Anna and spent time with her over the last few years. Anna and James grew up in the same neighborhood. He did what he could to watch out for her. But that was my job now.

It felt good to let that thought roll around inside my head. I wanted to be responsible for Anna, Joey, and Matty. I cared about all of them. I didn't like the idea of another man being in their lives, even someone who was a friend only. I wanted to be the one they went to when they needed things. The one they called for help.

I would be.

"Who needs a drink?" I asked them.

"I do. Got one for me?" Brantley Pierce asked.

"Always. How are ya?" Brantley and I played baseball together in high school. He was two years ahead of me, and I learned a lot from him. He wanted to be a teacher even then, and the high school was lucky to have him as the base-ball coach and the cross-country coach, too.

"Good. Bored out of my mind, though. I didn't know I was missing the party on Thursday nights." Brantley looked down the line and tipped his beer to the others. Life in a small town meant even if they didn't know each other, they knew each other.

"Don't you have like twelve jobs? How are you bored?" Knox asked.

Brantley shrugged. "I'm single in a town where I've either dated most of the single women or I'm teaching their kids. I coach so I'm not sitting around my house breaking shit so I can stay busy."

"You definitely broke enough shit when you bought it," Knox teased.

Brantley chuckled. "That's what happens when you buy a fixer upper and have no skills. Speaking of which, his drinks are on my tab. I think I still owe you a few dozen drinks for all the help."

"I'll take that," Knox said.

"When does baseball practice start?" I asked Brantley.

"Not until March. I might lose my mind."

"Got any good prospects?" I asked.

Brantley nodded. "Some real good ones. A few that'll probably get scholarships if they decide to go to college for baseball. Hey, you should come out and help. Big time athlete like you."

I shook my head. "It's been a long time since I've seen a field."

"Then it's past time. You were a third baseman, weren't you?"

"A lifetime ago."

"Doesn't matter. You did something some of these kids are dreaming about. It'll be good for them to see it's possible."

"Yeah, but I got hurt. Blew out my knee and had to give it up."

Brantley shook his head. "Doesn't matter. Shit happens. Some of these kids need to see it to believe it, and some need to see there's life after baseball. Either way, it'll be good to get you on a field again."

I nodded. "I'll think about it."

"He's got a date," Knox told him.

"Yeah? Anyone I know?"

"You know Joey Charlotte?" James asked.

"Of course. He played for me last year. Lots of talent but

not a lot of confidence. I'm hoping this year that changes since he's a junior and has a year of varsity under his belt."

"Hud's dating his mom," Ian told Brantley.

Brantley's brows went up. "No shit. Anna's always willing to do whatever she can to help everyone out. I like her a lot."

"So does Hudson," Knox said.

"You're all children. I'm gone. Spending some time with my woman," I said, tossing the bar towel in the bin.

They cackled like the teenagers they were acting like.

"His woman. Wait till Anna hears that one."

"He's so whipped."

"He's a lucky son-of-a-bitch."

I waved at that one. I nodded to Jonathan and headed toward the back so I could get to my truck on the square without interference.

I pulled up in front of Anna's building two minutes early. I got out of the truck and headed to her door, not wanting to be late. As soon as it opened, none of it mattered.

Anna wore jeans that hugged her ample curves and showcased her thick thighs and round ass. She had on boots that came up to her knees and a sweater that covered half her butt. A coat was draped over her arm and a purse was slung across her body. Her hair fell in soft waves instead of the ponytail she usually wore. And her eyes were outlined in something dark that made her look mysterious and sexy and all I wanted to do was fall to my knees and thank God the woman thought I was good enough to take her out for a night.

"Damn," I breathed.

She huffed a laugh and smiled. "I was thinking the same."

I wore jeans, too, and a brand new shirt that Finley made me buy a year ago. I'd never worn it because I didn't have anywhere to wear a button-down shirt, but the look in Anna's eyes said Finley was right, and it was a good shirt.

"Are you ready to go?" I asked Anna.

She nodded and reached for the door. "I'm leaving," she shouted into the apartment.

Footsteps pounded toward her, and both boys grabbed her from either side. They squeezed her tight like she was the most precious thing in their world and they didn't want her to go.

I understood the feeling.

Joey looked up at me and nodded once. Matty looked up at me and glared. "You better be nice to her."

I nodded solemnly. "I promise."

Matty pointed two fingers at himself, then two at me. "I'm watching you," he said in a menacing voice.

I nodded again, trying not to laugh. It was sweet how much they adored their mom, and I was not going to laugh at that.

"All right," Anna said. "We'll be back in a few hours. Be good. And go to bed on time."

"Yes, Mom," they said together. It was obviously something they'd heard more than a few times.

Anna turned and flashed me an anxious smile, then ushered me out the door. She locked it, then followed me out of the building and to my truck.

"Can I kiss you now?" I asked when I opened the door for her.

She exhaled like she'd been holding her breath since I arrived. "Sorry. Yes. I wasn't sure how that would go."

I hated that she didn't think it would go well, but I wasn't confident in it myself, so I didn't blame her. I leaned in and kissed her softly, no tongue, adjusting my position until she sighed and sank against me.

"I think I needed that."

I smiled and brushed her hair back. "Me, too. Are you ready for dinner?"

She nodded. "I'm starving."

"Good. Me, too."

I jogged around the truck and started it up. We sat for a minute while it warmed up, then headed toward our first stop of the night.

"Are you going to tell me where we're going?" Anna asked once we'd pulled onto Saint Lawrence Parkway heading north.

"I thought you were open to being surprised."

"I am, but I'm also curious. Especially since we're not going into town."

I reached over and grabbed her hand. "I figured if we went into town, everyone would be watching us and you might be uncomfortable. I decided to go somewhere a little different. If that's okay."

"Oh. Um, yeah. Of course."

That didn't sound too sure. I glanced over at her, but she was staring out the window into the darkness.

I kept chatting. "When Finley was pregnant, I would bring her up here for her appointments. I didn't feel right going in a lot of the time, so I just dropped her off and drove around. I found this little place on one of my visits and have been coming up here ever since. It's small and really not much to look at, but the food is amazing and the people are even better."

"Really?" she asked.

I nodded. "I guess I should have asked you where you wanted to go, but I thought it would be good to have a little distance between us and the rest of the nosy people in town."

"You weren't trying to hide me from your friends?" Anna asked, sounding small and scared.

I barked a laugh. "Hide you? Never. Sorry. I shouldn't have laughed at that, but I promise you, no. I was at O'Kelley's tonight, dressed like this. They all know we were going out."

"All of them?" she squeaked.

"Is that a problem?" I asked, parking outside Thai Cafe.

She exhaled loudly. "No. It's not a problem. I'm just... This is all new for me."

I squeezed her hand. "For me, too."

She smiled and sighed. "I hadn't thought about that."

"Are you ready for dinner?"

She nodded and looked up at where we were. "Ooh, I love Thai food. The boys hate it so I don't ever get it."

"Good. It was a risk, but I hoped a good one. Let's go in. You're going to love this place."

She got out and hurried to the door. When she stepped inside, she gasped and looked around. It was a dark restaurant with candles on every table. Sconces lined the walls, casting soft glows all around. The floor had tile at the entryway but carpet where the tables were. It had a cozy feel without being too closed in.

"Hudson," Mrs. Woo, one of the owners, said. "How are you?"

"I'm good, Mrs. Woo." I hugged her when she came closer. "It looks like a good night."

"It is. You picked a good time to come. It's starting to quiet down. We have your table ready. Who is this?"

"This is Anna."

"Nice to meet you, Anna."

"You, too."

"How did a nice woman like you end up with a guy like him?"

Anna laughed and let Mrs. Woo lead her toward the table.

"He caught me off guard and won me over."

"Ah, that makes sense. The good ones tend to surprise you." Mrs. Woo stood next to the table closest to the kitchen. "We have a special menu for you tonight."

"You didn't have to do that," I protested.

"Oh, please. It's not every day you make a reservation. We knew Anna was someone special if you brought her all the way up here."

"You act like we came from another planet."

"Maybe I just miss you and want you to come back again soon. If I spoil you, you'll visit more often."

I kissed her cheek. "I will. I haven't been good about a lot of things lately. But I'm hoping to hire someone soon and I'm going to take some time off."

"You better," Mrs. Woo said. She turned to Anna. "This one fell asleep one day. Right in the middle of his lunch. He gives back to everyone and doesn't take anything for himself. Make sure you get him to take a day off sometime, okay?"

"I will do my best, although I have to admit I'm not always good at that either."

Mrs. Woo groaned. "Ah, you two! You need to be better. Take care of yourselves. Otherwise, you won't get to enjoy your retirement age."

"Like you are?" I teased her.

"You know we love it here. And we are closed half the week, so there."

I grinned at her. She was right. But it didn't make it easy to do.

"Okay, you sit. I'll bring out the first course. Anna, how spicy do you like your food?"

"A little spicy is okay."

"Me, too. I'll have Mr. Woo make sure it's all perfect. Then you can both come back and see us."

Anna smiled and nodded. "I'd like that."

"Good." Mrs. Woo disappeared into the kitchen, but we could still hear her shouting through the door.

"She's wonderful," Anna said.

"I agree. When I came in here the first time, she took one look at me and told me she'd have the chef prepare something that would perk me right up. I didn't know then that the chef is Mr. Woo. I'm still not sure what he made me that day, but it did the trick. I've been coming here ever since."

"It's nice. Very homey."

"Especially if your home includes a nosy, sarcastic Thai woman."

Anna laughed.

"Thank you for agreeing to a date."

"Thank you for asking."

We shared a smile. I reached across the table for her hand and rubbed my thumb over her wrist. "It's going to be hard to keep my hands off you all night."

"Who said you had to?"

"Well, I didn't plan for any private time, so I think it's best if I do."

Anna shook her head. "I don't know what you were thinking."

I laughed. "I was thinking I wanted to show you that I'm not just in this for the incredible sex, although that's a really nice perk. I want to get to know you, too."

She smiled and ducked her chin. "I want that, too."

"Good."

"So, what did your friends say when you told them we were going out?"

"I think James was going to kick my ass. I assured him I was in this for the right reasons. Everyone else was more surprised that I was dating. Except Knox. He already knew, apparently."

"I don't think I know Knox."

"He owns Al's Hardware."

"Oh, okay. I don't know him, but I know who you're talking about. How did he know we were going on a date?"

I shook my head. "Town gossip runs straight through his shop. I think the old men in town talk more than the women."

Anna snorted. "I believe it. There are men in my neighborhood who sit around on each other's steps and talk about everyone in the neighborhood. The women are too busy working and doing other things. The men sit around and run their mouths."

"You sound like Knox."

"He's right."

"Well, we're not going to worry about any of them. We're here to get to know each other and have a good first date."

"Does it really count as a first date if we've already slept together?"

"I'm counting it. I plan to take you on a lot more dates, no matter how many times we've slept together."

Her cheeks turned pink at my declaration. She nibbled her lower lip and looked up at me through those dark lashes. The look in her eyes went straight to my cock.

"Anna," I groaned.

"Are you sure we can't rearrange some of our evening?"

"I think we might have to if you keep looking at me like that."

"Then I guess I'll have to do that."

I groaned and leaned over, cupping the back of her head and bringing her to me. I pulsed my tongue between her lips, enjoying the little gasps she made. She reached up and fisted my shirt in her hand.

A throat cleared, and a plate thunked down on the table. "This is a family place," Mrs. Woo admonished us. "Save that for dessert."

We smiled and nodded. "Yes, ma'am."

20

———————

MRS. WOO WAS TRUE TO HER WORD AND BROUGHT US AN incredible four course meal. But for all the food and how delicious it was, Anna was still my favorite part.

I couldn't keep my hands off her as we ate. I loved the way she enjoyed her food. When she was trying something new, she closed her eyes and focused on the food alone. She would smile and tilt her head and breathe deep, like every bite was special and needed to be savored.

I was more than ready for dessert.

"That was amazing," Anna gushed to Mrs. Woo when she brought over the check. "I don't think I've ever enjoyed a dinner so much."

Mrs. Woo grinned widely. "You're too sweet. I'll tell Mr. Woo. He's the master behind all of this. He loves to cook and share his gift with people. I just like to talk."

"Well, you make the perfect pair. You help people feel comfortable and welcome, and he feeds them until they can't move."

Mrs. Woo laughed loudly. "It's a good combination."

Anna laughed with her. "The best."

"I hope you two will come back sometime."

"We definitely will," Anna said, meeting my gaze with her smiling one.

Mrs. Woo caught my eye and nodded. I grinned. She approved. That was good to know. Not that it would have changed my mind about Anna, but Mrs. Woo was important to me. And she was a good judge of character.

Anna groaned when it was time to stand and rubbed her belly. "Oh, my God, I think I ate too much. I couldn't stop."

"I feel that way whenever I come here. Everything is so good."

"It was amazing. Thank you for bringing me here."

I smiled at her. "You're welcome."

We made our way across the icy parking lot and rubbed our hands together. She blew warm breath into her hands. I blasted the heat that wasn't yet warm and took her hands into mine, rubbing them together and blowing my breath onto them.

Her gaze collided with mine. She sucked in a sharp breath. It was no longer cold inside the truck.

We leaned toward each other at the same moment, stretching across the console that separated us. My hand dove into her hair, tilting her head to give me access to her eager mouth. She grabbed my jacket and tugged me closer. My hip hit the console, the hard plastic digging in to the point of pain, but I didn't care. I had my hands on Anna, and after the torture of watching her savor her meal, I wasn't sure I was strong enough to stop until I was able to savor her.

We kissed like teenagers, hands roaming on top of clothes and heat blasting all around us. I cupped her hip and honestly debated skipping our second stop of the night, or just worshipping Anna in the back of my truck. But I promised her a date, and I wasn't going to let my dick take over and ruin that. For either of us.

I pulled back, panting for breath and hating myself for not continuing. She was breathing just as hard and chewed on her lip. We didn't let go of each other, our hands keeping our faces close together.

"We have another stop," I pushed out through my ragged breath.

"Please tell me it's your house."

I chuckled at her pleading voice and shook my head. "Not yet."

"You're torturing me."

"Trust me, you're not the only one who feels tortured."

"Good," she said.

I chuckled and extracted myself from her. The windows were fogged up and the entire cab was steamy from our make-out session. I turned on the defrost and wiped the glass in front of us clear, then headed toward our second stop.

Anna looked sideways at me when I parked in front of a church. "Do you think I need some religion in my life?"

I chuckled. "We're not here for church."

She saw the people heading toward the back door and raised an eyebrow at me. We were younger than all of them by at least two decades. "What is this?"

I smiled. "You'll see."

She was a good sport and got out of the truck with me. I reached for her hand, and she willingly grasped mine. We followed the others into the door at the back of the church and down the stairs to the basement.

"Bingo?" she gasped.

I nodded. "Don't let these kind looking people fool you. They will dab you to death if you fuck up their bingo game."

She snorted a laugh and tried to cover it with her hand.

"Are you playing or gawking?" a woman said from behind us.

We stepped to the side to let the woman pass with her walker and bag of bingo dabbers. She had every color of the rainbow in there, and probably a few more.

"This is insane."

"It's fun. Come on." I tugged her toward the entrance table and paid our way in. It was a quarter for each board. They let you play as many as you wanted, but once you played a board, it was done. I handed over a twenty and took the stack they gave us. It was another dollar for each bingo dabber. We got two for each of us.

Anna just stared at the scene with wide eyes and a smile.

We found two empty seats at a table in the middle. Most of the tables up front were full. We joined three men and a woman, all of whom nodded once, then went back to their game without a word to us.

"This is intense," Anna whispered.

"They're cut-throat here. Pay attention and don't talk during a game."

The woman across from us glared in our direction. Another number was called, and she focused on marking the ten boards she had in front of her.

Anna turned to me with wide eyes and a grin. I tried not to laugh.

We joined in when they started a new game, each of us only using one board for our first turn. We got the hang of it and added a second board for the next game. Anna came close to bingo on the third game, but one of the men at our table won before Anna.

They took a break after six games. People got up and

talked to the others they knew. Coffee was served and cookies appeared out of nowhere.

"Want anything?" I asked her.

Anna shook her head. "I'm still stuffed from dinner."

"Me, too."

"This is fun," she admitted.

"Good. I was hoping you wouldn't be opposed to it."

She nodded. "Can I ask you a question?"

"Sure."

"You said you're not good with numbers, right?"

I sucked in a breath and nodded. "Yep."

"You don't seem to be having trouble with this."

I shook my head, feeling itchy all over. I didn't like talking about my disability. Not because I was ashamed but because most people didn't really get it. They thought I should try harder or focus better instead of understanding that nothing worked to make sense in my mind. If I was tired, I was hopeless. And the more numbers, the worse it always was.

"Something like this is more patterns than anything else. I can look at what's called and match it to what's on my board. My brain doesn't see these as numbers, even though they are. They're more like pictures."

"That's interesting. Does it help you with the numbers?"

"No. It's just different."

"Oh."

I didn't ask why she was asking. I wasn't sure if she was trying to figure out how to make me smarter or what. I wasn't going to change, and if she was trying to figure out how to change me, maybe we weren't as compatible as I thought.

"Did you know Joey's dyslexic, too?"

"He is?"

She nodded. "I wasn't sure if you knew. I thought that's why you were telling me you were. It took his teachers a long time to figure it out. For years, they told me he was just not that smart, but I knew he was. He just couldn't understand numbers and some letters."

"The same thing happened to me. I was held back in elementary school because they thought I wasn't smart enough to move forward. I had a really good teacher one year who figured it out and was able to teach me some ways to understand better. They know a lot more now and have tools that make it easier, but it's still not easy."

Anna shook her head. "It's not. As a parent, either. I feel like I've let him down. Constantly. I should have figured out what was going on so I could have gotten him the help he needed sooner."

"That's not on you. A parent is supposed to think their child is perfect. And Joey is. So's Matty. It took me a long time to accept that just because my brain works differently than other people's doesn't mean I'm not smart."

"You're very smart," she said.

I smiled. "Thank you. And so is Joey."

She nodded and looked down at her hands. "Can I ask you another question?"

"Sure."

"Do you think he'll be successful in college?"

I took a minute to consider my answer because I didn't want to assure her it would be fine when I knew it would be harder than for most kids. "College isn't easy. Even though I knew what I was facing, I didn't reach out for help until I was failing and my coaches forced it on me. And even then, I fought it. People can be cruel. But there are resources, so if Joey's willing to accept help, I think he can be very successful."

Anna sighed heavily, like that had been weighing on her.

"You were worried?"

She nodded. "Right now, I can help him. Not always, but some. Enough to try to explain things if he's struggling. When he goes to college, I won't be able to do that."

"He'll be okay. He's resourceful."

She smiled. "Yes, he is."

"Five minutes!" the man at the front of the room announced.

"Want to grab anything before we get started again?" I asked her.

She shook her head. "Thank you for letting me ask you questions. Joey doesn't know this, but his dad always said he was stupid. The last time he visited, Joey was starting to learn to read and Nick rolled his eyes and got frustrated when Joey would guess the wrong word. I never want him to know, but I've always felt bad about that. He deserves better."

"He has better. He has you. He doesn't need his father."

She smiled. "Thank you."

I leaned down and kissed her softly, letting myself enjoy the moment as the people around us settled into their seats for another round of bingo.

The woman across the table slammed her cane against the side and shook her head. "None of that here. We're in a church."

Anna and I shared a grin and nodded. We got our cards ready and waited for the round to begin.

"I CAN'T BELIEVE I WON," Anna said with a laugh on the ride home. She beamed with excitement, the same excitement that was on her face when she realized she had bingo.

"I almost had you," I said.

She laughed. "Yep, but you didn't."

She waved her five dollars in my face, brushing my cheek with her reward. I laughed and shook my head. It was good to see her so happy.

"So, does that mean you'll let me take you out again? You had fun?"

Her laughter faded, and I worried I pushed her too far. I glanced over and she had a dreamy look in her eyes. "Yeah, I had fun. Thank you."

"Good." I paused. "You didn't answer the question."

She laughed. "Yes, I'll let you take me out again. But next time you don't have to spend so much money."

"Quarter bingo pushed it over the edge?" I teased.

She laughed again, the sound filling me up. I wanted to hear that sound every day. "You know what I mean."

"I know money is an issue for you. I need you to understand it isn't for me. I have a successful business, and I've been single most of my life. Hillary had a small life insurance policy through her work, so I inherited a little money, which I used to buy O'Kelley's. I own my home outright, and my truck, and I have no debt. I know that's not what you're asking, but it's important to me that you know I'm financially secure, not like Trent, but secure, and I enjoy spending my money on people I care about."

She gasped, quietly. I knew it was because I said I care. I reached over and grabbed her hand, needing to feel her skin against mine.

"I care about you, Anna. And Joey and Matty. You're important to me."

"Thank you," she whispered.

We drove the rest of the way to MacKellar Cove in silence. She didn't pull away from me, and it wasn't awkward. Just the kind of comfortable silence you only could find with someone you trusted.

"Do you want me to take you home?" I asked. I hoped she said no, but I wasn't going to push my luck.

"No." One word. No explanation was needed. I got the message. All of me got the message.

I pulled into my garage and closed the door behind us. The wind whistled through the cracks, but we were protected inside. I let us into the house, the entrance from the garage opening to a small mudroom. My heart beat hard, and my palms started to sweat.

I took off my coat and helped Anna out of hers. We both took our wet boots off, then padded in socks around the corner to the kitchen. I stopped at the island, unsure what to do next. Whisking her to my bed felt like a dick move, but we'd been dancing around ending up in bed all night.

"I love your house," she whispered.

"Thanks. It's been a lot of work, but I love it."

"You remodeled it?"

I nodded. "It wasn't bad when I bought it, but it was outdated. There was a wall here between the kitchen and dining room. The fireplace was shiny black tile with a gold mantel. The bathrooms had green fixtures and cheap vinyl flooring that was peeling and coming up. It took me years to get it to how I wanted it, but it's been worth it."

She nodded and chewed on her lip. Her gaze drifted around the space, taking it all in. When she looked up at me, she smiled shyly. "Why am I so nervous?"

I laughed and moved toward her. "I don't know, but I am, too."

She breathed a laugh. "I'm not sure if that makes me feel better or worse."

"I can show you around the house and then take you home. Or not, if you want. Nothing has to happen. I didn't plan for this."

She nodded and stepped into my arms. We stood there for a long moment, then she stepped back and smiled. "Lead the way."

I led her back toward the mudroom and showed her the two guest rooms and the bathroom for those rooms. Both were set up with double beds even though they were rarely used. We went back to the kitchen and looked at the open dining and living rooms. She loved the rock I'd used for the fireplace when I redid it, and said she hoped to see the deck out back when the weather was nicer.

I liked that thought.

The only room left to show her was my bedroom. I'd never brought a woman into my bedroom. The few I'd slept with over the years, we either went to their place or used one of the guest rooms. But taking Anna into my room felt right.

My heart pounded hard again, but this time I knew it wasn't anxiety. It was anticipation. She ran her hand across my soft gray comforter. She peeked into the bathroom and gasped at the oversized tub. Then she turned back to me.

I leaned against the dresser and watched her. I wasn't going to pressure her. If anything was going to happen, it would be up to her.

She sat on the edge of my bed. My heart beat faster. She looked up at me. "Hudson."

I pushed off the dresser and crossed the room to her. I cupped her jaw and lifted her face as I ducked to meet her in the middle. She gasped as our lips touched, letting me in. I swept my tongue through her mouth and tangled with hers. We didn't fight. We alternated who had control.

She lifted my shirt, pressing her hand flat to my stomach. She sighed and slid her hand around my back, pulling me down as she laid back on the bed.

I leaned my weight onto her, pressing my erection to her center. She spread her thighs wider and wrapped her legs around my hips.

"Please," she whispered against my lips.

"Are you still nervous?"

She shook her head. "Only that you might have changed your mind."

"Not a chance."

She surged up and kissed me, pulling me onto her again. She tugged at my shirt, lifting it to expose my skin to hers.

I spread my hands over her body. We moved together to stand, our hands on each other, pulling, stretching, yanking clothes off until nothing stood between us.

"Condom."

"In the nightstand. But I'm not ready for that yet."

She looked up at me, her eyes hooded with desire. I wanted to lick every inch of her, taste her body and know her soul. One night wasn't enough. It hadn't been enough the first time, and I was sure it never would be.

I didn't think I'd fall in love ever again. I was partly going through the motions when I said I was ready to date again. I missed having a partner, someone to share my days and nights with, but I didn't think I'd find someone I couldn't get enough of. Not again. Not ever again.

Anna Charlotte stormed into my life and made me crazy. She pissed me off and yelled at me and challenged me, and made me love her and her kids. She made me want to be a better man. She made me a better man.

And I intended to show her exactly how much that meant to me. One kiss, one touch, one fuck at a time.

21

ANNA

THE LOOK IN HIS EYES WAS ENOUGH TO MAKE ME WET. NO MAN had ever looked at me the way he did. Every time he made me feel like my curves and lumps and bumps were perfect. Like my thighs weren't too thick and my hips weren't too wide. Like he couldn't imagine me being any different than I was. If that wasn't enough to make me want him, the way he drove me wild was.

He kissed me, and I swore I felt it in my toes. My entire body tingled. His hands slid over my body, squeezing and caressing and lighting me up. He gently pushed me backward until I hit the edge of his mattress.

"On the bed," he said. His voice was rough, not cruel, just unsteady, like he was as close to losing it as I was.

I sat down on the edge and started to move up, but he grabbed my ankle. I looked up at him. His gaze was low, between my legs. Where I hadn't shaved in decades and couldn't see to do it, anyway. He'd already been there and didn't say a thing about it, but that time wasn't planned. This time...

Was he going to be disappointed?

"I can't wait to taste you again," he growled. "If you'll let me. What time do you need to be home?"

I shook my head. "I don't have a curfew."

He grinned and grabbed my other ankle. "Good. Because we never had dessert."

He pulled me to the edge of the bed and dropped to his knees. I couldn't see him over the bump of my belly. He dropped my ankles and skimmed his hands up the inside of my legs. I trembled at his touch, closing my eyes and letting my body feel the excitement building.

One finger traced my entrance, drawing out the moisture pooling just inside. When he opened me, it was like a floodgate. I felt it seep from me, trailing between my legs.

Then his tongue was there, licking me clean. I jumped, the gentle touch a surprise.

"So good," he whispered.

He licked to my entrance and dipped his tongue inside me, pulsing in and out a few times before he traced my folds to my clit. His hands pressed my thighs wider, giving him more space to work. His thumbs brushed where my thighs met my entrance and sent shockwaves through my body.

I was tense and ready. Anticipation coursed through me, readying me for the pleasure I knew he was going to deliver. When he pressed a thick finger into me, my body drew him in deeper and pumped around him.

"Fuck, Anna. You're already ready, aren't you?" he asked, his lips brushing my flesh with each word.

"Hudson," I moaned.

"I want to hear you tonight, Anna. I want you to scream my name. I'm not stopping until you're so far out of your mind you shout. Are you ready?"

"Hudson."

He didn't wait for me to say anything else. He added a

second finger to the one that had been pumping in and out of me while he spoke, thrusting them deep inside and setting off the first tremors inside me. He had a way of sending me over the edge in an instant. My body was craving him, begging for more from him, and ready to accept everything he gave me.

My first orgasm was small, but Hudson was far from finished. He added a third finger, stretching my entrance to the limit and fucking me hard with his hand. My core burned. Sparks shot out to all areas of my body. Years of quiet orgasms on my couch kept me from opening my mouth and letting all those feelings out.

He licked my clit and sucked hard when he felt me pulsing around him. I panted and writhed. I bucked against his face. I pleaded in whispers.

And he kept going. Harder. Faster. Deeper. My body accepted everything he gave me. He pressed my thighs wider when they closed on his head. Then he pushed me to my limit.

"I love seeing you like this," he whispered. "Watching you lose your mind. My hand full of your come, my face soaked in it. I can't wait to feel you come on my dick. God, I'm so fucking hard right now. I want to stroke myself and come with you, but I want to be inside you. I want to feel you lose yourself with me buried deep inside you. You're so beautiful, Anna. So fucking beautiful. How did I get so lucky?"

His whispered words, the conviction in them, drove me to the edge. I heard him, and I believed him, and I lost all sense of everything except him.

He punctuated his words with licks and sucks, sending me higher and higher with each thrust of his hand inside me. And when he bit down on my clit and sucked it hard into his mouth, I lost the battle I wasn't trying to fight and screamed his name.

"Hudson! Oh, fuck. So good. So fucking good. Yes. Yes. Yes!"

I couldn't stop the moans from tearing out of my throat or the way my hips bucked against him and demanded more. He sent me up a second time, not giving me a break between orgasms. My heart pounded. My body shook. Every inch of me burned like I'd walked through fire.

Colors burst behind my eyelids, and all the air in the room disappeared. I couldn't breathe. I couldn't think. All I could do was ride the wave and pray I didn't die in his bed. Because I wanted more of that.

When I blinked my eyes open, he was standing. He was positioned between my thighs, his hands running up and down the sensitive flesh that trembled at his touch.

"Are you with me again?" he asked softly.

I nodded. "I've never come that hard."

"Good. Ready to come again?"

"Hudson..."

He thrust into me in one stroke, his body meeting mine the only thing that stopped him from going in deeper. I moaned instantly, my sensitive flesh dancing around him.

"Oh, God."

"Fuck, Anna. I'm dying here. I want to go slow, but—"

I looked him dead in the eye and said, "Fuck me, Hudson."

Those words broke something in him, and he lost it. His hips pounded hard, sending me up and up and up until I teetered on the edge once more. His gaze bore into mine, our eyes locked and holding.

His face twisted. His mouth pinched. His eyes closed for a second, then opened and met mine again.

"Anna," he grunted.

"Hudson."

He knew. He knew that meant I was close. I was ready for him. He didn't have to hold back because I was right there, hanging over the edge, just like he was.

He reached between us and pressed his thumb to my clit, and I lost my fucking mind. My already sensitive body jumped into mid-air, knowing Hudson would catch me and keep me safe.

He came with a shout, my name a roar as he pumped his hips, then stilled deep inside me and pulsed with his orgasm.

My breath left me in jerky pants. My thighs shook like they were jelly. My channel quivered in the best possible way. And the man above me looked at me like I was everything he needed in life.

He leaned down and kissed me hard. His breath puffed against my cheek while I tasted myself on his tongue. He held my head still, even though I had no intention of pulling back from him.

When he released me, he held me tight, our bodies still connected. His hand ran up and down my spine. His heart pounded beneath my ear. We stayed that way until he adjusted and slid from my body.

"I'll be right back," he said, walking bare-assed to the bathroom.

I watched him go and wondered how I'd ever go back to a life without Hudson Grant in it.

I shook the thought away. I wasn't going to go there. Not now. Not when I was still with him. When it ended, I would figure it out. I had no choice.

He came back and leaned over me, kissing me once more like he couldn't get enough. "I feel like I'm addicted to you. And not just sex, but you. I feel more like myself when I'm with you than I've felt in a long time."

I smiled up at him and cupped his jaw. This beautiful, kind, amazing man was addicted to me. Damn. "I feel the same way."

He kissed me again, then pulled back and said he should get me home.

I didn't want to leave. His big bed and his private bathroom and the kitchen that was the size of my entire apartment called to me. I'd never lived in a place like his house. And it was all his.

It was another reminder that we came from different worlds. Even though we had the same zip code, we were worlds apart. He lived the life I'd only ever dreamed of living. Stable, solid, secure. Those were words that never described my existence.

By the time he dropped me off, I was struggling to remember why he would want to be with me. He walked me to the door to the building and stopped.

"Are we okay?"

I nodded.

"Something changed. Are you sure?"

I wasn't sure I liked how perceptive he was. I laughed. "I was just thinking your world is so much different from mine."

"How do you mean?"

"It's nothing. I'm just being weird. I had a really good time tonight."

"Anna? I don't want you to think you can't talk to me."

I smiled. "I know I can. It's just hard for me to trust that. I've never had anyone in my life I could rely on."

"That's not the case anymore." He pulled me in close and kissed the top of my head. He said all the right things and did all the right things. I wanted to believe it was real and it would last, but I'd learned to wait for the other shoe to drop. To wait for the shit to fly and for it to end. It would. It always did. I just hoped I'd survive it this time because the more time I spent with him, the more time I wanted to spend with him.

"Will I see you tomorrow?"

"What's tomorrow?"

He shrugged. "I don't care. I just want to see you."

I laughed. "Sounds good."

He kissed me again, then opened the door for me to go into the building. He stood there until I unlocked my door and let myself into my apartment.

I leaned against the door and sighed. That weird feeling I had? It was happiness. I wasn't sure the last time I felt it, but it was there. And it was starting to fill up all the space inside me.

I just hoped it stayed because if it didn't, all that space would feel really damn empty without the Hudson provided happiness there.

HUDSON WAS busy with interviews over the next week, and I was busy with work. We texted or talked every day, and managed a few stolen sexy moments, but we hadn't managed to go on another date yet.

"How are things going with Hudson?" Finley asked one morning. She was putting in an order for more books and I was helping her with inventory. She hadn't asked much about Hudson, but I was sure she was curious.

"Good. For now."

"What do you mean?"

I shrugged. "I really like him. He's not who I thought he was at all. He's really good for my kids, and we have a lot of fun together."

"But?"

"But he's going to get bored. Or realize I'm not worth the effort. Or find someone else."

"Why would you think that?" Finley asked, ignoring her computer.

"It's what happens."

"Not always. We're surrounded by women at book club who have happy, healthy, secure relationships. Why can't you have one?"

"I just don't know if it's in the cards for me."

"It is. I know it is. I've never seen Hudson like he is with you. He doesn't date, at all, and he's crazy for you."

"That's what I'm talking about. He hasn't dated since his wife died. He might want to figure out what else is out there."

"He's not that kind of man. He didn't date a ton before Hillary. He knows what he wants. And that's you."

"I guess."

"What do you want? Do you want to be with him?"

"Yeah, I do. I've never dated anyone like him. I really like him."

Finley smiled, that look where her eyes went soft and crinkled around the edges and she looked like she couldn't get enough of the happy. "Good. Trent and I are still talking about that marketing job. It would mean some travel, but I think most of it will be done remotely. I think it'll be really good."

I nodded, unsure why she kept mentioning it to me. She said she had no intention of letting me go, but when they brought in someone to handle marketing, she might change her mind. I wasn't brave enough to ask her if that was the plan. Not yet. "It sounds like it'll be a good option."

"Yeah? That's good to hear." She went back to her computer. "Do you want to grab us some lunch? Hudson said he could have something ready in fifteen minutes."

"Are you matchmaking?"

"Definitely."

I chuckled and shook my head, but we both knew I would do as she asked and go see him. Finley smiled when I pulled on my coat and headed for the door.

"Thank you!"

I waved. "I'll be back soon."

"No rush on my part."

I shook my head as I walked out.

The wind whipped around me on the quick walk next door. Not a lot of people were out, even though it was a Saturday. Joey was working, and Matty was spending a few hours with Hudson, so I knew we wouldn't get much time together, but I still wanted to see him.

O'Kelley's was warm. It was quiet still, but a few groups were having lunch and enjoying the warmth of the place. Matty was at the bar. I didn't see Joey, but that didn't concern me.

Hudson was standing on the other side of the bar from Matty and looked up when I walked in. He smiled at me and said something to Matty. I walked toward them, my gaze locked on Hudson's.

"Good afternoon," he said.

"Good afternoon. I heard you were making us lunch today."

"I am. Matty and I were just talking about that. He wants a burger today, too."

"Thank you. Put it on my tab."

Hudson shook his head. "Employees eat for free. Joey didn't eat earlier this week when he worked so he has a free meal banked."

"You don't have to do that."

"It's policy. I do it for everyone."

"Thank you."

"You're welcome. I did want to talk to you about something, though. If you have a minute to come to my office." He raised a brow.

"Sure," I said, my pulse skipping faster.

Hudson led the way. As soon as I stepped inside, he closed the door and pushed me against it. Our hands roamed quickly, grasping for each other in a frenzy to grab on to as much pleasure as we could in a few minutes.

"I've missed you," he growled against my throat. "I want to be inside you right now."

"Oh, God, yes," I moaned back.

"I also wanted to talk to you about something."

"What?"

"I'm in this, Anna. You and me. This isn't a fling for me. I want you and Joey and Matty in my life."

"Did Finley say something to you?" I blurted, taking a head-clearing step back.

"No. Finley didn't say anything. I just want you to know that. I know it hasn't been long, but I'm the kind of person who makes quick decisions and jumps in. To show you I'm serious, I want to pay for Joey's college."

"You what?" I gasped.

He smiled. He thought I was happy about his offer. That my gasp was a good thing.

"Yeah, I mean, I have money, and it's just sitting there not doing anything. We can set up a trust or something so you don't worry that I'm going to stop paying at any point. Eventually, I'd like to do the same for Matty."

"What... Uh... I..."

A crash outside the office drew our attention. Shouting followed.

Hudson moved me from in front of the door. He yanked it open and took a step back.

"I found these two going at it in the closet," Jonathan told Hudson.

I looked past him and saw Joey. Shirtless. He was standing in front of Tierney, who was also shirtless.

"Joey?" I shouted.

"Shit," he breathed. "Mom, this isn't what it looks like."

"It looks like two underage kids taking advantage of me," Hudson growled.

Joey's gaze snapped to Hudson's, then sank to the floor. "I'm sorry."

"You should be. This is a place of business, and there's no excuse for anything like that. She's not an employee, and I could lose my license for having a non-employee in employees only areas. You both need to get yourselves together and get out of there. Now."

"Yes, sir," Joey mumbled. He bent down and grabbed his shirt, then handed Tierney hers. Her cheeks were bright red, and she didn't look up at any of the adults.

They left the closet and headed back toward the bar. Jonathan shook his head and grabbed a mop, then followed the kids.

Hudson hung his head. He exhaled loudly, then stepped back into the office and closed the door again. "I probably didn't handle that well. I'm sorry. It doesn't change my opinion of him. I still want to pay for his college. He's a smart kid with a bright future, and I—"

"You're not his father. You're his boss. You have no right to do something like that. How could you think I'd be okay with it?"

"You said you can't afford college for him, and you're not sure he'll get a scholarship. If he doesn't, or even if he does, I want to help. I can pay for it easily. The money isn't an issue."

"It is for me. I will not be indebted to you. I will never do that. You're not going to promise me something like that and then use it to get whatever it is you want from me. Jesus, I was just telling Finley you weren't who I thought you were, and then you go and prove me wrong. You're exactly the kind of man I thought you were. And I'm done."

22

HUDSON

I GAWKED AT HER BACK AS SHE STALKED AWAY. WAS SHE serious?

"Anna," I called out.

She didn't stop.

I followed her down the hall and into the bar. She stopped at the bar where Charlie had her food ready. I caught up to her before she could turn to leave.

"What the hell was that?" I demanded.

"That was you being an asshole."

"Excuse me? I was trying to help you out."

"I don't need your help! I don't need anything from you. I can't believe I thought you understood. That I thought you were different. But no. You're just like every other man who thinks he can make a decision and the little woman is just going to go along with it. Screw you, Hudson Grant. And your insulting offer to control me."

"Seriously? That's what you think I was doing?"

"Are you honestly going to stand there and tell me you weren't? That you don't see money as a tool to solve all your problems?"

"Of course I do. That's what money is."

She scoffed. "Said like someone who's never had to worry about money."

"That's not true."

"Really? Because normal people don't pay for college for someone else's kid. He's not yours. He's never going to be yours. Stop trying to pretend you're their father. Just because you don't have your own kids doesn't give you the right to claim mine just because we've slept together."

I sucked in a breath and took a step back. I nodded once. "Good to know where we stand."

She glared at me.

"I guess we're done if that's how you feel."

She inhaled sharply and nodded. "Yep. You're off the hook."

"Lucky me."

"Come on, Matty. Let's go. You can stay with me today."

"But, Mom—"

"Now, Matty."

Matty slid off his stool and trudged behind her out the door.

And out of my life.

"Are you okay?" Jonathan asked.

"Yeah, I'm fucking great."

"Was she pissed because Joey was in the closet?"

"Nope. Probably. That isn't why she left. We're done."

"You'll figure it out. You two were good together."

"We're over. She made that clear. I'll be in my office."

"Hud—"

"I need to get ready for the interviews on Monday. The top three for the business manager job will all be here in the morning."

Jonathan nodded and let me go. It was better that way. For everyone.

I was better off alone.

I WAS a miserable asshole the rest of the weekend. I locked myself in my office and told everyone I was getting ready for the interviews. They all knew I was just avoiding people. Not that they minded when I snapped at everyone at least once.

Monday morning, I mainlined coffee and tried to wake myself up. I hadn't gotten any sleep. My brain felt like mush. My eyes were scratchy, and my skin was too tight on my body.

The first interview was set for ten o'clock with the others right after. By the middle of the day, I'd have someone chosen and I could...

Who the fuck cared? I would have all the time in the world and nothing to do with it.

It didn't matter anymore. I hadn't heard anything from Anna. Joey barely said anything to me on Saturday when he left, and he wasn't supposed to work again until Wednesday. If he actually showed up. I wouldn't be surprised if Anna made him quit.

Again, none of it mattered. I was done with her. We were over. She made it clear what she thought of me. I had no interest in killing myself to get her to change her mind. It wasn't worth it. If she didn't want to be with me, and she didn't, then I didn't want to be with her.

I just wish I'd found out before I fucking fell in love with her, but oh, well. You live and learn, and I won't make that damn mistake again.

My back hurt from sleeping in my guest room for two nights, so I tossed a few painkillers down my throat and washed them down with the dregs of my coffee and went to O'Kelley's.

The bar was closed and dark, like it was supposed to be. I unlocked the door and set about flipping chairs off tables and getting everything ready for when I opened. Jonathan and Danielle were both going to be there at ten so I could focus on the interviews and not get pulled away to handle something in the bar.

I went through inventory, forgetting my count a dozen times before I even made it through the first item on the list. Fuck it. I'd have to figure it out later.

I made myself more coffee and drank the shit black. It tasted like sucking an exhaust pipe, but it woke me up a little.

Just before ten, I unlocked the back door. Danielle came in a few minutes later, following shortly after by Jonathan. He took one look at me and shook his head. He'd already learned not to comment on my appearance. Or my attitude. Or my ability to focus. My brain was even more fucked up than normal since I wasn't sleeping.

Right at ten, I opened the front door. A woman in a clean white button down and a slim pair of black pants walked in. She smiled and shook my hand and followed me to the office for interview number two.

Rachel was a good candidate. She had a business degree and an incredible track record. She was currently working as a business manager for an attorney's office in A-Bay.

"Why do you want to move up here?" I asked her.

"I probably wouldn't move. It's only about twenty minutes, which is very doable even in winter."

"Why are you looking to leave your current position?"

"I'm always open to new opportunities. My current job has a lot of things that I like, but a more casual environment where I can have a more flexible schedule appeals to me."

"Are you okay with working around a bunch of drunk people?"

She blanched, her perfect smile faltering just a touch.

Did she seriously not consider that part of the job?

"Well, I'm not a big drinker. And the office manager is someone who will be dealing with mostly background stuff, so I doubt I'd be around drunk people all that often."

Her snooty attitude reminded me of Anna for a split second, and the asshole caveman part of my brain decided she wasn't right for the job. I couldn't risk even a hint of Anna invading anymore of my life. Not when she was everywhere and in everything and I was already dying because I had to let her go.

"Actually, you're around drunk people all the time in this job. It's in a freaking bar. What do you think people do here?"

She sucked in a breath. "Okay, but people aren't always drunk."

"I think they could be. And you should probably plan for it. If you can't handle being around drunk people, you probably shouldn't apply for jobs in bars, you know? I mean, that's kind of dumb, if you ask me."

"Well, I didn't ask you, but thank you for your opinion." She stood and grabbed her too big bag and slung it over her shoulder. "Thank you for your time, Mr. Grant. I think this interview is over."

I nodded at her and didn't feel the slightest upset to see her go.

The second interview was almost as successful. That guy lasted a little longer, but he still walked out. He wasn't willing to get in the middle of a fight between two drunk people if he needed to.

What the fuck? It was half of my job. I needed someone who could handle shit like that.

The third candidate showed up ten minutes early. He was pressed and polished and looked all wrong for the place on arrival. His gray suit with a blue tie would be dirty in minutes, and his perfectly parted hair would get messed up just as fast. Hell, I wanted to mess up his hair just to prove it.

I knew from his resume he was the most qualified with a lot of experience managing restaurants and bars and some experience with businesses, too. He was also older than the other candidates and already lived in town. He was my top choice, when I actually gave a shit.

"Hudson, good to see you again," Arthur said, approaching me with a hand out.

I shook his hand. "Yep."

He stood there for a second, his gaze tightening. "Should we sit?"

I sighed heavily. "Yeah. We'll go to my office."

He flashed a smile I knew was forced and followed me down the hall. I closed the door while he sat in one of my guest chairs. I needed to burn those, too. Anna sat in them. The couch definitely had to go. Maybe I should sell the entire fucking bar.

"So, um, thank you for giving me another opportunity," he said.

"Yep. Glad you could come in." I glanced at my desktop and grabbed his resume. "I guess we should get started. First thing is what can you do for me and this place that the other candidates I already spoke to can't do?"

Surprise flashed across his face at my gruff and direct question. He folded his hands together and composed himself before looking at me and pressing his lips up into a tight smile. "Obviously, I don't know who else you spoke to, so all I can tell you is what I'm capable of. I have years of experience as a business manager in restaurants, bars, and offices. I've adapted to every situation I've been in. I have my own systems that I bring with me and use to make a place that's already successful even more successful. For me, this job isn't just about taking things off your plate or making your life easier, it's also about making the business more profitable."

"Assuming you care about money," I growled.

His smile faltered again before he stuck it back on. "True. But I have yet to meet a business owner who doesn't. It doesn't really matter what you're selling, you want to make money."

"Not everyone cares about money."

"Um, yes. Okay."

I rolled my eyes and looked at my notes again. "How do you handle conflict? Are you willing to jump in when drunk assholes start throwing punches or would you be too afraid to wrinkle your suit?"

He rolled his lips in and pressed them together. He sucked in a breath, then tilted his head. "Conflict is always a part of any job. I'm not afraid of conflict. I'm typically the one who gets blamed when things don't go as planned, so I'm used to it. As for jumping into a fight, I can't say it would be my favorite part of the job, but I wouldn't want anyone to get hurt."

"Not worried about your suit?" I asked. Yeah, I was an asshole.

He smiled. "Not at all. I take it you don't like men in suits."

"Don't know that many. I tend to prefer hanging out with men who are less concerned with their appearances."

Arthur nodded again. "Good to know."

"How do you work under pressure?" I asked, continuing the interview.

"Well, most of the time. I will usually step back and evaluate a situation before I jump in. I believe there is always a solution to every problem, and it's easier for me to find it from the outside instead of the inside, so I tend to think things through a bit before trying to fix them in the wrong way."

"But you'd jump into a fight? Which is it? Do you jump in or sit back?"

"It depends on the situation," he snarled. Clearly, the questions were getting to him.

"Tell me a time when you would jump in."

"If someone is going to get hurt, I would always jump in."

"What if it's just two guys talking shit to each other? Or a guy being inappropriate to a female server? You'd let that continue?"

Arthur sighed. "No. Physical pain isn't the only pain there is."

"Ah, so you're sensitive. That's good. Men are too afraid to share their feelings."

"Sure," Arthur said through gritted teeth.

"Where are you going to be in five years?"

"Professionally, I hope to be running my own business."

My brows shot up. "Yeah? Doing what? Boxing?" I laughed at my own joke.

Arthur clenched his hands into fists. He took a deep breath and let it out slowly. "I'd like to develop a business management firm that handles things like I'd be doing here, if I got the job, but centralize the work so small businesses don't have to pay a salary for an entire person plus benefits. They would have the option to hire someone on a per hour basis and pay a fee for the person, but they would be full-time employees for me."

I was slightly impressed. It sounded like a good idea. If something like that already existed, I would have hired someone sooner than I was.

Maybe.

But it didn't exist.

"Do you think you can get it up and running in five years and still do a good job working for me?"

Arthur nodded. "Absolutely. I would never let my responsibilities slide for my employer. That wouldn't be fair."

I snorted. "Fair. Life's not fair, dude."

He linked his hands together and rested them on his lap.

I asked him the standard bullshit about disagreeing with coworkers, fixing mistakes, owning up to his mistakes, and being challenged. He answered everything with tight lips and tense answers.

But he lasted longer than the others.

When the hour was up, I stood with him. "Well, you made it. First one today."

He didn't reply. "Thank you for the opportunity."

"I didn't say you had the job yet."

He drew in a sharp breath. "I will make sure not to wait for your call. Good luck, Mr. Grant."

I waved as he strode toward the door and pushed his way out.

I went back to my office and closed the door. I knew Arthur was the one I needed to hire. He had the best experience. And he was the only one who didn't get scared off and leave the interview.

I went through all my notes on all of them and reviewed their resumes. If I was actually going to hire someone, I needed to make sure it was the right person. I had employees to take care of, and even if I wanted to burn the shit down, I knew I wouldn't actually do it.

Since Goldie was the one who sent me all the candidates, I called her to thank her for her help and let her know I was going to make an offer to Arthur.

"Hello?"

"It's Hudson. I just wanted you to know I decided to hire one of the people you sent me. Thanks."

"You're welcome, Hudson. Who did you decide to hire?"

"Guy named Arthur. He's the best one."

She chuckled. "I agree. Arthur is very talented and has amazing experience."

"Yep. It should be good. Anyway, wanted to tell you."

"How are you?" she blurted as I was about to hang up the phone.

I snorted. "I'm fucking fabulous. Did Anna tell you to ask me?"

"No. I'm at work, not with Anna."

"Cool. Don't care."

"Hudson, what happened between you two?"

"She decided she's done. I'm not going to beg her to change her mind. She's done, I'm done. All good."

"You don't sound like you're all good."

"Hey, you know what? I don't need you to pile on right now and tell me she's right and I'm wrong and I'm not worth her time. I just wanted to be nice and thank you for bringing me candidates."

"Hudson—"

I hung up before she could say anything else.

Before she could call back, if she was going to, I called Arthur.

"Hello?" Arthur said. Screaming kids echoed in the background. Someone told them to be quiet, but I could still hear them.

"Arthur, it's Hudson Grant from O'Kelley's. I wanted to talk to you about the business manager job."

"Okay."

"I'd like to formally offer you the job. I know you're working right now, and it'll take a few weeks for you to put in your notice, but I'm hoping I can get you to start working as soon as possible. Maybe by the end of February."

"Uh, yeah, thanks, but no."

"Excuse me?"

"I don't think O'Kelley's is the right place for me."

"Why not? You seemed interested after your first interview. Why did you come back for a second one if you were just going to say no?"

"Honestly, Mr. Grant, I had every intention of taking the job. I want something closer to home with hours that can be flexible. The money was in line with what I think I deserve. Everything was great until today. Quite frankly, you were a jerk, and I've worked for enough jerks to know that if you act like that during an interview, it's only worse when I'm your employee. So, thank you, but no."

"Arthur—" He was already gone.

"Fuck!" I shouted. I threw my phone and watched as it hit the wall and fell to the floor with a thunk. I closed my eyes.

I did what I told myself I would never do. I fell so far into Anna that I lost sight of everything else in my world. I lost sight of my business and I fucked everything up.

I wanted to blame her, to hate her for one more thing, but the truth was, I made those choices. I fell in love with her. I put her and my pain from losing her ahead of my business. I chose all of that. And I was going to be the one to pay for it.

But it told me I was done. Done trying to have something I wasn't meant to have. Done trying to create a life that involved more than my bar. Just fucking done.

23

ANNA

"Dammit," I hissed as I wiped a tear from the cover of a book I was supposed to be shelving. The stupid hero had the same crooked grin as Hudson. I stared at him a little too long and a tear leaked free.

I shoved the book onto the shelf and grabbed another one. I didn't let myself look at the covers, just the spine, so I knew where it needed to go. I couldn't get distracted. Not again.

I thought my husband leaving me with two young kids and getting divorced while saddled with thousands of debt I didn't spend was bad. Nope. Not even close to being betrayed by a man I could have, maybe, possibly, started to see a future with.

It was my fault, though. I thought he saw me as capable. Instead, he showed me that he saw me as a charity case. Not good enough. A failure of a parent since I not only couldn't afford to pay for my son's college, but I also raised a kid who was going to sneak off to screw around with his girlfriend when he was supposed to be working.

All of it burned. Not because it wasn't true, but because

it was. Joey and I were barely speaking, Matty was mad because he couldn't hang out with Hudson anymore, and I just cried constantly.

I never should have gotten involved with him. I shouldn't have let my whole family get involved with him. My pride wanted to tell Joey he had to quit, but we needed the money. Just one more thing Hudson was right about and Hudson was doing.

When Joey first started working there, I didn't like it, but I let it go. I let it happen and accepted what Joey was getting paid so we could dig ourselves out of the hole Nick had left us in. Joey was a big help. His income kept the lights on some months and made sure the boys had enough to eat. I was grateful for it, but I was foolish for letting myself get involved with Hudson.

No more dating. I was done. I deleted my Book Boyfriends Wanted account and was focusing on keeping my shit together while I was around others and crying myself to sleep every night. Six nights. I didn't cry that much when Nick left me.

I finished shelving the books and took the empty box to the storage room to break down and recycle. I grabbed another to put those books on the shelves when Finley stepped in my way.

"Can we talk?" she asked.

My throat tightened, and my palms dampened. I hated those words. When they came from a boss, it always meant I was about to lose my job. A job that supported my family. A job I thought was secure.

Did Hudson tell her to fire me? I couldn't imagine he would, but I didn't really know him. I thought I did, but I was wrong.

I set the box down and forced a smile. "Sure."

"Let's sit."

Even worse. The boss never asked you to sit unless it was really bad.

I followed Finley to the seating area where she hosted book club. Obviously, I wasn't invited to that anymore. God, I was so stupid. I'd lived in MacKellar Cove my whole life and in the last few months I let myself think I could actually be a part of the town. I was so wrong.

"Okay, so this is hard for me to say, but—"

"It's okay," I told her. God, I was so pathetic, reassuring my boss that it wasn't a big deal for her to fire me. "I know you have to let me go."

"Does that mean you're saying yes?" she asked, all excited.

"To what? To Hudson? No. I already told him no. I haven't changed my mind."

"Wait, what are you talking about? Did Hudson offer you a job?"

I snorted. "No, he offered to pay for Joey's college. Why would he offer me a job?"

"Back up. What are you talking about? I'm so confused right now."

"You're firing me because Hudson and I broke up."

Finley jerked back. "Whoa, what? Are you kidding me?" She shook her head. "No. Okay, I'm... I need a second to process all of this. First, why do you think I would fire you just because you and Hudson broke up?"

"Because he's your people. You're good friends. And it's a small town. You're either on the inside or the outside, and I'm on the outside."

"Oh, Anna. I'm so sorry you feel that way. You're on the inside with me. I adore having you work here. And I adore your boys. I think of you as a friend."

"You're my boss, Finley. I know that means we can't really be friends."

"That's not how I function. I don't want people in my life and in my business that aren't people I trust. I turned my entire world over to you when George was born. You asked me for a job, and I threw my arms around you and suffocated you because I was so grateful. I always feel like I come on too strong, but with you, I always felt like I wasn't clear how much you meant to me."

Tears filled my eyes. She sounded like she meant it.

"You are as important to me as Blake and Karissa and Trinity and everyone else. You're part of my crazy, wild, messed up family. It's why we invited you to thanksgiving. You're family to us. And that's why I wouldn't even consider anyone else for the marketing job."

"Marketing job? What are you talking about?"

"With MacKellar Investments. I told you about it. Doing marketing for all the bookstores in Trent's hotels."

"You want me to do that job?"

"Of course. There's no one else that would be better at it."

I snorted. "That's not anywhere close to true. I don't have a degree in marketing, or anything else. I have no experience. I'm just a cashier and stock person."

Finley closed her eyes and leaned forward. She grabbed my hand and squeezed it. When she looked up at me, her eyes were glassy and sad. "Anna, you're the reason we're making money this year. I've never been overly successful. I love this place, but I don't have a business mind. I was considering closing the doors not long ago. Goldie helped me out with a few events, and then I got pregnant with George. Those events made it possible for me to stay open until the spring when business would pick up, but I was sure I would have to shut down the shop for good when George arrived. If it wasn't for you stepping up to work here, to run this place, and all your ideas to get people not only in the door but to the online shop, I wouldn't have had a choice."

"All I did was showcase the store."

Finley nodded. "But you did it in a way that I never saw to do. You were clever and creative. You designed displays that made sense and you were smart about the way you did everything. You coming onboard has nearly doubled profits."

I sucked in a breath. I knew things were good, but I didn't realize they were that much better. I felt the first burn of pride in my chest. Finley created an amazing store, but she was giving me the credit for making it more successful. "Thank you."

"Thank you. I know sometimes my life looks picture perfect from the outside, but when I got pregnant, I was terrified. Even when I hired you, I had no idea if Trent would ever truly step up and help me. I saw how strong you were and how amazing your boys are, and it gave me a tiny bit of confidence that maybe I could be a decent single mom."

My throat tightened. "Thank you," I whispered.

"Trent has more money than God, and I know I don't have to worry about anything right now, but a year ago, I did. A year ago, I was struggling to make ends meet. I know you feel the same and have for your entire life. And I'm not judging you for that. You've been dealt a shitty hand. But this job is something you earned. I'm not giving it to you, you've worked your ass off and proven to Trent and me you're the only person who should be in charge of marketing for all the bookstores."

That kind of job was like a dream come true for me. I'd always loved marketing, but until Finley, I never had a boss who let me try things. Finley encouraged me and let me fly. And now, she was letting me go even higher. But...

"This is too big of a job for me. I really appreciate it, but I think you'll regret hiring me."

Finley shook her head the entire time I spoke. "No. Anna, no. You know this store. You know what I stock. You are always looking for new authors, up-and-coming authors for readers to try. You know what sells and what doesn't. You are smart and you get this market. You were the one who had the idea to put bookstores in Trent's hotels. I never thought of that. This entire project is because of you. Trent and I agreed we don't want anyone else."

"But—"

"You are more than qualified. You are the best person for this job. I know I haven't done a very good job of making it clear I was offering it to you, but you're the only person we considered. The travel is minimal. You'll have a store manager in each location to handle the day-to-day stuff. If you want to move, you can do that, but I hope you'll stay here and use this store as your home base."

"This is... It's a lot, Finley."

She nodded. "I know. But we're going to start small. Five stores in the first year. Trent has ideas about where he'd like them to be, but we want you to make the final decision. He'd like to get started on the construction in the next month or two."

Excitement filled me for the first time in a very long time. I was going to build something amazing. It would be a new challenge and a new project, something unique and special and fun. My first thought was to call Hudson and tell him, but of course, that wasn't an option.

I bit the inside of my lip to pull back the emotion. He wasn't a part of my life anymore. Which made taking this job an easier choice. Maybe we would move. Maybe starting over some place else would be better for all of us. Some place where no one knows us.

Joey would hate me for moving him right before his senior year. Matty might be okay with it. It wouldn't be easy, but maybe it was better.

"I'd be honored to take this on. Thank you, Finley."

"Really? Yay! I'm so excited. I thought for sure you were going to say no."

I laughed with her. "I like the idea of a new challenge. And I'm going to talk to the boys about moving. That might be a good idea for us."

"Really?" Finley said, her excitement dulling.

I nodded. "I need a fresh start. It'll depend on the markets you're looking to move to and if I can afford it, but—"

"Oh! I'm so bad at this. Trent has a salary for you. Technically, you'll be working for him with this job. It'll come with full benefits and a salary. Hang on." She hurried into the office.

Full benefits? I'd never had a job with full benefits. Or a salary. My heart skipped at the thought.

"Here it is," Finley said, waving a sheet of paper toward me as she came back. "All the details of the job offer from Trent. He's an official kind of guy, so he has everything in writing. He wants to set up a meeting with you to answer any questions you have and go over everything in detail. And you can negotiate the salary. He expects it, so don't worry about asking for ten percent more. Or more than that. Whatever you think."

I stared at the number on the page and thought I was

going to pass out. His offer was more than twice what Joey and I made together last year. On top of that, it came with full benefits, a retirement plan, and travel expenses for any trips I needed to go on. Trent also put...

"A car allowance?" I asked, looking up at Finley.

She nodded. "Apparently it's something he has in every contract for his executive vice presidents."

"Executive vice president? Finley, this is too much."

Finley put her hand on mine again and waited until I met her gaze. "It's not enough for you, Anna. You've earned it."

"I don't know if I can handle all of this."

"You won't be alone. I'll always be available to talk, you'll have an assistant, and there will be a manager in each store. You will have a hand in all of those people, and they will all be working for you. This is a big job."

I stared at the paper again. That number was a big number. The kind of number it would have taken me three years to earn in any other job I'd ever had. Maybe four years. "What about Matty? And Joey? I don't know if I feel comfortable leaving them if I have to travel. I don't have anyone who could stay with them."

Finley smiled. "Yes, you do. Anna, you're not alone. Not anymore. I know you don't like accepting help, but Trent and I will take the boys anytime you need to travel. We have plenty of space. And Hudson—"

"Is not an option," I said firmly.

"Why did you two breakup?"

"Because he doesn't think I'm capable of taking care of my family. This proves it."

Finley chuckled. "I've never known a more capable person than you. How could you ever think you're not capable of taking care of your family?"

"Hudson said he wanted to pay for Joey's college. Because I can't afford to. He decided to be the savior and swoop in and take care of it. He wanted to control me."

Finley shook her head slowly. "Oh, Anna. I'm so sorry. Hudson is the kind of person who goes big when he cares about someone. There are no small measures for him. He loves with his whole self, and when he can't say the words, he tries to show it and it comes off as overbearing."

"He doesn't love me."

"Yes, he does. He's been a miserable asshole all week. He wouldn't tell me what happened, but if you two ended things, that makes sense. I thought it was because the guy he wanted to hire turned him down, but now I get it. Regardless of that, I know he loves you. And I know him offering to pay for Joey's college was his way of showing you how much you mean to him."

"I don't believe that."

Finley smiled sadly. "Hudson jumped in when I got pregnant. He insisted on driving me to my appointments, and he was willing to be in the room when I delivered. He brought me food and made sure I was taking care of myself. He was everything I wanted Trent to be. He even told Trent off. He never once said he loves me, but I know that's why he was doing it. Hudson doesn't have family. Hillary, his parents... he's been alone for a long time. I think he's rusty when it comes to saying the words, so he goes above and beyond to show people he loves them. And you and your boys are at the top of that list right now."

Tears rolled down my cheeks. "I really don't think that's true."

"Listen, no one knows this, but Hudson sponsors a scholarship. It goes to one kid from the high school every year. It's always a kid whose parents don't really have the money to pay for the kid to go to college. He works with the school to collect applications and he goes through them, but since he knows so many people in town, he knows which families need the money. The scholarship makes a huge difference to the kid who gets it."

"Are you serious?"

Finley nodded. "Hudson is always giving back. He always wanted kids, but since he doesn't have his own, he sponsors other kids to help see their dreams come true. I really think that's all he was doing with Joey, but without the secrecy."

"I messed everything up, didn't I?"

Finley shook her head. "No. If I know anything about Hudson, it's that he will always forgive someone. But only if you mean it. Do you want to forgive him for the money or for the man?"

My face twisted as I held back my tears. "I never wanted the money."

"What about the man? Do you want him? Because I love you, but I love him, too. I'm not going to push you back to him if you're not really in this. I've never seen him so upset. Trinity said James told her when Hillary died is the only other time Hudson's ever been this far gone. James is worried about him. I am, too. But if you're not as miserable as he is, if you're not in this, I'm going to ask you to leave him alone and let him figure out how to get over you."

I stopped fighting the emotions I'd been fighting all week and let Finley see how broken I was. I covered my face with my hands and cried like I'd been doing every night. As much as I hated what Hudson did, I believed what Finley said. He was trying to show me what I wasn't ready to hear.

"I haven't told anyone I love them except my boys. Ever. My parents never said the words to me. I probably said them to Nick at one point, but growing up without hearing those words made me not know how important they were. When Joey was born, I knew what love was. That was the first time I'd ever felt it. I felt it again with Matty. And again with Hudson."

"Good," Finley said through her own tears.

"I don't know how to tell him."

Finley shook her head. "I don't either, and it's not going to be easy. But you deserve happiness. Both of you. And I think you can have it together."

"I hope so."

24

HUDSON

I SHOWERED, SHAVED MY HEAD, PUT ON CLEAN CLOTHES. I WAS not going to fuck things up a second time. I couldn't. Too much was on the line.

I got to O'Kelley's early and paced in my office. I was stressed and tired and tense. After today, it would be better, but until it was over, I was on the edge of my sanity. I needed it to be a good day.

At exactly ten o'clock, I unlocked the front door. I stepped back and waited. I had to play it cool. Not because I was, but because the situation was delicate.

The door opened, and I drew a deep breath. This was it.

Anna stepped inside the bar, and all my confidence shattered. I sucked in a sharp breath, one that drew her attention to me. Fuck. Not like I could have hidden from her, but just no.

"What are you doing here?" I barked.

"I wanted to talk to you."

"I'm busy," I said.

She glanced around the vacant bar but didn't comment. "I wanted to apologize for the way I acted."

"Great. Apology accepted. Have a nice life."

"Hudson—"

I couldn't do it. Not today. Of all fucking days, today was the day she decided to show up? To make amends or whatever the fuck she thought she was doing?

I walked from behind the bar and headed toward my office. It wasn't much, but maybe she wouldn't follow me.

I didn't even get to close the door.

"Anna, I don't have time for this right now."

"What do you have to do that's so important?" she asked, her eyes narrowing.

I raised a brow at her. "You don't get to ask about my life anymore. You made it very clear you didn't want to be in it, so get the hell out."

"Mr. Grant?" a man said from the door.

Anna stepped aside and turned to look at a very pissed off Arthur.

Of course.

I held his gaze for a long moment, already knowing he was going to walk out and never come back.

"Hello, I'm Anna," she said, stepping toward him.

"Arthur Hill."

Anna looked back at me like she expected me to explain who Arthur was and why he was there. It was none of her damn business, so I kept my mouth shut. It only got me in more trouble anyway.

"Well, it's nice to meet you. I'll let you two talk."

Arthur nodded to her as she moved around him. When she was out of the office, I exhaled loudly.

"Mr. Grant—"

"Please, call me Hudson. And please let me explain that before you say anything. I know I can't ask you anything personal, and I have no intention of doing so, but what you just walked in on is very personal. Anna's son is one of the busboys here, and we were involved. Anna and I, not her son. She's the first woman I've been involved with since my wife died seventeen years ago. I'm clearly rusty with women because it ended."

"I'm sorry, but I have to say speaking to her like you did is likely the reason."

"Hardly. She ended things with me after I offered to pay for her son to go to college."

"That was generous of you."

I scoffed. "She didn't agree. She thought it was a way for me to tie her to me or hold it over her head so she had no choice but to stay with me. She thought it was a method of control."

"Was it?"

I shook my head. "I would rather be without her than have her feel as though she had to stay with me. That's not love. That's obligation."

Arthur tilted his head. "Why did you tell her to get out?"

"She said she came to apologize. We haven't spoken in nine days. I wanted her gone before you arrived so I didn't mess up another conversation with you."

"Nine days? In other words, two days before our last interview?"

I nodded.

"That's why you acted the way you did? Because of her?"

I nodded again. "That's no excuse for my behavior, and I apologize for it. My wife was my world, and when she died, I never thought I'd meet another woman I could see myself building a life with. When Anna decided she was done with me, I couldn't really handle it. I took that out on you, and others, and even if you still aren't interested in the job, I wanted to apologize in person for the way I behaved."

Arthur looked at me for a long moment. His blue eyes narrowed, and his lips turned up slightly. "I've definitely had my fair share of heartbreak and bad days because of a woman. I'm fortunate now that I have a wife who understands me and lets me be me, and three kids who are our entire world. They're why I wanted to take this job. It would mean a better balance for my family."

"I understand. I'm sorry I didn't give you a better impression and you decided working for me wasn't in your best interest."

He rubbed his jaw and considered me. "I may have been too quick to judge."

"Really?"

He nodded. "Love has a way of tossing us upside down and ripping out our insides and making us grateful for it. I can't blame a man who let love in and got beat up in the process."

"Does that mean you'll take the job?"

Arthur nodded slowly. "Yes, I will. But I have one condition."

"Name it."

"Hear her out."

"Who?"

"Anna. Let her say what she needs to say and really listen to her. She didn't look like a woman who was here to rub salt in your wounds."

"Just seeing her rubs salt in my wounds."

"If what she has to say doesn't soothe some of that, you can let her go. But if it does, maybe you'll find a way back to each other."

I rubbed my head and sighed heavily. Everything inside me was raw and sore. Just being in the same room with Anna hurt. The last thing I wanted to do was have a conversation with her. And the only thing I wanted to do was have a conversation with her.

I finally nodded. "I'll talk to her. I can't promise anything, but—"

"Give her a chance. That's all I ask. And I'm happy to see my first impression of you was accurate. I think this will be a great place to work."

"Thank you, Arthur. I'm really looking forward to having you here."

We talked another fifteen minutes about the job and when he would start, then he left. I'd heard movement and voices in the bar, so I knew it was well in hand and I could take a few minutes to process seeing Anna.

I tossed my ball cap on my desk and rubbed my temples. The sight of her lingered in my mind. Her jeans were fitted, hugging her curves and making my mouth water. Her pink shirt rested on the top of her breasts and hung loose to her hips. Her hair fell in soft waves. She looked good. Not happy, but good.

I hoped she was. As much as it hurt to let her go, I wanted her to be happy. I accepted that as the truth. She decided I wasn't the right person for her, and I wouldn't fight her on that, so I wished her well. Inside because I wasn't strong enough to say it to her face.

A knock on the door had me lifting my head. She was standing there, looking like a dream I conjured. "I thought you left."

She shook her head. "Can we talk? Please."

It was that one word that did it. That made me agree when I knew it would crush me. I promised Arthur, but I intended to put it off for a while. Until being in the same space as her didn't hurt so badly.

I nodded.

She sat in the chair Arthur had just vacated and fidgeted with her sleeves. I wasn't going to give in and start the conversation. I felt like an ass, but she was the one who came to me.

"I wanted to tell you how sorry I am for judging you the way I did."

She looked up at me, and I nodded.

"It wasn't fair. I..." She swallowed roughly. "I've never known what it was like to have someone actually care about me. To have someone want to do something for me or my boys without expecting anything in return—"

"I never said—"

"I know. I know. My own parents took money from me and deserted me as soon as they could. My husband told me he never really wanted me or to have kids and felt trapped. None of them ever told me they loved me. And they didn't. But whenever they did something nice, my entire life, it's been because they wanted something from me."

"I didn't want anything. And I definitely didn't want you to feel like you were stuck with me. I would have created a trust or something. So Joey and Matty would be able to use the money without you even having to talk to me if that was what you wanted."

She shook her head. "It's not." She breathed a laugh. She pursed her lips and swallowed roughly. "God, it's not what I want. I've missed you. But I know I don't have the right to say that to you. I have never loved someone I didn't give birth to. I never knew it was possible for me to. Not until I met you. And I will always carry that with me. I will always love you, Hudson. Thank you for that gift."

I swallowed around the lump in my throat. She smiled sadly at me, then made a move to get up.

"You're leaving?"

She looked at me, eyes shiny with unshed tears and a smile that said she knew it was the end. "Just like I didn't want to accept anything from you that came with strings, I'd never ask you to accept anything from me that did. I didn't tell you I love you because I expect you to forgive and forget and fall back into me. You are an amazing man, and I'm honored to have been a part of your life for a little while. That's why I wanted to talk to you."

"So, you're still done." It wasn't a question.

"I'll never be done with you, Hudson. You're a part of me now. A piece of my heart will always belong to you. I'm terrified of that piece because it's tender, but that piece gives me strength I never knew I had."

"And that's all you want. Is a piece."

She huffed a laugh and wiped at the tears that fell from her eyes. "No. I want all of you. I want a life with you. I want to tell you about the job offer from Finley and Trent and talk to you about Joey's college options next year and have family dinners and vacations and wake up to you every morning and go to sleep next to you every night. But I don't have the right to ask you for any of that."

"So you're just going to walk away and not give me a chance to tell you if I want any of that?"

She closed her eyes for a minute, giving me a chance to study her. God, she was stunning. It hurt to look at her from across my desk and not touch her. It was downright painful. But I had some things to say first.

She lifted her gaze to mine and smiled. It was one of anxiety and fear. Two things I hated to see in her beautiful brown eyes. But I understood. I hadn't given her any reason to think I was about to do exactly what she thought I wouldn't do.

"Tell me about the job."

She blinked and drew back. "The job?"

I nodded. "You said Finley and Trent offered you a job. What is it?"

"Um, well, it's Vice President of Bookstore Marketing for MacKellar Investments. Finley's going to open bookstores in some of the hotels, and they want me in charge of the marketing for them."

"That sounds like a great job."

"It is. I'm really excited about it. It'll be some travel, but the pay is amazing, and I'm going to be in charge of a team that will run each store. I've never been challenged like this. Or trusted. I owe Finley and Trent a lot."

"I'm sure they feel as though you earned the job."

She smiled. "That's what they both said."

"Then you know it's true. What are you going to do with the boys when you travel?"

She drew a breath. "If school is out, they'll come with me. If not, Finley and Trent said they could stay there."

"It'll be hard to have them leave their own beds, though. I think they should just stay home when you go."

She shook her head, letting her brown strands tumble over her shoulders. "Joey's not old enough for that. I know they're good kids, but I wouldn't be comfortable leaving them home alone."

"What if they aren't alone?"

"I couldn't ask Finley to sleep at my apartment. I can afford a nicer place with the new salary, but I'm not going to have a place as nice as hers. And I wouldn't ask her to leave her own son."

"What if all of you moved into my house?"

She gasped. Our gazes collided and held. Hope drifted between us and hung on the edge of her lashes in the tear that hovered there. "Hudson."

I groaned. "You know you can't say my name like that and expect me to keep my hands off of you."

She squeezed her eyes shut, and the tear fell.

"I love you, Anna. I want all the things you said you want. I want you and Joey and Matty in my life. And if you want, I want all three of you in my home. Tonight. Tomorrow. Whenever you're ready. Because I've been ready since the first night you came to my house. I've missed you so damn much."

"You have?"

I nodded. "Hell, yes. I never meant to make you feel like you owed me anything. Or to make you feel like you weren't enough. You earned that job from Finley and Trent, and the salary and everything else. You are amazing. And smart. And strong. And everything I never thought I'd find again. I'm scared, too, but I know we can do anything if we have each other because living without you sucks."

"It really does," she said through her tears. "Are you serious about all of this?"

I opened my top drawer and pulled out a keyring. I spun it on my finger and moved around the desk to kneel in front of her. "I'm not proposing now, but this ring is as good as a proposal to me. This is a key to my home. Three actually. One for you, one for Joey, and one for Matty. I want the three of you to move in with me. Make my home yours."

She cried harder and wrapped her hand around mine. "I'm sorry I ever doubted your intentions. That I let my past destroy our present."

"You didn't. We will have more hurdles, but we'll get over them together. If you're willing to try."

She nodded. "Yes. Absolutely. Please."

I surged up and sealed my lips to hers, pressing her back into the chair. Her arms wound around my neck and pulled closer until I was kneeling in front of her. I set my hands on her hips and squeezed.

"Fucking hell, I missed you," I whispered against her lips.

"I missed you, too. And I love you."

"I love you, Anna. Thank you for giving us another chance."

"Thank you for accepting my apology."

I chuckled. "I owe my new business manager a thanks for that."

"New business manager?" she asked, pulling back to look at me with a quirk of her brow.

"The reason I couldn't talk when you got here this morning. I made a mess of his interview and he declined the job when I offered it to him. I begged him to come in so I could apologize and try to explain, then you showed up and I almost messed it up again. Arthur convinced me to listen to what you had to say and give us a chance."

"You wouldn't have if he hadn't said that?"

I shook my head. "I'd never have been able to resist you. I was hurt and angry at myself, but I can't say no to you. I love you too much for that."

She pushed me back, a scolding look in her eyes. "I don't want that. This has to be a partnership. Where we can be honest with each other and push each other and challenge each other to be better. If you're not going to push back when I'm being ridiculous, I'm going to feel like I'm manipulating you or taking advantage of you."

"You can take advantage of me anytime you want," I teased.

"I'm serious," she said, scowling. "I love you, and I know you're not a pushover. You have to be able to say no to me."

"Are you going to say no to me?"

"Absolutely."

"Even when I kiss you right here?" I kissed the side of her neck.

"Yes."

"What about here?" I licked her earlobe.

"Yes."

"And here?" I nibbled her collarbone.

"Oh, yes," she moaned.

"Wait, I'm confused. Are you supposed to be saying yes or no?"

"I don't care as long as you don't stop. Please, Hudson."

"Now that's all you really need to say."

"What about I love you?"

"That works, too." I jumped up and pushed the door closed, making sure it was locked before I went back to my spot on the floor between her thighs.

"Are you comfortable?"

"Not as comfortable as I'll be when I'm buried deep inside you."

"Hudson."

"I'm really happy to hear you say my name again. Especially like that."

She smiled as I lifted her shirt up and off. "I never stopped. And I never will. I love you."

"I love you," I said. It was more than three words. It was a promise. And the keyring on her finger was only temporary. I wasn't going to wait long to make her a more permanent promise.

EPILOGUE
GOLDIE

"Paul, grab that box," I hissed to my teenager.

He shoved his phone in his pocket and rolled his eyes like only a teenager can. I swear, it was like his eyes were double-jointed. Or whatever the equivalent was for something that wasn't a joint.

I pasted a smile on my face and followed him into the house. It was gorgeous. I was a little surprised when Anna told me she didn't make any changes to it and that it was all Hudson. Then again, he loved her, so I knew he had good taste.

"Thank you guys for helping," Hudson said as he passed us on the way out the door for more boxes.

Paul grumbled something that was, thankfully, unintelligible, and I plastered my smile on and prayed Hudson wasn't offended by my highly offensive teen.

Hudson snorted and kept going. Maybe he was already used to it. I could only hope.

"Kitchen?" I asked Anna when we came around the corner and found her standing in the middle of the dining room.

"Yes. Please. Thank you so much. Both of you. Paul, you should go check out Joey's room. I think Hudson said we're almost done. You can take a break."

Paul didn't wait for me to agree before taking off in the direction Anna pointed.

I sighed. "I'm sorry. He woke up in a mood today. I probably should have left him home."

Anna chuckled and shook her head. "Trust me, I get it. Everyone says boys are so easy, but boys have just as many moods and attitudes as girls."

"Tell me about it. I swear, there are days I want to ask Paul if he's PMS'ing."

Anna snorted. "I've asked Joey that. He got even more angry. But it was funny. How many times has that been the assumption from men?"

"Too many."

We shared a smile.

"How's the new job going?"

"Tiring. But amazing. I won't complain. And thank you for offering to be a back-up for Hudson while I'm gone next month. I've never been away from the boys for longer than an overnight at a friend's house. It's going to be hard."

"You'll be busy with work and back home before you know it. Trust me."

"You're used to it, though. It's not normal for me to travel. Or to have a decent paycheck."

"You've earned it. Enjoy it. And put it toward college. Or a wedding."

Anna rolled her eyes. "I'm starting to wonder if he was joking about wanting to propose right away."

"You've only been back together a few weeks. And you've been busy getting ready to move and starting your new job.

And he's been getting Arthur settled into the business manager job."

"So, Arthur is Patrick's brother?"

I nodded and tore the tape off a box.

"He's pretty cute."

"He's married," I said.

"I'm not looking. I'm just saying... do good genes run in the family?"

I choked on absolutely nothing. My first instinct was to say hell yes, but that would mean admitting I'd noticed Patrick was gorgeous. He was, but there was a line I wasn't willing to cross with my assistant.

"All choked up just thinking about him?" Anna asked.

I glared at her. "We've already talked about this."

"Yes, and you said he's attractive but not an option. I'm still wondering why he's not an option. Because he seems like a damn good one to me."

"You're all happy and bubbly and think everyone else can join you. I want to, but Patrick is almost fourteen years younger than me. When I was his age, I had my son. I'm too old to be starting over."

"Who says you need to start over?"

I shook my head. "Patrick's a flirt. That's all. He likes to flirt and tells me how beautiful I am, which is part of his flirting. It doesn't mean he has a thing for me."

"It doesn't mean he doesn't," Anna said firmly. She raised a brow when I opened my mouth to argue.

"We're not talking about Patrick. We're talking about you and Hudson. When do you think he's going to propose?"

She sighed heavily. "I don't know. But I can't worry about it. If he changes his mind, it'll be okay. I have a job I really enjoy, and I feel more financially secure than I've ever felt.

I'm moving in with the man I love. That's enough for right now."

"Good for you. I'm still a little impressed you moved in with him so fast. I love that you did because you love him and he loves you, but I thought you'd debate it for a long time."

Anna shook her head and stared at Hudson as he walked in with a large box. He winked at her and kept going past the kitchen. "I love him. I know it's a little fast, but I don't want to spend another night apart from him. I talked to the boys about it, and they were on board with moving here instead of finding our own place for a little while. They love Hudson, too."

"I'm really happy for both of you," I told her.

"Thanks. I am, too. It's a good feeling."

I smiled and handed her a glass to put away. Love looked good on her. Hell, it looked good on everyone. When I had it, it looked good on me. But Charles and I drifted apart and when he left, it wasn't a big shock. I wanted a partner, but I was willing to accept a partner in name only. He wasn't. He wanted love, and he found it with his new husband.

I was happy for them, as happy as you could be for someone who lied to you about who they were and fell in love with someone else. I missed having a partner, and I was lonely. But being lonely wasn't enough of a reason to give in to the flirtations between Patrick and I. Even the ones that got a little hot and made me wonder if Patrick was more serious than he let on.

At the end of the day, I was still his boss. And that meant there was a line I couldn't cross. A line that was dangerous to us both. A line that I dreamed about crossing when no one else was around.

THANK **you** for reading Hudson and Anna's story! Hudson has been a favorite of mine since I started this series, and Anna was exactly the kind of woman he needed. Someone who wouldn't be impressed by him owning the bar, or want anything for free from him. She kept him on his toes, and brought him hard to his knees.

The next book in the series is Goldie and Patrick's book. When she hired him, she never thought the cute, young man would be someone she would be attracted to. He's too young, too pretty, and too tempting. When they're paired on Book Boyfriends Wanted, Goldie learns there's a lot more to him than meets the eye. Read His Curvy Boss today!

CAN'T GET ENOUGH of Hudson and Anna? He was serious when he said he wasn't going to wait long to propose. Sign up now to read their bonus epilogue!

COLLEGE GRAD, Paige is on a break with her best friends. She's newly single, and the perfect way to get over her ex is with the sinfully sexy Dante. Five days is long enough, and they go their separate ways. Until Paige walks into her new job and finds Dante is her new coworker. Read In Front Of Me today.

ABOUT THE AUTHOR

USA TODAY Bestselling Author Mary E Thompson spent most of her childhood wishing she had a few less curves. She hid in the pages of books because her favorite characters never cared what size her clothes were. Now, neither does Mary, and she writes stories that celebrate women like her. Real women who have curves, chase dreams, and find love, because we should all be happy, no matter our dress size.

Mary spends her non-writing time with her husband and two kids, watching too much TV, cheering for her hometown football team (Go Bills!), and hiding chocolate from her family.

Visit https://MaryEThompson.com/ to sign up for Mary's newsletter, **Romancing the Curves.** Subscribers get free ebooks and other fun stuff, like exclusive, members only content and giveaways, plus are the first to know about new releases and sales!